FATHER NUÑEZ AND THE NIGHT THAT TOMBSTONE BURNED

Flicker was doomed.

He had escaped the fiery hell of the burning Tombstone jail only to be cornered by the lynch mob in the San Pedro Saloon.

I could not accept the vision of the untamable Flicker driven to earth by such peasants.

I heard the piteous neighing of a horse trapped in the flames of the jail stable. Freeing and mounting the terrified brute, I spurred him into the street. With a yell, I drove through the mob and crashed through the swinging doors of the saloon.

I saw that Flicker was alone and defended only by the mob's fear of him. His very voice echoed the last controls of desperation.

"¿Quien es? ¿Quien es?" he called hoarsely. He saw, then, that it was only the small crippled servant of Rome.

"Nombre Dios!" he said to me. "I prayed for help, and God sent *you!*"

Bantam Books by Clay Fisher
Ask your bookseller for the books you have missed

BLACK APACHE

by
CLAY FISHER

BLACK APACHE
A Bantam Book | November 1976

ISBN 0–553–02825–1

Published simultaneously in the United States and Canada

Bantam Books are published by Bantam Books, Inc. Its trade-
mark, consisting of the words "Bantam Books" and the por-
trayal of a bantam, is registered in the United States Patent
Office and in other countries. Marca Registrada, Bantam
Books, Inc., 666 Fifth Avenue, New York, New York 10019.

PRINTED IN THE UNITED STATES OF AMERICA

To Dr. Phil Welton

*True listener for
the mission bells far off*

Translated from the Spanish, the original journals of Fr. Panfilo Alvar Nunez, O.F.M., an entry dated A.D. *1879, Barranca Rio de Naranjas, Durango y Sinaloa, Méjico.*

Apache-language passages may differ from texts phoneticizing from American Chiricahuan sources.

The Indian term *black robe* was initially employed to designate the Jesuits, in Sonora. Later, it came to include all orders of the priesthood, from brown-robed Franciscan to white-clad Carmelite.

It was always consistent in Indian meaning, however: The "black robes" of any color went much unloved in that wild land and dangerous time.

CONTENTS

Flight from Casas Grandes

A FOREWORD

*The story of the black Apache is a tale of two men:
Sergeant Flicker and Father Nunez.*

*Both were of a kind to remember—the kind Shake-
speare meant when he vowed their antics would make
the angels weep.*

*Flicker was a renegade American soldier under
charges of rape, murder, and desertion. Nunez was a
crippled Mexican priest unfrocked by his church for
gross rebellion. Both men were in unlawful flight to
avoid prosecution. Arrest for the soldier meant death
by the firing squad. For the curate a possible lifetime
in the iron cages of excommunication. Each understood his own peril; neither would submit to capture
alive.*

God arranged the crossing of their trails.

*Nunez wanted to build a chapel for the hostile
Apache Indians. He saw it as a church no white man
might attend, and he wanted to build it in the wild
heart of Mexico's Sierra Madre Mountains of the
North. His Franciscan order absolutely forbade it.
Nunez, being Nunez, absolutely ignored his order. Soon
came the response from the Franciscans: Stay where
you are, we are sending a bishops' committee to arrest
you.*

Nunez did not wait.

*He went over the wall of his mission at Casas
Grandes, outward bound in his search for the one man
he knew could save him and the dream of an Apache
church.*

He was looking for a legend.

The Índios reducidos, *the tame Indians, called this man Soldado Negro, Black Soldier; and sometimes he was known as Mirlo, Blackbird. The Mexican's called him Trasfuga, the Runaway. The* mestizos, *the lowly half-breed people of the* monte, *called him the Black Apache, and they feared—or revered—him more than any bronco of the pure blood.*

The Americans up in Arizona called him many things but mostly, "that damned nigger Cherry Cow (Chiricahua) son of a bitch."

The army at Fort Bliss, Texas, called him Robert E. Lee Flicker, first sergeant, cavalry, and listed him "deserter."

The sheriff of El Paso called him "wanted for aggravated rape and murder" and had his likeness nailed up on five-hundred-dollar-reward posters from Fort Davis to Camp Grant in the Arizona Territory.

The press of the time used all of the above, with but one paper printing a semblance of fair treatment: the El Paso Daily Outpost.

Charged with the brutal rape-slaying of the daughter of post sutler Albert Thompson, Sergeant Flicker steadfastly denies his guilt and tells an entirely different story from his accusers.

Outpost reporter John Brown Stokes found the black prisoner a tragic victim of the divisions following the late conflict. Sergeant Flicker, says Stokes, was the first Negro from a Southern state to be appointed, postwar, to the United States Military Academy at West Point. Reporter Stoke's full story is exclusive with the Outpost, including the R. E. L. Flicker biographical summary beginning elsewhere in this issue.

It was October, 23, 1868, that the Outpost *spoke in lone voice against the public preclusion of guilt in the*

*Flicker case. The black sergeant never saw the news-
paper account but he foresaw the shadow of its dire
prophecy: Untried, he was already convicted, and he
knew then what he must do, and swiftly.*

*In the chill fog of earliest dawn, Sergeant Flicker
broke barracks and fled across the Rio Grande. He
had but one passion, one rage of purpose remaining.
Vengeance against those he believed had betrayed him
because he was black. For the next ten years, living
among the hostile bronco Apaches of the Sierra Madre
del Norte, he waged war on both governments, Mexican and American, and the blood price was on his
head north and south of the border.*

*It was this outlawed American army deserter whom
Father Nunez set forth to find in 1879, the eleventh
year of Flicker's Mexican exile.*

*How the two men found each other, and so found
themselves, is the story of* Black Apache.

1
THE BANISHMENT

My name is Father Nunez. Once I was a priest of
the people, fully cloaked in the authority of my order,
that of the monks of Saint Francis of Assisi. Now, God
save me, the Franciscans have cast me out. The
cruel Bishop Galbines will not hear me, and Emi-
nence Cardinal Mendoza, down in Ciudad Chihuahua, has sought a papal dire warrant for my arrest.
Should he succeed, it will mean imprisonment and
secret trial, with God alone knowing the penalties but
any monk able to guess at them. And tremble.

In the happy years before my banishment, I had
found and restored the original mission that had been
built at Casas Grandes half a century gone and left in
ruins by the Apaches shortly thereafter.

I had toiled like a human dog, as well, to win over
for God these same Apache Indians. For the first time
in my church's history, I was succeeding. There were
no conversions, no Catholic Apaches, true. But Nunez
was being a friend to the untamed ones and making
friends of them. Then, entirely through no fault of
either priest or Apache, events conspired to once
more bring the wild riders to destroy the mission. Full
blame for this second loss was inevitably put by my
superiors upon my forbidden efforts to solicit the
trust of an implacable foe. What a sad waste and
wrongness for us all.

Yet one may not criticize his church here.

The Apache were in fact known as *los bárbaros*,
the barbarians. My own people feared them hysteri-
cally. In consequence of that dread, my flock also
turned against me. The personal crusade of their
pastor to entice and tame—it was whispered even to
train!—the red wolves of the Sierra Madre was not
alone *malo* but *loco*.

1

And so. they prayed. the time of Crazy Nunez upon their blighted parish would soon be done.

Yet, strangely, my advertised failures and my church's published bans notwithstanding, no new padre appeared in Casas Grandes to take my place. Neither did any bishops' soldiers arrive from the south to denounce Panfilo Alvar Nunez, the outlaw priest.

It became a singular time of waiting.

The days fled into years. Years through which I labored alone to once again raise the mission, my parishioners refusing to help their mad *cura* another useless time. Mercifully, I lost count of the winters of solitary devotion. In the end I had rebuilt but the rudest of quarters for myself, a village housekeeper, and an Apache child I had been rearing at the mission before its demolishment. But then, on that last day of which I tell, one of my flock, loyal yet, brought me dread word.

The years had been long but my order had not forgotten me. One of the justly feared bishops' committees of the Franciscans was finally en route to Casas Grandes to arrest me for my crimes. Its grim members were in fact but a day's mule ride away. And pressing their wearied mounts.

I grew pale at the news.

Were I now to wait, I would be carried off by the bishops' committee to those unlit dungeons from whence no rebel priest returns—an unthinkable thing. One course of desperation remained to me. I must seek a miracle from the hand of God to guard me against the nearing peril.

And it came to pass, even so. The hand of God did intercede. The visitation came as I rested in the darkling sunset of that final day. A day I had squandered as ten hundred others in exhorting my parishioners to labor with their beleaguered priest. To join him in the burro-headed effort of rearing up yet one more church of the Virgin for the Apache to tear down.

The nature of the miracle requires a turning back to another, older sunset of the years before. The sunset that had seen my beautiful mission pounded into its present ruin by the artillery fire of perhaps the most sinister figure in Mexican-American frontier history.

I speak of the renegade Negro West Point officer turned Apache messiah, Lieut. Robert E. Lee Flicker.

It is with Flicker that it all began. That was when the miracle was poised, put in place.

Qué cosa maravilloso, what a thing of wonderment!

Even the hand of God is sometimes black.

2
THE LIONS OF YESTERDAY

When I came home to Casas Grandes from my small part in the rescue from Flicker's Apache of the young son of the governor of Texas, I was a popular hero.

Ben Allison, the famed Texan *pistolero,* and myself had achieved a wide and generous notoriety. Our dangerous ransoming and safe retrieval of the boy were trumpeted in the press of both lands. We were lions then.

But that was yesterday.

Now, this decade later, the lesser lion was grown older and his keepers jaded with him. When the unforgiving monks of the bishops' committee came next day, they would make short work of my guilt. I would be found wanting and marched away in peremptory arrest. I would be a priest as ruined as my broken mission.

At this prospect depression whelmed me over.

I must flee, but where, how, toward what future and what friend?

Allison, alas, was years since disappeared.

He had vanished the same day of our defeat of Flicker, riding off into the haze of cannon smoke that was still drifting from the Negro deserter's shelling of *Misión Casas Grandes*. Deserted, I had no power to replace that of Allison's great cap-and-ball revolver. But still I knew there must be a better way than bullets to prosecute my salvation of the barbarian Apache. What I required of course was a miracle, and none had come forth.

Angrily, I cursed aloud and hurled the heavy tile in my hand against the mission bell, long since fallen from its tower to lodge amid the sharded adobes of my garden patio.

The tile caromed off the ancient bronze with a deep gonging vibration. The bell, thus tolled, commenced to shudder with an unnatural intensity. Suddenly, it broke through the crust of rubble to plunge into a tunneled room beneath the ruins. A cloud of debris swirled upward. Borne aloft on the dust, a parchment fluttered and fell at my feet. Its legend caught my eye: *Mapa de Mina Perdida del Rio Naranjas.*

Merciful Father, what was this?

Had the bell's cave-in released the true map to the fabled lost mine of El Naranjal? The ghost mine whose odd name meant "the orange grove" and which—legend hinted—the Franciscans owned in specious title to one Blasco Salazar, civilian citrus rancher? The spectral bonanza camouflaged thus by an orange grove planted to hide it from taxation by the central government?

No, how might such treasure fall to me, a ruined priest? It was beyond thinking. But as I continued to peer at the map, it became not beyond thinking. Indeed, I was looking upon the very *carta* of the folklore. Two centuries of antiquity lay in the hand of a spoiled half-breed priest who must soon be fugitive or lose his freedom to the subterranean cages of Bishop Galbines.

It was then the realization invaded me; here was my miracle.

With the gold of El Naranjal, I could escape Galbines. Escape him and so remove myself to build entirely another kind of church than yet imagined by

Rome. A church built for the wild Apache alone. It would not be in Casas Grandes but the inner ranges of the Sierra Madre. No white man might attend it, not even any Mexican, and Nunez would have done a thing no other priest of the cloth had dared to dream before him.

Pardiez! I would raise up an Apache chapel.

All I need do now was follow the ancient map to the phantom canyon of the orange grove. There awaited me a treasure second only to the fabled lost Tayopa mine of the thieving Society of Jesus. *Madre!* it fevered the brain.

Who found the wealth of El Naranjal controlled not alone his redemption as a priest, he would rule all of Chihuahua, even of Sonora. There was no bishop in Mexico who could say him nay. The committee be damned. Fornicate Bishop Galbines. Even Saint Francis take heed. Nunez had the power now. He held it in his single hand that clutched the parchment *carta* of the mine.

The thought twisted my senses awry.

I leaped atop a mound of rubbish in the ruins of my bombarded church.

"I shall find it! I shall find the gold!" I shouted. And when the earless adobes and broken shards of mission tile answered not, I tucked brown Franciscan robes and galloped down the hill toward the village of Casas Grandes, screeching, "It is mine, damn your eyes! The gold is mine, do you hear? All of it! all of it! all of it!"

3
THE WIFE OF THE SHOEMAKER

Long before I reached the town and Bustamante's flyblown *mercería,* I regained my good sense. Rather than waving the treasure map, I hid it quickly in my robes. In place of running and shouting, I sat

down on a roadside boulder and prayed. After six
Hail Marys, I felt improved. Now for some straight
thinking.

Patently, I could not dash into Bustamante's mar-
ketplace yelling that I had found the map to El
Naranjal. Every wastrel and daydreamer in Chihuahua would hear of it within three days. Yes, and
every evil person, too. I understood my position.
Hereinafter, I would need to travel in the full shelter
of my priest's habit. It would not be easy, but I did
have armament.

No sensible servant of the Church goes about a
frontier land without weapons—concealed naturally
—against the uncertainties of the road. I now, therefore, sought my Jeruselem blade, my Writ of Holy
Scripture, that is to say my Bible. The Book never
failed when called upon with proper devotion.

Scanning the way to make certain no parishioner
observed me, I removed the flask of grape brandy
from the hollowed-out Bible and took a smacking
pull. I then put mind to problem of moment: What
did a veritable pilgrim require to outfit himself for
finding a lost gold mine?

Before all things of course must come a chief of
soldiers to protect the expedition. All things else—
including an Apache ambassador to get us through
his fierce people in safety, a mining expert who
would know the gold country when we reached it,
and perhaps a cook and keeper of the pack mules—
must wait upon the finding of our *capitán,* our
jefe de soldados. Without such a one to guard against
the barbarians and outlaws of that wild land (who
would kill travelers for no more than a pound of
bacon, a mold of bread, or *pellizco* of salt), not one
step could be taken.

Praise God, I knew such a leader; I would seek
out the black lieutenant, later sergeant, Flicker. But
to find Flicker I needed a certain Apache named
Kaytennae. So then, let first things be first. Where
was Kaytennae?

Arising from my rock at roadside, I went into town
and sought out the handsome, ripe-bodied wife of

my storekeeper friend, Mayor Bustamante. She, Dolores, was a creature surrendered in totality to the cross. Even an unfrocked priest could command her. When I told her that I wished a discreet conference with the Indian wife of Refugio Baca, the town shoemaker, fat Dolores put down her metate, left cornmeal in grinding bowl, and departed at full waddle.

Presently, I was with the summoned girl in the darkest backreach of the Bustamante barn.

Ay de mí! here permit a word about Charra, Baca, the young wife of Refugio, known to the Apaches as Josana.

This was a child of tenderest years but a completed woman, no matter. She appeared to be of mixed Apache and Anglo blood. She had been left on the steps of my church by passing Indian raiders whose number had included the child's mother. The fleeing war party was almost certainly of the Chiricahua of Cochise, from Arizona, and were being hotly pursued by veteran Mexican cavalry troops. There was blood all over the stones of the entryway to God's house, and I always assumed the mother to have been mortally hurt—Apaches unfailingly know if they will die—and thus to have left her child with Father Nunez rather than to see it end upon a Mexican bayonet.

In any event, the Mexican Nednhi Apache of Chief Juh would not accept the infant, it being a female, and *mestizo*.

I, Nunez, had been forced to employ a whore of the village, just then wet from a stillbirth of her own, to nurse the foundling. Both the woman and the orphaned waif lived with me at the mission until the child was off the breast.

At this time the villagers were commencing to whisper of my inordinately kind treatment of a street woman, admittedly a creature of superb animal graces, and I had to discharge her. It was my understanding that she removed to Fronteras, where the Anglos were more numerous and business therefore more prosperous.

Left with the Apache girl, I naturally attempted to rear her as my own daughter. Yet all too soon were the summers fled. Little Charra was no longer little Charra. Her nubbins became overnight as noble as any in North Chihuahua. When, all swiftly, the remainder of her grew to match the remarkable breasts, my parishioners once more demanded some less earthy housekeeper for their humpbacked priest.

Outraged that the simpletons dared imagine that Nunez would be fevered of such worldly evilments as a child-woman's bobbling teats or jiggling buttocks, I immediately sent the girl down the hill to the Bustamantes. They prudently married her off to *zapatero* Baca, the middle-aging shoe-leather prince of Casas Grandes. By all reports Baca was delighted with his Apache wildcat, but Charra had a pagan sensuality not to be assuaged by the banked fires of middle years. To the present day she had remained a sultry, hot-minded she-creature, more true to her barbarian blood than to her mission upbringing.

I had not, to that same present day, taken occasion to visit her since sending her to live with Bustamante and his fat wife. This was not for lack of interest in the child but only in deference to the tiny minds of my parish. Men, and more so women, will forever mistake gallantry for gonadal ambition in their priest. It is one of the burdens of the cloth. But I bore it then as I bear it now, true to my vows and to mine own self. Let them think what they will. I, Nunez, know what I have done.

Besides, what harm is there in honest admiration for a buttock's bounce beneath its cling of skirting? Or in the appreciation of the manner, say, in which a woman's nipple will erect itself in response to frank and open salute from the eye of an inspired male beholder?

Pah! small lives made small minds.

I, Nunez, was a free man.

4
THE WHORE OF FRONTERAS

I found a stub of candle in the barn of my friend Bustamante and struck a sulfur match to it and lit its charred wick. In the waxen light I saw the dance of the devil in the eyes of Charra Baca watching me and waiting for me to speak. Drawing deep breath, I not alone directed Beelzebub to get him behind me but also the Lord of Hosts to shore me up from in front. It was no real question of Nunez falling upon this dark angel, *quita!* It was simply that the look of her was of that feral nature to drive a man's mind from his beads to his codpiece. An ordinary man, that is. For myself, the tempting tried my mettle but did not untemper it. Nunez had reared this child of desire; he was her only father.

"Listen, Charra," I said quickly, "I need to find your cousin Kaytennae. Is he still with Juh's people?"

"No, Kaytennae went to live with the Chiricahua of Warm Springs, up in Arizona. He thinks they are his true people and that he won't be an orphan anymore."

I frowned, displeased. "It is strange he did not come see me; he was as an own-son to me."

"He is an Apache, father."

"Well, Charra, and so are you an Apache."

"More so each day, father. I am leaving Baca, going home to my mother's people. I would have told you."

"But, here, girl! You cannot do that. You are married to Baca, a good man."

"No, father, he is not. He cannot arouse me, nor elevate himself. No good in any way. I am going."

"Where will you go, God's name?"

"Arizona. Kaytennae found his people there. Perhaps I can find my people there also. You know,

9

father, you always told me my mother was of the Chiricahua of Cochise."

She had me there. But no matter. I had already conceived a better way out for Nunez.

"Well, I must say you are one lucky girl," I smiled. "I am by coincidence myself bound for Arizona and will thus accompany you on your way."

"Us," she corrected me. "My mother is going with me. She finds business failing in Fronteras. There is a new place up in Arizona. A mining camp. Very big one, they say. They call it Tombstone."

A mining camp! Here was my answer to locating the expert in mineral work that I wanted for El Naranjal's exploration. Plus the bonus also of Charra leading me to Kaytennae in the process. God was in command.

"Your foster-dam does not concern me," I lied. "I have been in her company many times."

"That is what the villagers whisper, father."

"Hush, you vixen!" I ordered. "Do you dare mock me?"

Charra turned lovely face to me. "No, father," she murmured. "You are all the father I know. I do but tease you, as my mother did."

"Will you stop calling that low trollop your mother," I complained. "Your mother was a noble Apache, even perhaps a warrior woman. She died to bring you to my doorstep. Do you then still call that damned whore 'mother' in her place?"

There was a flurry in the outer darkness of the barn, and a familiar rough voice attacked me.

"And what damned whore are you calling a damned whore?" it demanded. "Why, you rat turd of a spoiled priest, I ought to tell the girl a few of those prayers you taught me while I was suckling her at your little Mission of the Virgin, eh?" Zorra strode in out of the murk where she had been hiding. Arms akimbo, she struck the pose I recalled so well, a bastard posture half accusatory, half sexually inflammatory. "Well, priest," she defied me, "will you apologize, or must I begin reciting my catalog of blackmail?"

Belatedly, I sought to defuse her temper, which was memorable.

"Neither course should be necessary with old friends such as we," I shrugged. "How many times have you called me a damned priest?"

"Ahhh," she sighed, letting the anger flow out of her still matchless figure. "You little humpbacked son of a bitch, you still can make my parts turn warm. You know it, too, damn you. Come here to me, you rotten, ruined padre, you."

Before I might elude her, she grasped me to her monumental bosoms and delivered me a buss of such suction and succulence as to render me giddy for three drawn breaths.

"By God!" she testified. "They may have taken away your order, padre, but they left your ardor. You bastard!"

"Mother," Charra reprimanded, "be still. Father Nunez may have lost his church but he is not to be taken in this lewd manner of yours. You do him a dishonor to remind him of days we all would forget."

"Hah, speak for yourself, stripling wench. Who wants to forget such days? And the *nights!* Eh, Nunez?"

"Dear sweet Jesus," I pleaded with them, "will we three go together to the United States, or will we not?"

Zorra peered at me through the candleshine.

"Why," she murmured, "if you see no priestly stain in traveling with a prostitute, where is our reason to delay?"

"If you would but desist in calling yourself such a woman," I admonished her, "no one would ever guess your guilt. I would know you for *una dama grande* anywhere."

"Ah, Rat Turd, you could always mold me."

"And you, Charra?" I said, wincing to the endearments from the fallen lady of Fronteras. "My little girl of yesterday. Does it suit you that I join you to find Kaytennae and to visit the great new mining camp? How was it you called it? Headslab, Arizona?"

"Tombstone," Charra said. "It is in the country of the Cochise people, my people." She looked upon me in a way very close to love. "Of course you may travel with us, father," she agreed softly. "But don't you think you should discard your robes of lost office? You know, travel as an ordinary *hombre del monte,* like all the other *mestizos?* After all, you are no longer a priest."

Indignantly, I drew myself up to my full five feet and one inch. "As long as the cloth and the charity of God's patience endure me to do so," I declared, "I shall go as Father Nunez. The people may desert me, the Indians make sport of my misfortunes, the very tides of fate engulf my broken body, yet so long as the Lord my God suffers me to serve him, I shall travel in his name

Zorra gazed upon me with unhid admiration. As honestly, she delivered me a blow athwart the shoulder bones that well-nigh restored the straightness to my bent spine.

"By Christ," she said. "A sort of God's padre, is that it, little priest?"

I nodded in pained acceptance.

"Yes, that's it. God's padre."

And we blew out the candle and stole from the barn of Bustamante, outward bound upon the finding of Kaytennae.

Who would lead us to Sergeant Flicker?

Who would, *por supuesto,* take us to the gold mine of the orange grove?

5
AWAY TO ARIZONA

As befitted a cloistered savant I was of notably simple mind about the real world. I had never been to the United States of America and as we trudged north past Janos, the last Mexican settlement, I kept asking my two ladies when we might expect to see the line separating that great country from Mother Mexico. Eventually, Zorra made abrupt halt.

"Damned fool priest," she fumed, "there is no line

to see. When we come to *Estados Unidos,* it will seem
no different than *Méjico.*"

"How will we know when we are there, then?" I
asked.

"When we see Anglos, father," Charra answered for
her bellicose dam.

"Aye," Zorra nodded. "You know an Anglo when
you see one, don't you, Nunez?"

"Hah! Nunez know Anglos? Who do you think it
was that saved all those Anglos when Flicker bombarded my mission?"

"I cannot imagine. Who?"

"It was I, Nunez, you hussy. Naturally, with a bit
of help from Kaytennae."

"Lah! A *bit,* you say? You should hear how Kaytennae tells the same story!"

"Never mind; hush, woman. An Indian will forever
extend the truth in his own favor."

"Just like a priest, eh, Nunez? Telling lies all day
and drinking the altar wine all night. *Mierda!*"

"Mother, don't talk like that to father," Charra Baca
scolded. "Priests don't make up those lies they tell.
They are all written down in the Holy Book they carry.
They can't help it that the church employs them to trade
those lies to the people for their small coins and dear
belongings. It is no different than the comancheros selling us rotted buffalo hides or rancid back fat. Or the
scalphunters offering our dead Indian hair in the mar-
ketplace at Ciudad Chihuahua. Or the Americans letting their Apaches raid down here, steal our Mexican
horses and herds of fine beef animals, and drive them
back up to Arizona for sale."

"God's name!" I exploded. "What is this idle chatter
you spout? Am I to be compared with One-Ear Kifer?
Or with some stinking Comanche half-breed who sells
putrid hides in Santa Fe? Or with the damned *Yanquis*
who protect Del Shay and Loco and Nana and Victorio
and those other murdering Arizona Apaches? *Santissima!*"

Zorra yawned in my reddened face.

"Go to hell and come on," she said. "It's getting late.
We will never get to Tombstone at this pace."

She took up her cudgel-stick and trudged onward. My flame-haired foster child, Charra Baca, smiled at me and patted my hand and told me to forgive the fallen one and to follow her to Arizona. Grumbling and threatening, I did as advised. After all, I had no useful knowledge of the land beyond Janos and Rio Casas Grandes. Now that the security of these remembered haunts lay behind us, I was in reality lost.

Not so my twain of disparate females.

Zorra had plied her art as far afield as San Diego, in California. Charra, her nursling cub, had also been to *Estados Unidos*. She had run away as a very small child to go with the Nednhi Apache of Chief Juh on a tribal visit to American Apache kinfolk near mighty San Carlos Reservation. She knew Sonoita, Tubac, and other familiar place-names in that country of Cochise and the Chiricahua of southern Arizona. Or so, at least, she said.

I was to learn to my sadness that her memory did not match the maps of the United States. But for the moment there in the traildust outside Janos, what argument might I make against the widely traveled pair who were my raffish guides? I was of no more worth there than back amid the broken adobes of my mission, in Casas Grandes. I was but a spoiled priest fleeing the authority of his faith. A purblind fool who knew nothing of the harsh world waiting beyond his vestry's walls.

One thing, however, I did know.

I would be quite content to lose Zorra in Headstone, Arizona. And to then leave Charra Baca with the Cochise people whom I prayed might indeed prove to be the blood of her lost mother.

The very moment that I had located Kaytennae and he had found Flicker for me, I was finally and doubly done with these women. A brazen Mexican prostitute and a wild seventeen-year-old Apache Eve were scarcely the trail companions of choice. Certainly not on an expedition of outlawed men through chartless mountain wastes to find and purloin the Franciscan gold of the orange grove.

So, rearmed by determination, I tucked up my habit

and opened the tarantula's scuttle of my crippled stride
to gain again the sides of my temporary comrades.

"I will be of no further trouble to you in the matter
of asking when we will be in America," I assured Zorra.
"I will leave it all to you."

"Good," answered the courtesan of Fronteras, not
slowing her long gait. "You see that little pile of rocks
back there where we passed the paloverde grove? Squint
hard. About five miles back there."

"What of it?" I demanded, seeing no pile of rocks
and not even any stand of paloverde trees. "This
cursed desert is full of rock piles."

"Not like that one, priest. The Mexican soldiers from
the garrison at Janos put it there for a marker."

"A marker of what, God's name? The grave of some
Gila monster or great horned toad?"

"No, Father Rat Filing," answered Zorra the whore.
"The marker beyond which the American cavalry will
know it has passed into Mexican territory."

"What! you monstrous bawd!"

"Yes, Humpback. We have been walking in Ameri-
cano dust for the past two hours; this is Arizona."

I made her no reply.

It is a wise man who knows when both ears of the
jackass have been awarded him.

6
THE BATTLE OF ALAMO HUECO TANK

We had not entered Arizona as my guides had permitted me to believe. Rather, we had come into the
United States through a little corner of the New Mexico Territory. Indeed, one cannot, except that he be a
bird of the air, enter Arizona from Chihuahua. I
should have understood this. I knew that there was a
mule road of good quality going by way of Penuelas
over the Sierra to Agua Prieta, in Sonora, just at the

border of the Arizona country. But by the time I remembered this fact, we were lost in the Alamo Hueco Mountains of New Mexico.

My guides had separate explanations.

"Quita!" Charra said, frowning all about her. "This does not seem to be the same way that I came with Juh and the Nednhi to find the Warm Springs people. These bastardly rocks are strange to me."

"De ahí!" scowled Zorra. "Stand aside, you simple-witted she-mule. I shall take the lead."

"You!" Charra cried out. "Who was it told Father Nunez we were in Arizona?"

"Arizona, you say?" Zorra was gripping hard on her knobby mesquite walking stick. "Who was it said those Warm Springs Apaches lived in Arizona?"

"Not I," Charra denied. She backed off a step, eyeing the mesquite stick. "It's the Cochise people who live in Arizona. That's all I said."

"Liar!" Zorra swung the mesquite stick with a lunge, but the girl danced lightly free. The older woman regripped the stick. "You said Nunez wanted to find Kaytennae, with the Warm Springs people. That's in New Mexico, and far into it. That's why I didn't say anything when I realized you were taking us into New Mexico, instead of Arizona."

"Now who's a liar?" Charra incautiously challenged her foster-mother. "Wasn't it you who told Father Nunez where we were? He didn't ask it of me. I said nothing to him. And what did you answer him, whore mother? All I heard was Arizona."

Thhwwaacckkk!

The mesquite stick caught the girl across the lovely slant of her left buttock, from the side. Charra yowled like a dog kicked by a burro, and she instantly attacked the woman who had suckled her at the breast. They were rolling in the rocks and sand like two cats before I might even think how to dissuade them.

Then I spied the mesquite stick where it had fallen from Zorra's grasp. I at once seized up the cudgel, hesitating to employ it, fearful that I might injure one or the other of the combatants. But when women fight it is like no other fighting in the world. There is no zest in it, no sense of the good contest hardly fought to the gallant conclusion. Women do not fight for fun. They intend to kill one another.

So I laid into the whirling bundle of their forms with the knobby mesquite stick. But the damned stick struck a boulder and broke into two equal pieces. The broken pieces struck Charra and Zorra with force enough to halt their snarling battle, but only by turning its fury onto myself. Each of the screeching females grabbed a half of the shattered mesquite staff and came, fire-eyed, for Father Dunce Cap.

In terror, I held up my silver cross, crying, "God's name! halt!" I may as well have employed the *cruz* to turn aside the lightning forks of the Mexican Sierra Madre. With a perfect rain of welting blows descending on my shoulders and the bony processes of my priestly buttocks, I fled into the higher rocks. At bay up there, I prepared to die as a man. Or as well as a man can die who must be cudgeled to his end by two women. However, the Lord finally intervened. Zorra, in her eagerness to be first at the kill, tripped and fell all the way down out of the higher rocks, hitting Charra in the course of her tumbling flight, landing them both back down below and full into the *tanque,* or desert water hole, where we had stopped to rest.

They surfaced spitting and coughing from the water, then began to laugh wild as loons at sunset. All in a moment they had seemingly forgotten Father Nunez and were stripping off every stitch of their hot and sweated clothing down to the very fluff and tufting of their delicious parts! *Santissima!* For mortal shame!

Down the mountainside I raced, determined to threaten them with eternity in hell, or at very least a penance of a hundred confessions. Or six months of Hail Marys to purge them of this gross sin of disrobement before the eyes of a priest.

But, at the side of the splashing tank of desert waters, Satan sprang from the rocks behind me. Entering into my poor body, he thrust out the wrath of God and installed the wit of Beelzebub.

With a cry of plainest despair, I also ripped away the brown and dusty smother of my robes, kicked off mule-hide *guaraches,* leaped, with the idiot's laughter of a demented coyote, into the water of the *tanque* fair between the two full-teated, white-buttocked demons of my temptation. It was the finest swimming I ever had, although I cannot remember if it ever came to bathing.

Our spirits were cleansed, however.

That, I recall.

7
WE ACQUIRE YOUNG GRASS

Refreshed, we went on. We at last knew that to reach Arizona we must travel westerly. But, making our way out of the Alamo Hueco Mountains, we were confronted by the even more forbidding Animas Range. We were lost among its peaks for five days. Finally, we were rescued and redirected by an ancient Mescalero woman left by her people to die. As she had been waiting for the Dark One nearly a week, feeling all the while stronger, she seized upon our predicament to alter her own fate.

"Listen," she said to me, interested that I spoke her Apache tongue, "I haven't time to wait here any longer. I will go with you. A priest in Janos once nursed me to health and asked nothing. So I owe you something."

"No, no," I interrupted. "We priests are vowed to such things, Little Mother, and never for hire."

"Pah!" she denied. "Most of you black robes are cheats and liars. But I like you; I am going to call you Broken Back."

I entreated her to withdraw the honor, but she insisted that if Broken Foot was good enough a name for the great Apache chief, Nana, then Broken Back was surely sufficient for a homely poor cripple of a Mexican padre.

"Aye, but Nana does not permit that name to be

used in his presence," I objected. "I understand he is very sensitive about it."

"Well, of course, *cura*. Nana was crippled by an accident as a child, and he is a proud man."

"So am I also a proud man and a cripple."

"True. They ought to have shot you when you were hurt."

"*Quita,* woman; I was born this way."

"Hmm. Your mother should have drowned you, then. The Apache would never permit a mother to keep such a damaged thing."

I conceded the point. In return, the Mescalero squaw promised to guide us safely out of the Animas badlands. Resting until the sun went down, we set out once more to find Arizona. At first rest halt, two merciless hours later, the old lady limped over to me. Peering into my face, she squeezed my arm. "Don't feel bad about that name I gave you," she said. "Do you know how I am called? Old Croaker," she answered herself. "Isn't that a poor and shameful name? Once I was called Young Grass."

Touched, I looked back at her.

The moon was rising. By its wan first light, I could see the bony, wrinkled features. She was crying silently.

I looked away respectfully.

"Young Grass," I told her, "I did not hear that other name."

She rubbed sniffingly at the tears, anxious that I not note them. "Small man," she replied, "be you also of good spirit; I will get you a better name soon."

Turning at once away from me, she addressed the two others of our party with some roughness of embarrassment.

"*Ugashe,*" she ordered them. "Stir yourselves. It is time to go."

Charra Baca and her foster-mother arose with groanings of stiff muscles and blistered feet. I also abandoned my resting rock and once again the three of us followed the old lady westward. By dawn we had crossed over the Animas Range through San Luis Pass and were descending. We lay up through the fiercest heat of that day, went on at nightfall, now climbing once more. By midnight, we were near the summit of the Pedragosa Mountains, and were at last in Arizona.

"Tomorrow," Young Grass announced, "we will come to beautiful Whitewater River. From there, you will not need Old Croaker anymore."

I thought to hear her sniffle, to show some little hitching in the voice. But I was wrong. There was even ardor in the manner with which she wheeled on my two women, who had already found sitting rocks to groan upon.

"Here, you two gourd-breasted weaklings!" the Mescalero *anciana* upbraided them. "Get up from your fat backsides. We are wasting coolness hours. *Ugashe, ugashe!*"

She made effort to belabor them with her walking stick, but the motion only caused her to fall down. Unruffled, she gazed up at the early moon.

"My, but isn't this a pretty evening?" she asked.

And, with the opinion, she got unsteadily back afoot and tottered on in the lead singing a cracked and very much off-tune Apache happy song.

8
FLICKER IS NEAR!

All through the remaining "coolness hours" of the march onward into Arizona, the ancient Mescalero crone continued in her anticipations of the blessed valley of Whitewater River. She was a poetess, a gifting not uncommon among her desert kind. Those bred of that hot, harsh land had to see in it a loveliness beyond its too evident cruelty in order that the spirit might survive.

Even so, even knowing of this Apachean trait of gilding the cacti lilies, so convincing was Young Grass in these lyric praises of the Whitewater that I kept repeating, "Praise God. Celebrate his name. Press on."

But that was only because I had never seen the lovely meadows of the beautiful Whitewater River, in Arizona.

With the pearling gray of dawn we came to this stream, and Young Grass announced it as the place of her birth, hence of her naming. We looked about in the growing light. The Whitewater River flowed only with sand and the naked upshoulderings of its bedrock channel. There was no visible drop of water in it and already, even before the sun, one could see the shimmer of the heat lines wriggling above its bone-parched course. Of ground cover there was only the thinnest hairing of a brown and coarse salt grass growing in some of the river flats where accidents of previous flooding had deposited a trace of soil to bind the footless sand. "My God," I said to our Mescalero guide, "this is the grass of your naming? This the place of such a lovely baptismal? What did the shaman annoint you with? This pea gravel that cuts our sandals?"

"Ahhh," the old lady said softly, "your eyes are not long enough. Come on, we're almost there."

She went ahead, turning up the seared channel, moving now like some ancient mustang mare that has smelled the water of a hidden *tanque* and will reach it ere falling. Following her as best we could, we came presently around a sweeping bend buttressed by high red cliffs. The walls opened out before us. *"Miran!"* the old woman cried. "Do you see it? There, where I point with my stick."

We peered hard, seeing nothing.

"Loco," Zorra muttered beside me. *"Más loco."*

The old lady heard her. "No," she said, "not crazy. Smart. Come along, *mujer,* I forgive you. After all, you carry no Apache blood." She scuttled forward once more, bearing to her left, toward a nearby dark opening in the red rock walls. Charra was suddenly quickening her pace to come up with the Mescalero woman. "Aha!" Young Grass said. "So finally you show your mother's strain, eh? You see it?"

"I smell it!" Charra cried. "Water!"

"Yes, and more. Grass, wood, everything. Follow me, *chiquita.* I will teach you how to be a whole Apache."

We all hurried after her and soon had crawled up

into the dark opening in the wall. Going under a low natural rainbow rock, we came out upon the most astonishing of secret Apache oases. It was of about two hectares of level rich earth, thickly overgrown with meadow grass and harboring a grove of silverleaf poplar trees. Through the foliage of the poplars we could see the glint and sparkle of a body of water. We ran forward through the thick grass, laughing like children. Within minutes we were laving our weary bodies in the basin of the *tanque escondido,* the hidden Apache water hole.

This ancient camp of the desert was called *Hueco Perdido,* Lost Hole, Young Grass said. The centuries had collected there the seeds of grass and cottonwood and other desert flora. Even many Apaches did not know of its existence. As for the whites, untold numbers of them had died of thirst down at the crossing of Whitewater River, not quite a mile from this Arizona Eden.

We rested there for twenty-four hours.

It was during the rest that we discovered the real treasure we had found in our Mescalero grandmother, Young Grass.

Firstly, the home of the Warm Spring Apaches at Ojo Caliente was not far from the old lady's Mescalero Reservation at Sierra Blanca. Young Grass knew well many of the Warm Springs kinfolk. When questioned about Kaytennae, she had exclaimed over the youth at length. A remarkable young man indeed. He would go far in the affairs of his people. No doubt of it whatever.

What? Could Young Grass take us to see Kaytennae at Ojo Caliente? Well, she could take us to Ojo Caliente, yes. But we would not see Kaytennae there, no. He had gone with some wild Apaches to raid an ammunition camp over by Fort Huachuca. The times were uncertain. Victorio had fled again to Mexico, killing many Arizona settlers on the way. Indeed, Young Grass believed Kaytennae might be trying to get that ammunition for those same Victorio people who had been badly hurt by the pursuing cavalry.

"The White Eye settlers are angry again, too," the ancient crone finished. "They never could see the same humor in an Apache burning their barns and houses as in white men putting the torch to Apache jacals and rancherias. Kaytennae will be in great danger. He will need strong help from Yosen."

Yosen, also Ussen and Ysun, was the Apache main god. The use of his name made me fearful for Kaytennae. I asked Young Grass anxiously who the raiders were that had recruited him. Her reply brought me hard around.

"A black chief, up out of Mexico," she said. "I forget his name. Of middle years, handsome, fine pride, fierce."

"My God!" I cried. "Flicker!"

"Why, yes," nodded Young Grass, pleased. "That was the name. Do you know him?"

"Too well!" I said. "But never mind that. How was it that Kaytennae went with him?"

"Flicker needed a guide, someone who knew where the Huachuca dump was. Kaytennae agreed to go."

I then told the old woman of my kinship with the Apache Kaytennae—how, when he was a boy, I had nursed him against certain death and won him through to happy life. When she learned this, her gap-toothed smile embraced me as a brother.

"Padre Jorobado!" she proclaimed, "Father Hunchback! Of course. Now it comes to me. Damn the ruinations of the mind which ride apace and always on a faster horse with each winter's approach and passing. I apologize, Nunez. We hear you are half Indian yourself. The *mestizo* padre they call you, *anh?*"

"*Anh,* yes," I agreed, answering in Apache. "My mother was full-blood, an Opata, captive of the Nednhi."

"Juh's people," Young Grass said, as to herself. Then, to me, "Yes, I will help you find Kaytennae. At least I will take you to where Fort Huachuca is."

"We shall search where you direct us," I assured her earnestly. "We must find Kaytennae, as he alone can lead us to Flicker."

The withered crone nodded. "Ah, that black one," she said. "Like a wild horse, a king of wild horses. He stirs the blood with danger. He is a man of men. *Hijo!*"

"Flicker is all you say," I replied, "but now I had better tell you our story, mother. The truth of why we are here looking for him and for Kaytennae."

"Go ahead, Padre Jorobado. And be careful. I have the power of smelling liars."

"How do they smell?" I inquired, in humor.

She did not smile for return.

"They smell like priests," she said. "Tell your story as if you were someone else."

"Eh? What do you mean, *mujer?*"

"You know what I mean, small man. Speak with open words, not as a damned black robe."

"Ah," I sighed resignedly, *"Índios!"*

"Excrementos mulos," the old lady said calmly, "mule droppings."

And so we left it.

9
I CONFESS THE GOLD OF
EL NARANJAL

Quickly, I told Young Grass of my dream to build an Apache church with the gold of El Naranjal. I described for her, as well, my knowledge of the lost mine's location, "five days down the great North Barranca of Durango, three days travel toward Sinaloa and the sea." One had but to find *Barranca del Norte* to be on the road to Naranjal, I explained. And, once on the road, he had only to listen for the sound of the mission bells far off, and follow them, to find where the yellow metal waited. I then conveyed to the ancient squaw my immediate purpose of reaching Headstone, Arizona, with my companions. "Do you know Headstone?" I concluded. "Charra says it is near Fort Huachuca."

"Tombstone," Charra Baca corrected patiently.

"Call it whichever you will," Young Grass shrugged. She was masticating poplar bark for its sugar and she spat expertly of the juice to drown a passing small bug.

"I know where the new mining camp of the gray metal is over there, Jorobado," she returned to me. "I can find it for you."

"And find the Chiricahua people for me?" Charra cried.

I made a gesture, interrupting. "First things should be hewn to, girl," I reminded her. "The beginning goal is to locate Kaytennae. Let us pray that Young Grass really knows where Fort Huachuca is."

The fierce-eyed old Mescalero squaw drew herself up. "Damned black robe," she said. "I know everything about the soldiers in Arizona, all their camps. I can show you where every horse apple of the American cavalry has dropped since Red Beard Crook was out here the first time."

"How near are we to Fort Huachuca, then?"

"Thirty miles, a pony ride."

"And Headstone?"

"Tombstone," Charra repeated faithfully.

"Twenty miles," Young Grass said. "Only a good walk."

I took in a deep lungful of the sunshine-heated redolent air of the oasis. The excitement of the nearness of these places was building in me like altar wine. God had sent this ancient female Moses of the Mescalero to lead us out of the Arizona wilderness. Victory was to hand.

"Father, thy name be exalted!" I shouted aloud, startling my companions. "We shall press onward with dark."

"Let's go now," Charra Baca suggested, catching some of my fever. "The day's heat is not too great."

"No, no," Young Grass said, alarmed. "The black robe is right. We travel only by dark into that country."

"Why so?" Zorra demanded rudely. "Damn such delay. I am losing money every minute that we sit here waiting for night. Hell, that is when I make my money."

Young Grass took interest. "What money is that, great teats?" she asked. "Do you dig for silver, then? A woman?"

"My mother is a whore," Charra Baca laughed, an-

swering for her scowling dam. "She fornicates with
men for money. You don't need a pickax to strike
gold, *anciana*."

"*Annnhh,* I see." Young Grass made a lisping, disap-
proving Apache sound. "But nevertheless we shall wait
for fullest night. Flicker's party of *broncos* will have
stirred soldier and settler alike. Much too dangerous to
go by day, fornicator. The white people would shoot
us all."

"*Cállate,* shut up, mother," Charra broke in to tell
Zorra when Zorra would argue further. "Did you ever
hear of a dead whore getting rich?"

Zorra lost her scowl, barked out her foxlike laugh.

Young Grass, however, retained her frown, and I,
seeing that our Apache guide was not pleased with this
low *cháchara,* made hasty reproof. "Enough of loose
converse, ladies," I warned. "We should all be at thankful prayer. God has led us this far well and safely. Hail
Mary."

"Pah!" Young Grass snorted. "Why don't you ask
this god of yours to guide you on from this spot? Wasn't
it this same black robe god that was leading you when I
rescued the three of you from walking in stupid circles
back among the Animas peaks? *Ih!* A poor god and
a poor guide, both things, I say."

It might have proved a bad turn in our pathway but
that Divine illumination lit it for Nunez.

"Ah, yes, Young Grass," I agreed gracefully, "but
didn't my God lead us to you, who then saved us?"

"Don't bother to reply to him," Zorra advised the
Mescalero crone. "You cannot trap a priest except that
you kill him first."

"Yes," Charra Baca said. "But we don't want to do
that. Who would be my only father, then?"

"Pony offal!" Zorra rasped. "You're not interested in
a father. It's the Franciscan gold. Don't you think I
was watching you when Nunez mentioned the old mine
to this Apache hag? *El Naranjal,* he said, and your
ears nearly flew away from your scheming head.
All that buried treasure of Saint Francis in the Ghost
Canyon, eh? Down there a mile deep where the Rio
Naranjas flows and the old hacienda waits two hundred

years silent in the sunshine? That is why you don't want your dear 'only father' to be harmed, you red-haired bitchling, you. It's the gold!"

"A lie!" Charra defended angrily. "I barely noted Father Nunez to speak of the gold."

"Estúpida!" Zorra exploded. "Don't you know that every thieving priest in north Mexico has a map to some old Sierra gold or silver mine of mother church? Hell, girl, they sell those maps for two *céntimos* in the streets of Ciudad Chihuahua to raise money for their damned orphanages."

"A second vile falsehood!" Charra cried. "I want only to find my mother's people and to be with them."

"Anh," croaked old Young Grass. "Among our people, if you are not somebody, then you are nobody."

"I am an Apache, *anciana,"* Charra said impulsively. "You will see. We are the same blood."

The Mescalero squaw raised her head. The seamed face studied the freshness of the young girl. The slitted pouches of the eyeflesh parted to show a moment's glitter of dead-black Apache pupil. "Never," was all she said.

And that was the ending of our happy day at Hueco Perdido, the lost water hole of the Apache people. It was to be the last day, too, of my black robe's sheltered innocence, both of heart and high purpose.

This was God's place.

Tomorrow we would be in Lucifer's.

10
GOING TO COCHISE

Young Grass halted us at midnight. We were well into the Dragoon Mountains, even by moonlight a pitiless and foreboding range. She had found water again, how-ever, with even a patch of scant grass beside it. "Goat Eye Tank," she said. "Apache water. Everybody rest here."

We took her at her word, dropping to the barren earth like so many lifeless stones. Young Grass would not let us go to the water hole but brought each of us a share of its precious fluid in the horse-gut *bota* she carried, asling, over scrawny dark shoulder. "We must leave the tank as it was," she explained. "This is not possible, should I permit White Eyes, like yourselves, to mar the edges of the hole."

"But, God's name," I protested, "it is solid rock. How might we damage it? And, for that matter, whereby do you call us White Eyes? We are one Mexican woman, one young Apache girl, and one *mestizo* priest of Mexico."

"As for leaving your sign on the rock, you would do it, believe me. An Apache would know I had brought you here."

"Do you say this is forbidden to others?"

"Yes, if the Apache knew I had brought you here, it would go unhappily for me." She paused, reaching to reassure me with her patting hand. "But do not fear, little priest," she smiled. "We are not apt to meet my people by night, and by day we shall all be far away from here. Coming in darkness and by only the light of the moon, none of you could ever find it again."

I conceded the unlikelihood of such a return to Goat Eye Tank, *quita!* And thanked the old lady for bringing the water in her pony-intestine bag to each of us. Then I said to her, "Now, when we travel on, will the way lie downhill? It seems to me we are on the divide here. Is this so?"

"Yes, Jorobado," she answered, "but we will not all go downhill. Two of us will climb upward from this place."

Nerves tightening, I sensed the Indianness here. Old doubts of red reliability leaped within me. A man who is even one-half of the white blood will never wholly trust an Indian, except that he continually forces himself to the chore.

"Mother," I said, "you have not told us something."

The Mescalero squaw rested on the long cudgel she employed as crutch and cane upon the march. Braced thus, she gestured to the north. "Do you see that dark headland rearing there?" she said. "That is where Josana must go to find her mother's people, and where I must go to guide her. You and the fornicator will go on to the mining camp, downward."

"You promised to guide us to Headstone," I charged. "We hold you to your Apache vow. Will you break it?"

"Listen, Jorobado," the old woman said, "you and the milk cow can find Headstone by yourselves. The girl would never reach the Chiricahua without me, and I vowed also to help her do that. Look again to the north."

A knowledge came to me, as I turned once more to scan the grim, great headland. "Cochise's stronghold!" I guessed excitedly aloud, and the old lady said, "Yes, it is where the Chiricahua will be in a bad time like this. I can take the girl there with safety. You would be killed in the pass."

"Indians!" I burst out. "Ingrates, all of you!" I glared at the withered Mescalero. "But for me, Josana would not be alive to look for her Apache mother!"

Instantly, the old harridan was contrite. She put bony hand gently to my indignant shoulder. "I will remind the Cochise people of that fact," she told me. "Perhaps they will honor it and not kill you when they find you still here at their tank in the morning."

When I stubbornly pursued the argument of her loyalty, Young Grass only shrugged that, should I persist in this *cháchara,* this chitchat, the sun would come and catch us all still sitting there. "On the other hand," she concluded, "if we all go now, we may each live a long time yet." She straightened, gripping the mesquite walking cudgel. "Come, Josana," she said. "We go north."

Without further word or other farewell for either Zorra or Jorobado, the ancient squaw limped off into the moonlight. We could see the tracery of the footpath going northward and climbing steeply even within our limited view. Charra Baca plainly did not know what to do. But God answered her quandary through his servant, Father Nunez. I embraced her strongly. "Go, daughter," I said. "You came to find your people. I came to seek the gold of El Naranjal. Our paths must divide here. Go with Young Grass, or you may never find your true home, your own people. *Vaya, Charrita mía.* Do not be afraid, for God has revealed this advice to me."

There were, of course, some salted tears, but the foster-mother Zorra enlisted herself on the side of God and Nunez, carrying the last hesitations.

"Remember," she encouraged Charra, "this is God's little padre. Didn't we name him that? Of course. I wouldn't trust an ordinary priest to confess an angel, but Father Rat Turd, here, well, he is in business for himself. If he says his God gave him the word, believe it. Hurry, now. That old bastard isn't waiting one step for you."

Charra ran off after Young Grass, sobbing the first three or four strides, then commencing to laugh and call out to the old lady to wait for her, that she was coming, and Young Grass would never regret guiding her.

It was at this point, the two of them having come together at a yon turn of their goat path of a trail northward, that I recalled something: The Mescalero crone had forgotten to describe for me the remaining trail to Headstone. I screeched as much out to her, begging her to hear me and to come back and fulfill her word to Padre Jorobado.

Well, an answer did come. It was thin with distance and twisted by echoing among the rockslides, yet I made it out clearly. It was the voice of Young Grass and what it told me was completely Indian, and particularly Apachean. "Go downhill," she shrilled, "or go to hell." Then, in a reedy croak of postscriptum that I held to be insufferably childlike in its Indian pride, "Young Grass and Josana are going to Cochise!"

Well, Zorra and I had to face it.

Go downhill or go to hell.

Mexican whores and half-breed priests weighed not a sucking pebble's gross in the Apache scale of human values. Zorra and I were worth less than two of those pony droppings the Mescalero hag had mentioned knowing by name throughout this southwest part of the Arizona Territory. But one thing I did know. Whatever we were worth right then, we would be worth considerably less come the new day, providing the Chiricahua caught us at Goat Eye Tank. Apache water was not priest water. Or whore water. I caught the eye of Zorra and nodded.

"Well, *mujer,*" I said, straightening as much as God had designed my backbones to permit, "let us go downhill. There is no visible trail, to be sure. However, I shall ask God to direct our progress. Perhaps he knows the way to Headstone."

"Downhill is better than hell," Zorra said. "You and God go ahead, padre. If he leads you over a cliff, I can always switch off and take the road to the other place. I understand that is downhill, too."

"Gird up your loins," I advised, starting out down the mountainside.

"You may be sure of that, Father Rat Filing," the insolent bawd replied, stumbling to come after me. "In my art, the ungirded loin earns a leper's fee."

"Be still," I commanded her. "Don't you ever think about anything but business?"

"Do you?" she answered succinctly.

I did not respond, but went sliding and falling down the rocky slot which I prayed was the trail to Headstone, Arizona. I knew Zorra followed me from her unmentionable cursing of the dark and body-bruising way. We continued the descent in excess of two brutal hours, coming out at last on a high, desolate bench overlooking a parched river valley out of which a wagon road climbed to pass along the bench southerly from our interception of it. In desperation we guessed this must be the route to the great new mining camp we sought.

"Praise His name," I panted to Zorra. "We are saved."

"You may be saved," she said. "I'm starved. Get out of my way, Nunez, I'm going into town and find work."

She did not wait, but set out at a doubled pace. Not relishing the dark and windy bench, I hobbled after her. And in this fashion, at three *ante meridiem,* in the hour just before moon set, we came to the fabled bonanza diggings of the Schieffelin Ledge, at Headstone, Arizona.

11
DOOMED IN TOMBSTONE JAIL

Approaching it, we saw the mining settlement to be in a state of high disturbance. It was lighted by lantern, lamp, torch, and bonfire. At first we believed it to be burning, and we commenced to run, fearful to find it in ashes. Drawing yet closer, we saw that people by the hundreds were in the dusty streets. Riders galloped the main thoroughfare. Men on foot crowded, shouted, cursed, and bellowed in senseless laughter. The air being restless, as it is at three in the morning, and set in our direction, we could smell the raw stink of the Anglo whiskey. Coming shortly to the town's outer edge, we made halt to consider our course. By chance we crouched beneath a large, poorly carpentered sign nailed to an ancient yucca stalk.

"Aha, Nunez," Zorra said. "Does it say Headstone?"

I glanced up. Of course the sign did not read Headstone. Rather, it proclaimed the place to be Tombstone. Charra Baca had been correct. I admitted this graciously to my companion. The maid of Fronteras was forgiving.

"*Mierda,* priest," she laughed. "What does it matter who is right about the name? We have found the place."

"A true thing," I agreed. "Now what?"

Zorra frowned quickly at the query.

"Listen, Nunez," she said, "here we part. It cannot help me in my business to be seen with a priest. Nor will it help the priest, either. So, good-bye. I hope you find your gold."

She departed my side before I might say her aye or nay. I called after her, but I had served my purpose in finding for her the new mining camp with its many rich Americanos. For another moment I shivered under the unpainted boards of the sign, then plucked up my

32

brown robes and scuttled after my onetime housekeeper of Casas Grandes. However, she had already outdistanced me. Nor would she respond to my cries. By the time I had taken to cursing her for abandoning me, I had come into the principal avenue of Tombstone, Arizona.

After that, I was given no opportunity to search for the foster-mother of Charra Baca. It was all I might do to save my own situation. Indeed, to preserve my life.

Within ten strides of the thoroughfare, I was run down by a four-horse hitch of freight animals. The wagon they drew passed over my body, but God lay with his servant in the cold mud of Allen Street. Tottering up, I was again knocked down, this time by a yowling Anglo horseman, fair into the noxious garbage of the gutter. Finally, I was chased up onto the whipsawn lumber walkway of the street, by the arrival of the Tucson stage. Here, with remaining dizzied strength, I fell behind an alley rain barrel.

This oak-staved sanctuary proved to be an unexpected confessional. From its harbor, I was able to eavesdrop on the streetside populace and to learn, all swiftly, the nature of the mortal sin that Tombstone planned.

Hearing it, I forgot my bruises.

This was not a joyous crowd that coursed the raw dirt roadway of the new camp; it was a mob: a mob that intended soon to take from the town jail a poor blackamoor of no means and no defense and to hang him by the neck! His crime, you ask? The excuse, rather, the mob gave to itself for murder most foul? Military desertion. And ten years past!

But the truth, the real reason—ah, God forgive them.

They were not going to take the "nigger," as they called him, from Tombstone Jail to kill him out of racial anger. He would not hang because he was a black man, which he was. Neither were they going to hang him for an army deserter, which he also and as surely was. They were going to "take the black bastard out and stretch him" because he had been that day apprehended riding with the Apaches.

Yes, he had been caught in the company of six Mexican hostiles and a lone New Mexican bronco. The "nigger Apache" had been captured when a stray bullet knocked him off his pony in a running rifle fight over near the Fort Huachuca ammunition depot. The Mexican Apaches had made their escape when their black comrade was shot. They were last seen riding south. Two of them were holding up the sagging form of the American *bronco* brother. The pursuing Huachuca troops reported that the American Apache appeared to be fatally struck.

At these final words, a chill came over me. I shrank farther behind the alley barrel. God save us, that was my black soldier Flicker they had in Tombstone Jail. And it was my Apache godson Kaytennae whom the troops had seen being carried, dying, from the field at Huachuca dump.

Was Kaytennae already dead somewhere in the freezing darkness along the retreat of the Mexican wild ones?

Would brave Flicker indeed be hanged before the sun came to warm the corpse of slim Kaytennae?

What, now, of the gold of El Naranjal and the Apache church that gold was to have built in the Sierra Madre? Was that dream also dead? Shot by the rifle bullet that had killed Kaytennae? Strangled by the hempen noose that would murder Robert E. Lee Flicker?

The questions coursed my mind without answers. I cowered deeper yet behind the rain barrel off Allen Street. I turned my face to Heaven. "Lord God of Hosts," I pleaded, "can you not send your twisted, unfrocked priest of Casas Grandes one more miracle to go with the map of El Naranjal? Let me pray and let thee answer me."

I stepped from behind the barrel into full view of the passing vigilante citizens of Tombstone. Kneeling in the mud of the roadway, I commenced aloud my litany in the Latin of my calling. I had scarcely begun the prayer when the Lord my God took action, sending two rude bullies of the town to come upon me from the rear.

My accosters bore large fowling pieces with the barrels cut off short, and each wore a star-shaped medallion of pewter marking him an officer of the civil law.

"Why, lookee hyar, Belcher," announced the first of them, a keg-bellied lout with greasy blond hair and the moustaches of an Eskimo walrus. "See what we done caught us." He raised me out of the mud. "I ain't see'd one in brown fur afore, but I reckon he's a mackerel snapper priest all the same. Ain't he, Belcher?" he frowned, worried.

Belcher, a lank brute, mean and dirty as a buried bone, was an educated man. "He's a Friscan'," he said proudly. "I see'd a hull passel of them in Californy. They ain't the power of the blackbird ones, but they're good enough for a nigger Cathlick, I reckon. Lower him down, Crench."

Crench set me once more on the ground, where I commenced to protest in English against the rough handling.

Belcher was impressed with my command of his tongue but was not to be turned from the mission on which his superior had dispatched Crench and himself. "Sorry, padry," he said, "but we got us a rush on. Nigger up to the jail's got about a half hour to live. Nigger knows it and asked the marshal for a priest. Marshal Karper, being a Christian man, said as long as we couldn't save the black son of a bitch's life, it was only fair to give the Lord a crack at saving his soul. You agree, padry?"

I nodded, standing to my full five feet.

"We are all sons of the same Father," I answered the hulking churl. "Black or brown, or even white. I am ready to go with you."

Both scowled hard at me. They seemed to realize they had heard something wrong, but they were unable to ferret it out in such short time. "All right," Belcher said. "March."

So it was they took me up Allen Street to confess the sins and clear the soul of the deserter American cavalryman, Robert E. Lee Flicker, doomed in Tombstone Jail.

And so it was that God sent me my other miracle.

12
CELL OF THE MAD DOG

The deputies of Tombstone conducted me rudely up the slough of despond. The mud of Allen Street sucked at my sandaled feet and my priestly spirit. It seemed that every misbegotten seeker after the silver metal whom God had ever created was obstructing our passage. The church, never popular in *Estados Unidos,* was fair sport. To see one of its servants humbled in arrest fired the populace. Nunez was hooted at, even spat upon. But he endured. Even elevated himself.

Such human curs would snap at the robes of Christ; I strode among them as a maned lion in the company of hairless jackals.

At the *juzgada,* my escorts cudgeled the rabble back from me with their fowling pieces. They would barrel whip them or jam muzzles, end on, into gut or kidney. The beast people fell away and we were safely through the plank doors of the prison.

My gasp of relief was premature.

God's name, the foul air of the place was unbreathable. We had come into a human zoo. The five cells visible to me were one *vara,* one pace, by two. Into each of these tiny cages as many as six captives were pushed and sealed by the strap-iron doors. There were no apparent provisions for defecation or urination. A single, sickly lantern lit the place into a half-darkness from whence issued the moanings, coughs, laughings, and puling and puking revulsions of the damned who were trapped therein. It was as a pesthouse in a time of plague.

There seemed in my view but one illumination of pride. Most of the inmates appeared to be Anglos, not my people. I made to inquire of the deputies about this.

"Oh, hell, reverend," Crench said, "we don't jail Mexes, we shoot 'em."

To which Deputy Belcher testified gravely, "Matter of record, padry. You're the fust greaser been in here."

Taking evasive measure, I demanded forcefully to see the doomed black man who had asked for a priest. For answer, Belcher, who seemed senior to Crench, said he would need to talk to the marshal about that. This he did by turning to a closed door and bawling, "Karper, come out! We got us your mackerel snapper priest hyar!"

The door flew open but no man emerged.

From the oblong of brighter lamplight within the revealed office, a strident voice fell, however.

"Damn you, Belcher," it stated. "How many times must I tell you it's *Marshal* Karper."

"Well, marshal, I reckon nobody knows better'n you that it ain't easy to remember it."

"Ha, ha!" Deputy Crench guffawed in support. "It sure ain't. Easier by a site to recollect otherwise!"

The voice of the marshal of Tombstone came again in menace. It held itself in that thin control that madmen affect, which of course renders them so dangerous. When the voice paused in its quiet violence, the senior deputy said, "Sure enough, marshal. You want to see this runt Mex padry we brang in?"

"No, the nigger wants to see him, you fool."

"He still in the pit? The nigger?"

"No, I had to move him. The dog was at him too much."

"Where's he at, then, the nigger?"

"I've got him safe, don't fret it. Just shove the padre in any cell you can. I got to get this thing figured out. That mob is set to batter in here any minute."

Belcher frowned into the oblong of light from the marshal's office. "Thought you wanted them to bust in," he said, "so's you could feed them the nigger."

"Yeah," Deputy Crench recalled. "You said thataway it wouldn't matter the nigger had maybe recognized you."

"I didn't say he had maybe recognized me; I said

he gave me a funny look. It twinged me somehow."

"Funny looks don't mean nothing," Belcher frowned. "Nigger didn't say anything, did he, marshal?"

"No, not a word. No name, nothing. Wouldn't talk."

"And you don't recollect him? Not from nowhere?"

"Never saw him before in my life. But it was funny, no matter. Like he'd never seen me either, but knew me anyhow."

"Well, then, play it safe," Belcher said. "Let them drunks out in Allen Street have the black bastard. We got too good a thing going hyar, marshal. Ain't nobody ever going to think to look for *you* wearing a lawman's star." Belcher tightened his grip on my arm. "What you want did with the padry? Hadn't we oughter quieten him, too?"

The deputies could see the man to whom they spoke, but I could not. Yet I felt a deepening fear of that voice, a fear out of the past. Who was this lawman in the inner office who was afraid that Flicker might know who he truly was? And whose cold voice stirred memories of terror in me?

Dear God, could it be the one ghoul of hell with cause to remember both the black deserter and myself?

I rejected the possibility.

Yet the voice twanging on in converse with the deputies would not permit me the escape.

It held an undeniable Mexican accent to its *Tejano* nasals. I was a master of tongues. No man could deceive Nunez on the dialects of the *monte*. This marshal, whatever his Texas speech or even breeding, had been born in Mexico.

I thought it again. My God it could be him. Still, it must not be. He was dead, and ten years dead.

Deputy Belcher leaned farther into the opening of the office door. "All right, marshal," he said, "but you ain't said what you want did with the padry here. Not sensible, you ain't. Shoving him in one of these front cells won't shut his mouth, nor his eyes neither."

"I got to think," Marshal Karper snapped.

"How about putting him in with the dog?" Belcher suggested. "Mebbe he could faith heal the mutt."

Something bothered me in this dog proposal. What

was a dog doing in the prison's punishment cell? Here was a second mention of the dog business, and I didn't care for it.

Crench helped me out. "Aw, you couldn't do thet," he objected. "Put the little feller in the pit? With that there slobber-sick dog? Thet ain't funny, Belcher."

"No, by God, it isn't!" cried Marshal Karper. "But it's a hell of an idea. Pitch him in there, Belcher. And for Christ's sake don't let the goddamn dog slip out past you. Doc Flett hasn't been over to see him yet. Happen he gets loose on the camp, and—well, just watch sharp you don't let him out. Hydraphoby isn't something you want spread around."

"Maybe he ain't got it," Crench offered helpfully.

"You fool," answered Karper. "That's why I got Doc coming over to look at him. I'm not going to blow his head off 'fore I know he's rabbied for certain."

"Hell no," Belcher agreed. "He's the best dog we done ever had to warn the gang of strangers or thieves."

"Yeah," said honest brute-man Crench. "We didn't never lose a single sack of hair with old Loafer guarding our fire. And him a cripple like you, reverend."

Karper's voice raged at the fool to be still, but it was too late. Hair? Sacks of hair? *Quita!* these *were* scalpers parading as lawmen in Tombstone, Arizona. And not just any scalpers. God save me; it *was* him in there beyond the oblong of brighter lamplight.

But memory is a street upon which men walk both ways.

As my mind went back, so did his in the office.

I saw his shadow move in there. Then his voice came to me. "Padre?" he said, in his hard-accented Spanish of the *monte. "Padre Jorobado?"*

It was the moment. I wrenched free of Deputy Belcher.

"Yes," I answered him. "The crippled priest of Casas Grandes. And that is you, Santiago. The bastard son of your bastard father."

He was coming to the office door now. I heard him moving. I saw the gaunt figure framed in the oblong of lampshine made by the partially opened door. He was there, staring out at me. From some unknown well of forgotten courage, I drew a reckless draft of anger against him. Perhaps God spoke through me.

"Damn your soul to eternal basting in the winds of hell, Santiago Kifer," I said to him. "You need have no fear that the black man will disclose you. I, Nunez, will do it for him."

He was emerged from the lampshine, then, standing over me in the outer corridor of the cells, menacing as the shade of Satan that he was. I marked the skeletal features. The disfigured face where Allison's pistol ball had shot it partly away. The remnant of the right ear, mummified. The long black coat, the black string cravat, and the narrow-striped *pantalones* of American design did not cover the horror of my remembering. Nor did the star of pewter metal snagged on the flowered vestlet hold ought of decent meaning for me. This was no brave Arizona marshal, no duly employed mining camp officer of the law. I knew this harpy eagle of the *monte*. He was who he was.

The devil eyes flamed at me. There was death in them. He knew I threatened his place here, perhaps his very life. He half drew the great pistol at his belt, and I believed he would sunder me with shot where I stood defying him. But he stayed the trigger's pressure.

The cells had come alive. The discussion of Crench and Belcher and the marshal's harried answers had caught the attention of the brute fellow prisoners of the vanished Flicker. Caged or not, these were witnesses. To ignore them—after what they may have heard of my charge to the lawman they knew as Tombstone marshal Henry Karper—was not Santiago Kifer's skulking way. He would kill me and still my tongue, yes. But not in front of witnesses whose number must contain camp citizens of good repute when sober. Kifer's hand fell away from the Texas pistol.

"Padre," I heard him say, "my deputies brought you here for a noble purpose, to ease the last moments of one of your faith. I can't let you in to see him now, for you are surely drunk, or daft, or both. I have not heard the name you call me, while my own good name is known from the Pecos Valley to San Diego. Henry

Karper has a reputation beyond reproach. Ask these beauties back of the bars how many of them Henry Karper has sent to Yuma Prison!"

There was an animal growling of hatred from the cells. Its nature affirmed what the marshal had said. These men, some of the more desperate of them, knew Henry Karper to be what Santiago Kifer said he was: a law officer of hard but certain repute in that abandoned land. Nonetheless, I was determined that this terrible mistake in a man's true identity should not be continued where Alvar Nunez might yet shout *I accuse!* against him.

Somewhere, somehow, in the intervening years, Kifer had changed himself in outward form. His air, his dress, even his crude speech of former times had been elevated. The alteration was amazing. The man was more than merely dangerous; he was a consummate artist of evil. But I knew him still—and he seemed to read my threatening thoughts.

His instant solicitude for a poor priest of Casas Grandes was a masterstroke of mummery. "I will tell you what, good father," he said to me, deliberately loud enough to reach the listening prisoners. "There's a cot in the corner of my office. Come in and sleep it off, then we'll talk."

He took my arm, but I whirled free of him to cry out to the pitiful wretches beyond to remember the name I had called this murderous masquerader—Santiago Kifer—and to bear it to the good people of the camp. "They will remember him," I shouted. "They must; this man is not Marshal Henry Karper!"

The prisoners shouted back angered, it seemed to me, but I could not be certain if in agreement or derision.

"Take him," snapped Kifer to Crench and Belcher, but again I managed to elude immediate silencing arrest.

"Brave friends!" I cried once more to the prisoners. "Find and free the poor black man. He will tell you that I say the truth. This man *is* Santiago Kifer. He is own-son to Dutch John Kifer. Bear this news to the camp on your release. Announce it on every street corner. Advertise it in each cantina, each tent of fallen woman."

Kifer lunged for me and missed. My wrongly shaped spine gave me a spider's deceiving speed of scuttle.

"Goddamn it!" he hissed at the deputies. "Take him!"

Crench and Belcher leaped for me. I went sideways as some tarantula in the robes of a Franciscan, another benefit of the humpen bones. The hulking deputies came together with a rattling crunch of their big bodies. I had an instant's freedom remaining.

"Bear my message to the people!" I exhorted the now shouting and threatening prisoners. "If you do, it will not be an innocent black man they rope upon that monstrous gibbet the devil built in Allen Street. It will be this one, this murderer who is not Henry Karper but Santiago Kifer, the Scalper of Sonora! Hang him high—!"

Now my time was done. Kifer hurled the deputies aside with his enormous sinewed power. He had me like a poor crippled rat. One hairy paw sealed my mouth, the other gripped my habit at the nape. He was arage.

"Fling open the pit!" he hissed at the stupefied deputies, keeping his voice in a white-faced whisper so that none of the cell-caged witnesses might hear. "Don't you understand yet that this damned hunchback could get us all swung?"

Crench and Belcher leaped belatedly for the door of the pit. This was a separate cell. It had no bars. Only a slab door similar to those of the animal pits beneath the Colosseum of Rome. The barrier, grating on rusted hinges, was wrenched back. Into its blind maw I was flung as a bag of shelled corn. The deputies slammed the door so forcibly and so close behind me that I was hurled by it against the far wall of the noisome hole.

The impact dizzied me; for a moment my mind ranged away and I did not recall the condition of my danger.

Then I heard it.

It was a low slobbering growl, the most terrifying sound of a life's experience on the frontier. The hoarseness of it, the fearful strangling in the throat, the unnatural croaking, all were classic. We saw too much of hydrophobia in my *parroquia* not to know the dread sound of it when manifested.

Particularly in a sealed pit but five feet in circumference and airless as the crypt of Lazarus.

My throat spasmed. The breath would not move within me. The carotid vessels of my neck swelled as to burst in rupture. It was sheer human terror.

And then the brute thing licked me.

13
I FIND OUR WATCHGUARD

When the dog licked me, my heart stopped.

I knew the saliva of a rabid animal was as deadly as the bite itself. Even more, in that it might enter some tiny scratch or pinprick of the skin, causing later death to some poor wretch who imagined he would survive. Such things were not in the general knowledge of the times, of course. But it must be remembered that we Franciscans were the patron order of the animals of the earth. And so we knew much of them, as we did of medicine, thank God and Saint Francis.

However, that is the calmness of memory.

In the dread fact of the moment, I felt the animal's fetid breath and drooling jaws come against my face. I remembered at the same time that past night on the mountain trail over the Dragoons. I winced again to the slash of the sharp branch that had laid open my cheek. The same cheek now laved by the mad creature's slathering tongue.

Fear almost broke my mind.

But the Saint of Assisi was by my side. The teeth of the brute did not rend my flesh. The hoarse growl and strangulated breathing receded for a skipping of three heartbeats. In their place came a sound that lit the dungeon as by a candle to Saint Francis.

The dog whined.

And its frightened weight pressed against me there in the blindness of the pit, its paw sought and found my hand, and it whimpered again, pleadingly. I felt the movement of its tail and heard its weakened thumping on the earthen floor. God's name, this dog was not crazed, except that he was driven so by hurt. Into my physician's mind came the one possible condition that might simulate the terrible disease of hydrophobia.

In writing of the symptomology centuries gone, Hippocrates had noted that the victim's behavior was the same as if the animal had caught a bone in its throat which then caused its growl to issue with that hollow fearsomeness, that lobar hoarseness, so dreadly familiar to the physician experienced in the actual disease itself. Once this pronounced croaking is heard, death is the only and imminent end.

The great physician of the island of Cos might have added, if indeed he did not: unless, of course, the poor brute did verily lodge a bone in its bedeviled throat.

Gathering myself, I addressed the dog.

"Friend Loafer," I said to it, recalling the cognomen from outer mention, "be you of good faith, and do not bite me. You may yet be restored of life, as was Lazarus from among the rocks of Calvary." I felt for the jaws and forced them carefully apart. "This is my hand I give you in trust. Use it well."

With that, I was down the agonized throat of the animal, and, the power of my order being with me, I found the obstruction with the last, desperate straining of my reaching fingertips. Hooking the object, I was able to turn it and bring it forth only because of a vast expelling urge by the animal itself. The big fangteeth raked my arm unavoidably. My blood mingled with that of the pitiful creature's torn throat. But the gasp of its life flooding back into the wasted body was a fee greater than any ever paid ordained doctor.

I threw both arms about Loafer and held him to my breast. He could not even whine now, so violated were the tissues of his gullet and voice box. But he could still speak to me. I heard clearly the grateful thumping of the tail, weakly spasmodic, yet, but telling Father Nunez that friend Loafer would live.

And so would Father Nunez!

"Perro," I said to him, "could I but thump my tail, its joy would outdo yours. Let us both pray."

The dog mumbled something from its tortured throat and relaxed its great head upon my shoulder. I cast up my eyes to the blackness above but do not recall what prayer I framed, if any. Sleep, the mother of all restorers, claimed us two travelers from afar.

I do not know what thoughts Loafer dreamed of me.

But I knew a fact of him before slumber drugged my weary bones and Morpheus eased my pain.

Among the company manifest or list of members needed for the dangerous, distant journey to seek the gold of El Naranjal, I had found my dog to guard our camp.

14
A LIFE FOR A LIFE

I must have dozed but briefly.

When I awakened, it was to sounds of clamor beyond the oak-and-iron door of the pit. Where the light would not filter nor the air of life enter but tricklingly, it seemed the noises of the outer jail seeped into the pit alarmingly. At first, my companion and I shared a common wonderment, I am certain. The dog woofed and sniffed. The priest of Casas Grandes sniffed and all but woofed. What the devil? Were they at last hanging poor Flicker? Had the outer *juzgada* fallen? Was the mob within the gates? Would its frenzied members release the little cleric in the solitary-punishment dungeon? Or might I be permitted by oversight in the excitement to languish my life away in that foul pit? *Quita!*

Well, I had the dog.

I clung to the animal as if he presented some connection with life greater than my own. Loafer responded by burying his heavy snout beneath my arm. It was as if he didn't care to listen. Or, even in that darkness, to see.

But another sense would not so easily be covered.

Suddenly, the dog was snorting like a frightened horse and snuffling at some alien odor that had come into our stale-aired hole. Then even I could smell it.

Smoke.

Dear Jesus, the *idiotas* had fired the jail!

Almost with the thought, I smelled the raw taint of coal oil mixed with the stifle of the smoke, and I knew the truth. Arson. The mob had decided to burn down the clapboard and adobe-shelled jail. The walls would stand, but all within them—if not released from the cells—would roast in the standing.

More sounds of desperation from the outside.

Above all the voices, I could hear a clear, strong baritone-bass which I remembered from the past. It was the deep roll of Flicker's rich African tones. My soldier chief was alive! And not only living, but in command out there. Of what? Not the entering mob, surely. Then it struck me. The black American renegade had somehow broken free of his special prison and was leading the inmates in revolt. It had been done in a manner to panic the jail staff and frustrate the hanging pack outside. Fire. The military use of the oldest weapon. Flicker had set that Tombstone Jail on fire. I knew it on pure impulse. Flicker, the master soldier. The artilleryman. The sapper. The arsonist. The black genius who had gone wrong because of being wronged. The bastard! The wonderful, wild, untamable African Apache! He was burning us free.

But wait.

He did not know Nunez was in Arizona, let alone in the dark pit of the Tombstone jail. And who would tell him so? Not Santiago Kifer, God knew. Not that wickedness masquerading as Marshal Henry Karper. And not his two henchmen deputies. Wherever they were, these three would not be moving to save a hunchbacked half-breed priest who could identify their leader as the scourge of God that he was—Santiago Kifer, the Scalper of Sonora.

I coughed on the thickening smoke, reached to find the dog, and he was gone from my side.

I commenced to yell at lungs' uttermost burst.

I shrieked for help in Spanish, English, Latin, Greek, Low Deutsch, French, the biblical Hebrew, and no less than four of the five main Apache Indian dialects.

Nothing came back to me, even of echo, from outside.

There was, however, something of echo from within the choking pit.

The dog was whining imperatively over across the chamber, and clods of earth were being flung through the blind dark to strike me in a veritable fusillade on face and breast. It came to me that Loafer had chosen an unseemly time to bury the bone that I had removed from his ingrate throat. Moreover, he had now added insult to the hurt by directing his digging into my gasping face. Even strangling on the clot of smoke now solid within the pit, I uttered a curse on the mongrel.

For answer, Loafer gave me back an eager but demanding "Whoof!" and a whine that said, in any language, *Hurry, fool human being! Follow me!*

In the instant of this strange transmittal from the mangy brute, I smelt a great gush of fresh sweet air. With it came some luminous gray of lesser darkness, let in by the same hole Loafer had dug through the dirt wall of the pit. Merciful Christ, the creature had saved us. Air, light, and the just-vanishing hairy quarters of a huge dog disappearing, butt on, into the seeming solid earth led me to leap after Loafer.

The exit he had made was small. But he was a large *perro* and I a very small *hombre*. I became stuck in midpassage but seized Loafer's tail, crying him on. The brute responded with a surge, and we both came spilling out of the solitary pit into a larger cavern beyond it.

Instantly, the sweet fresh air of first release became of a stench to suffocate life. Struggling to surface, arms desperately wound about the dog, I broke free of the substance with a mighty Anglo shout.

They had a word, the Anglo did, like none other in

any tongue. It expressed all of the human experience in just four eloquent letters. Its sibilance had no peer in the languages of all earth's lands. I employed it now, roundly, nobly, and as if on an instinct that had no reason to exist within a Mexican *mestizo* priest.

"Shit!" I screeched, long and bawlingly.

And so it was.

The splendid Loafer had tunneled us out into the *letrina* of the Tombstone jail.

15
SOLDIERS THREE, AND A TALL BAY HORSE

Many a different face may be put upon misfortune. The humility of crawling forth from a *juzgada* cesspool can in no real degree be forgotten. The dog and I were excremented lepers, offal-clad pariahs, call us what seems worst. Yet in the moment of our emergence we went unwinded by the populace. Even we ourselves were whelmed over by the greater tragedy; the Tombstone jail was a belching inferno of pillared flame.

We stood in the rear prisonyard.

To our right was a lean-to that housed the saddle mounts of those officers on duty. The four animals presently stalled therein, rope-tied to steel manger bars, were in a state of terror. Left as they were, they would surely burn to death or burst their hearts in lunging. Crying out for Saint Francis to attend me, I ran for the lean-to to free them. I was too late.

From the street a great uproar of shouting arose.

Around the jail a torrent of the townfolk poured in pursuit of three desperately fleeing men. In an instant all would be upon me. The thought broke like lightning in my mind that the runners were Santiago Kifer and his ugly deputies. I could see the Winchester rifle that Kifer carried and the shotguns of Crench and Belcher. Did they see me escaped and standing there, I was a dead man. Even pursued by the mob, such villains never permitted witnesses against them to live. Left with no other refuge, I leaped into the great iron stock tank beside the lean-to, submerging myself in the murk of its mossy waters. When I could hold my breath no more, I surfaced. The three devils were just swinging to saddle inside the lean-to. Even as I gasped for air, they pounded past me in their rush for freedom, scattering the people who tried to block them off.

Some gunfire popped and spat in the morning grayness.

The fugitives did not return it but drove their horses safely away into the shadows of the false dawn.

The angered townfolk shouted back and forth in their frustration at losing the guilty quarry. Western Anglo folk set vast store by their law officers. To be betrayed by a man like Kifer, to have hired a wanted criminal for their chief official, was an embarrassment calling for vengeance. Overhearing their outrage from my hiding place in the horse trough was a boon from God. It informed me of events vital to my own immediate survival.

Flicker and his escaping fellow prisoners had faithfully conveyed to the townspeople my accusations against the man masquerading as famed Marshal Henry Karper. This the prisoners had miraculously managed to do while still making good their own flight. Here the good Lord had also augmented Flicker's efforts to aid the freed felons. Flames from the jail fire, driven by freshening winds, had leaped to the newly erected hangman's scaffold in the middle of Allen Street. In subsequence, the very gibbet from whence the citizens had planned to "dangle the nigger" had gone up with a roar and vasty rush of whirled embers. Its fall had revealed Santiago and his deputies hiding beneath its platform, from whence they had dashed for the prison stable.

Now, as the crowd yet milled before the burning gibbet, a man came crying from Allen Street that some of his fellows and himself had "got the nigger cornered." They had worked this wonder of raw courage when the black man stopped to cover the escape of his fellow prisoners.

Flicker seemed doomed. He had seized a gun from the marshal's office, but the crowd believed him out of ammunition for it now. He was acower inside the hastily emptied San Pedro Saloon, across from the jail. The mob had front and rear exits covered. It remained only for some hero to fill himself with courage from the bottle and so lead the rush to "go in and get the black bastard out."

The vision of the untamable Flicker driven to earth by such peasants was a desperate one for me. I could not accept it. *Quita!* this noble savage must not die thus trapped in the house of degeneracy called San Pedro Saloon. But what might I, a man of peace, perform of rescue or salvation? God would need to answer that for me, and for dauntless Flicker.

Wondrously, He did so.

From the burning lean-to issued the piteous screaming neigh of the last, forgotten horse.

Sweet Jesu! a horse.

If a king might save his realm or lose it for want of such animal, why not Nunez?

That saddled mount in there represented the last best chance brave Flicker had to enter the Kingdom of Heaven another day than this one dawning now over Tombstone.

"Caballo, caballo!" I cried. "Nunez comes—!"

Leaping from the stock tank, I ran dripping into the furnace of the lean-to.

I do not understand to the present day if it were the shield of water-soaked habit, the luck of the damned foolish, the work of Saint Francis, or some capricious trick of Lucifer. But I was permitted to reach the terrified brute unscathed of flame. I was even able to free the animal and mount myself upon it with but casual scorches. As I tried to turn the beast, however, it went mad beneath me. The roar of the fire reached for us.

Here, a thing of fate obtained.

A spark storm, created by the intense heat, sucked the flames upward in a tower of ascending embers. The resulting vacuum momentarily cleared the area about the horse, and the creature could see the shed exit beckoning. Wildly, it lunged to escape, clearing the lean-to in one mighty crouching bound. I, burred as a Texas fever tick to the old *Tejano* saddle, perforce went with it.

We alighted running and, behind us, as we did, I heard the crash of the lean-to falling back into the vacuum. Fearing to look over shoulder, I fought desperately for the loose reins of my mount. Again, my fates were watchful. I found the bridle lines. Gathering them in, I was able to force the horse leftward through the scattering onlookers and so around the burning jail. In another few jumps, I had his head.

Into the firelit pandemonium of Allen Street I drove the creature, setting him with last strength toward the doors of the San Pedro Saloon. In truth, I held shut my eyes then. I do not recall a single instant of the passage of the crowd in front of the place, nor the shattering splitting of the wooden doors. I did hear my mount neigh shrilly and felt him take a hurtling jump as if to clear a last obstacle. Then we were both inside the San Pedro, with black Flicker hauling down the rearing horse with one hand and snatching me safely to floor from the brute's convulsing back with the other. Here, my mind was returning to me some little.

I saw that it was dark of lantern or lampshine within the cantina, that Flicker was alone and defended only by the outer mob's fear of him. His very voice echoed the last controls of desperation.

"Quién es? Quién es?" he repeated hoarsely, at the same time dragging me nearer to him to peer at what his hand had caught. He saw, then, that it was a servant of Rome, and not just any such.

"Nombre Dios!" he said to me. "You!"

He threw back that handsomest of heads. The broad black chest glistened of sweat and incredible musculature there in the ghostlight of the last saloon that these two men would drink in, in that life. Flicker boomed out his bass and glorious laugh, a sound such as I think none other had ever heard from his black lips. "You!" he roared again. "I shouted to God to send me help, and instead he delivered me you!"

"You're forgetting the *caballo!*" I said angrily. "God's Blood, can you tell me you can't use a horse!"

Flicker looked at me. He tightened his grip on the bridle reins of the shivering tall bay horse. One black hand snaked to the bar and returned with a bottle of Old Crow American bourbon whiskey. He smashed off the neck of the bottle against the wood of the bar's top.

"Here," he said to me, offering the ragged beaker, aspill. "Make it a deep pull, padre. Just leave a little for me."

I took the whiskey from him and drained four fiery gulps of it into my shaking and empty belly. Taking back the bottle, black Flicker gulped strongly of it, threw it with a crash through the long mirror behind the hardwood of the bar. In the same sweep of movement he was up on the horse and had hoisted me to cantle saddle skirt behind him. The horse crouched and squealed to the double weight, and Flicker wrenched its head about to face the outer street. "Hang on," was all he said to me, and he drove the tall horse forward.

The great bay window of the San Pedro Saloon was the only piece of glass its size within another thousand miles of San Francisco. Once United States Army lieutenant Robert E. Lee Flicker leaped our gallant mount through the window's precise center pane with a crash and splinter that showered its shards and slivers for a hundred *varas* across Allen Street. The crowd panicked, shouting and falling over itself. The magnificent bay horse wheeled to the left and thundered away, showering a blizzard of glass bits behind it. Out of the fires of that Gehenna that had so nearly burned us all, the big bay bore its clinging riders southward into the sage. All in the minute of the window's crashing, we were free of Tombstone, Arizona. And thank a forgiving God for that.

I do not know if they ever rebuilt that jail. I heard there was a newer one in the courthouse on Toughnut Street. *No me importa un bledo,* I don't care. We got away from the only one we knew about, and no pursuit came after us.

The only living thing that followed us out of the disappearing town was a ragged apparition of a watch-guard dog who galloped with a halting gait but of a spirit noble as the desert wind. We cried old Loafer on, black Flicker and I, and we laughed to see him come with his outrageous limp and bid him welcome with the laugh to our entattered company.

Soldiers three we were, an army not to be accounted small for all our poverty of number, and but one horse to ride. Kingdoms have been won and lost with less.

16
SPINNING IN THE WIND

After perhaps a mile of double riding, Flicker surprisingly halted the tall bay horse. He got down from the animal and gave him over to me. I could not fathom his impulse and admitted it. He answered that by running afoot some distance, he would conserve the horse and encourage the dog, which was lagging badly.

"Aha!" I said, touched. "What a quaint gallantry."

Flicker was amused. "You black robes will see things as in a Bible story, always," he said. "Now an Apache understands life better than that. He would see that I am not truly succoring the dog but rather sparing the horse which might, in the end, save my own life."

"But you are not an Apache, Flicker."

"What am I, then, father?" he asked softly.

"A soldier," I insisted. "The finest I have seen."

"A *nigger* soldier," he said, more softly yet.

"*Pardiez!*" I snapped at him angrily. "The word comes ugly to my ear; I don't care for it."

Here, the dog caught up to us and reared its shaggy height to lick and muzzle at Flicker in gratitude. At the same time it uttered a doleful whimper, as if to agree to what it had overheard, coming up.

"You see, father," black Flicker laughed, "the dog doesn't care for the word either. Doubtless he's heard worse in his own direction, but a dog knows how a nigger feels. That's why they like us."

"*Absurdo!*" I snorted. "You are as bad as my housekeeper, Zorra. Always calling herself a whore."

"And is she one, father?"

"But of course."

"Then so am I a nigger."

"Damnation!" I protested. "If you will not call yourself black, or whore, or half-breed, the world will make its own estimate of you."

"Half-breed?" he frowned. "Where did that come in?"

"It came in with me; I am *mestizo*."

"Ah, yes, I had forgotten."

"That is because I do not continually remind all mankind of the mixture."

"And what does that leave you, finally, father?"

"A priest, Flicker."

"And I am still a soldier, eh?"

I nodded that this was so, and he frowned over it for five seconds. At last he returned my nod and asked, "Did I ever call you half-breed, father?"

I glared at him, offended. "Did I ever call you nigger, Flicker?"

The black deserter shook his leonine head, handsome as any Roman senator's. "You are saying, then, that we are two men, nothing more?"

"A little more, if you will have it: two friends."

Robert Flicker straightened at the words. He released the horse's cheek strap. The dark hand reached for mine. I gripped it hard, deeply wrought. As the grasp lingered, Flicker, by some instinct of his African huntsmen forebears, tensed suddenly. He swung away from me to stare back toward the north, whence we had come. I saw the wild black eyes narrow.

"Friend Nunez," he said, deep voice rumbling, "kick up your horse and whistle on your dog. Yonder comes the sun, and not alone."

I looked where he gestured. A group of many riders was moving out from Tombstone. They were not that far behind us, the members of that straggling clot of horsemen, that one failed to note the winking of the new sunlight along the barrels of the guns they carried. Thinly, we could hear the yelping of the riders, in cry. The vessels of my temples constricted.

"*Una fuerza*," I gasped. "*Una fuerza armada*."

"An accurate assessment," black Flicker said. "I would call that an armed posse, anywhere. Now who in the world do you suppose they can be after?"

"Ah!" I said. "They are chasing the evil Santiago!" Flicker spat to wet drying lips.

"Do you see Kifer and his two pals, father? Look all about now. Take your time. Who do you see that the posse also sees. Mark the direction that it comes."

I felt a sinking weakness of the belly.

"It is ourselves," I whispered. "The posse comes this way. It comes for us."

"It does," Flicker said.

He knotted his left hand in the leathers of my right-side stirrup. "Put the horse in a lope," he instructed me calmly. "I'll run by his side as long as I'm able. After that, you must go as long as you and the horse can. They won't forgive you, father. Kifer is only a murderer of women and children. But you! You tried to help a black man. You robbed them of stringing up their murdering nigger son of a bitch."

He glanced at the oncoming horde of Tombstoners.

"Now kick that horse the hell out of here like I told you," he ordered me. "Hee-yahh!" he shouted at the bay, when I hesitated. *"Vamos, caballo!"*

The tall horse responded, charging away through the shoulder-high juniper. Flicker stumbled, nearly went down, regained stride, and flew beside the galloping mount as though a part of the animal. Behind us, the ragged dog Loafer struggled at his lamed gait to follow our retreat. I soon lost sight of him in the dust raised by our horse's hammering pace. Neither could I longer see the Tombstone posse. But, ah! all too soon and plainly, we could *hear* it—talking to us with its guns.

The leaden messengers splashed the rocks about us, ricocheting off over the thinning junipers in whining tangent to our flight. Some fragmented themselves, hurling bits of searing lead as though of miniature grape or chain shot in all directions. Flicker, the tall bay horse, and myself were bleeding profusely within the first minute. I could not comprehend such unreasoning rage.

"God's name, Flicker!" I cried down to the straining black runner at my stirrup. "What is this monstrous wrong we've done? What mortal sin is ours that men will seek so desperately to kill us for it?"

Flicker's eyes were rolling. His tongue protruded blue and swollen as that of a dying Spanish fighting bull's. The great muscles of his limbs quivered in spasm. Only the command of his unbreakable will drove him onward. Yet he turned the agony of his face upward in gallant attempt to answer me. He could not. In the very moment of the effort, his stride broke staggeringly, the horse was virtually dragging him, and I knew our race was run. Rent in heart, I called upward to our Maker to let the black man and me die as comrades in the mercy of a common bullet. Amazingly, Flicker heard my cry.

I could not believe it as I looked down and saw that tortured bleeding face in a grin that triumphed upward through the dust and pain of our last steps.

"Pray harder for that easy bullet, Nunez," black Flicker gasped to me. "God might accommodate us. That bunch behind us never will. They'll swing us slow and leave us spinning till the rope unravels."

The crashing of the posse guns grew deafening. Powder flame and rifle smoke stabbed our very ears and stank to clot our nostrils. Yet Flicker had one more gasp, one more grin. And the answer to my anguished question.

"About that mortal sin of ours, father," he confessed. *"It's being us."*

17
BLACK APACHE MAGIC

I had imagined we were dead. The flashes and sounds of the posse's rifle fire were now so near as to blind the eye and deafen the hearing. Only the thick dust thrown up by the careening horses prevented our immediate blowing apart. But I had reckoned without the wily resources of black Flicker one more time. The Negro

Apache had learned well from his red foster people in the ten years he had lived among them.

With his vast strength, he vaulted now to the back of the tall bay horse, wresting its bridle reins away from me. As he did, I noted that two possemen riding furiously abreast had broken out of the dust cloud. They were no more than four jumps behind us, and Flicker had seen them before I did. "Down!" Flicker yelled at me. "Lie flat to the saddle!" I ducked low and, with a wrench that nearly broke the poor creature's neck, the black deserter swung the bay horse completely about face, spurring the animal in the reverse direction to which it had been running. The maneuver put the bay exactly facing and precisely between the oncoming rush of the two posse mounts. All three animals were on the gallop. The Tombstone riders could not, in that desperate fraction of time, get their animals halted or even slowed. As they met Flicker and the bay, they moved apart just enough to permit the bay to pass between them. As this happened, Flicker held out his two arms, bridle reins gripped in gleaming white teeth. He looked like some black crucifix of Satan. One might be forgiven to believe the two possemen had some similar thought, at least in retrospect. Flicker's arms caught each of them across the swallowing bones of the throat. The sickening impact lifted the two Tombstoners completely from their saddles, their horses thundering out from under them. For a moment they seemed to hang by their chins on the Negro's extended arms. Then Flicker let them drop. The last I saw of them, they were bouncing like rag dolls in the dust of their fellow riders.

Flicker was not through with his Indian work.

Again, he spun the tall bay in the Apache reverse. Again, he drove the panting mount between the fleeing, riderless horses of the unsaddled Tombstoners. But this time he came between the animals from the rear, and so their paces were equaled to our own mount's pace rather than opposed to it.

In result, we were running with a good saddled fresh horse on either side of our failing tall bay.

Before I might realize Flicker's demented intent, he

had seized me up under the arms, swept me off our bay, and jammed me into the saddle of the right-hand running horse. As quickly, he himself leaped to mount the left-hand riderless horse.

"Whip up! Whip up!" he yelled to me, booming out his deep laugh. "We have the bastards beat!"

In the dust and confused cross-firing of the posse, we did indeed make it away from the revengers from Tombstone, Arizona. I followed Flicker. The tall bay horse, running loose, chose to follow me. By a kindness of the Master, there appeared another follower, also.

This one was in seeming pursuit of the loose bay horse. How the rascal had arranged to stay with the bay in all of the shooting and shouting, we never did discover. But it was the wolfish dog Loafer, as you have little doubt surmised, and the ragged pariah was thus rejoined and the soldiers three made whole again.

We of course, as the Arizona folk said, "laid tracks away from there."

There remained a little nervous running to do before the rifle bullets lost their trajectory and only stung when they struck. But once given our new mounts, the mining camp riders were simply no match for black Flicker and his Mexican Apache training. By the time we had hit a side-canyon trail down into the valley of the San Pedro, it was over with.

Issuing from the narrow cleft far below, we could still see the cheated Tombstone riders clenching their fists after us and screaming down no-doubt terrible threats.

"Don't pay them any mind, padre," Flicker grinned. "A man of the cloth ought not to listen to such language." He clucked to his horse and we resumed the canter of our course toward the cottonwood and willow timber of the Rio San Pedro. "Besides," my companion concluded, "it was I who sent for a priest—not those ingrates."

The statement intrigued me, returning my mind to my arrest on the streets of Tombstone.

"You are not of the true faith, Flicker," I said. "I wondered at the time why I was called to tend your soul."

Flicker turned in the saddle, his easy expression gone. "I had a hidden knife. I meant to take whatever priest they sent me as hostage," he said. "When the jailer came to let the father out of my cell, I would put the knife at the priest's throat and kill him if the jailer refused us passage to freedom. Opening the cell door would also be the jailer's last memory of life, should he hesitate or call out."

"It is difficult for me to accept this, Flicker," I protested. "An innocent human life, even two, for your own freedom?"

"You are forgetting the words of your Master," he reminded me. " 'All that a man has, will he give for his life.' "

"Yes, yes, I know. But, damn it, Flicker. You would have killed even me, your friend from the old times?"

"I don't know, father. You saved my life ten years ago. But if one of us had to die—well, I don't know."

"You know. You could not have done it."

"Your damned religion again," Flicker said. "Always imagining that others follow those ridiculous rules set down in that black book you carry so fondly."

He had reminded me that I still had my buckskin traveler's bag fastened to my crucifix belt. The thought raised up my spirits.

"Halt your mount, comrade!" I cried to the black deserter. "You were inspired to think of my book. It has a special content even you may profit by."

We were just without the sanctuary of the river brush, but my companion indulgently brought his horse to stand. I fished among the treasures of my belt bag and produced the Bible. "Herein lies a secret of the Scriptures unrevealed to no other man than yourself," I said. Let its confidence now be a measure in your mind of my regard." With that, I opened the hollowed-out Bible and extracted from it my flat bottle of grape brandy.

The flask was three-quarters full, and Flicker received its sacrament with gratitude. He left a lipful for me, and I drained it hastily. The black Apache renegade smiled.

"Father Nunez," he said, wiping mouth with back of sweated, dust-grimed hand, "God bless you till you're properly promoted. Let's get to the river. That grape of yours requires a benediction of water. Phew!"

He turned his horse for the willows. I put my mount to following. Far across the flats behind us a doleful howl echoed. It was old Loafer crying, Wait for me! Flicker and I only laughed and went on into the trees.

We would have done grimly better to await the dog.

Being with us, Loafer most surely would have smelled out the menace ambushed ahead. Perhaps, even from across the flat, he had scented the danger. Possibly, his doleful wail had been a warning, not a plea to tarry for his laggard approach. No matter. Man only proposes. The Holy Spirit disposes. And in that triumphant moment that Flicker and I rode laughing through the river brush, the Holy Spirit had disposed to our dire peril.

Someone had come to the Rio San Pedro before us.

18
FIGURES IN A STILL LAGOON

We broke free of the willows. Our horses halted suddenly, throwing heads and pointing ears. Before us lay the Rio San Pedro. And something more.

The river slowed just here. The long sweep of its bend formed an island spit half-mooned by a lagoon where an old channel had been. Cottonwoods and desert sycamores stood lordly there. The water ran purling over pebbled and bedrock bottom, clear as morning sky. In the lagoon's placid mirror I could see the drift of cloud puffs overhead. There was something else mirrored in the quiet glass of that lagoon: the figures of three men.

"Good day, priest," Santiago Kifer greeted me. "You're coming up in the world, I see. Got a man Friday, now."

I sat my horse, head down, staring at the mocking images reflected in the lagoon. Beside me, black Flicker did the same, and spoke to me below-voice. "Very dangerous fellows, father. Let them make every move. Watch the marshal."

Astounded, I whispered back to him, "God's name, that isn't the marshal; it's Santiago Kifer."

Nodding, eyes narrowing, Flicker said, *"I know who it is,"* and he raised his head, and so did I, and we let our glances play on the three evil men before us.

My companion's dark face was a mask, the eye-slits examining the imposter marshal of Tombstone, Arizona. No outward emotion showed to say what Robert Flicker knew of this wicked thing he studied there. When he spoke, the rich Negro drawl of word fell almost gentle to ear.

"You are the scalper," he said to Santiago Kifer.

Kifer laughed harshly, giving no other answer. His men echoed the mirthless sound. Flicker's eyes moved in the mask of his face to take in the deputies. He dismissed them with a curl of lip. The pit-viper eyes came back to Kifer. The voice was too soft now, ominous.

"Don't you know me, scalper?"

"Am I supposed to?" Kifer grunted. "One of your kind looks just like another. A nigger's a nigger to me."

"Try harder," said Robert Flicker. "Think back."

Kifer turned to me. "Padre," he said, "who is this nigger Apache? Do we need him where we're going?" He cocked his Winchester rifle as he spoke.

"Well, now, I'm not sure," I answered hastily. "Where are we going?"

Santiago Kifer smiled, and I would rather he had not. "Games are past," he said. "We're talking about the lost Naranjal mine, hunchback."

"You're mad," I suggested. "I know of no such mine. Ah, is that breakfast fire smoke I see beyond the willow trees? Would there be a cup of coffee for a poor crippled priest?"

Kifer's obscene smile widened. "Why, naturally," he said. "It's a long ride to 'somewhere between Durango and Sinaloa,' where the mine is, eh, padre? Come along. I'll have one with you. Crench, pull the nigger off his horse. I want the bastard tied to that sycamore."

"No coffee for Sergeant Flicker?" my black companion asked softly of Kifer. The scalper flinched, paled.

"*Sergeant* Flicker?" he rasped. "Well, well, well." His color improved, and he waved Crench away from Flicker. "Leave him on his horse," he nodded. "I want to see him bounce." Again, he raised the Winchester.

He was going to shoot Flicker off his mount. The black renegade could whirl the horse and run. Or he could sit on him where he was and gamble on God doing something to save him. And I knew what Flicker thought of God.

"Wait!" I cried out to Kifer, leaping from my own mount to plead with him. The scalper merely struck me a vile blow athwart the privates with the barrel of his rifle. Down I went, bawling like a castrated calf. But in the trice required for Kifer to thus tend to my appeal, Flicker came off his horse with the single bound of a black jungle cat. Before the scalper might turn from striking me down, Flicker pounced on him and wrenched the Winchester from his grasp. In the same motion, he drove the weapon's steel-shod butt into the scalper's mid-body. Kifer stiffened. His was the paralyzed look of a solar plexus blow. He could not move even to fall down. But others could, and did.

"Behind you, Flicker!" I yelled suddenly. "*Cuidado!*"

I was too late. The two deputies of Kifer had already slipped in behind the black rider. It was Belcher who struck him in the back of the skull with the flat of his shotgun's stock. Flicker went down soundlessly.

I was taken in an anguish of selfish grief. This was my chief of soldiers for the lost Naranjal expedition. How dare the devils! For once I acted fearlessly.

With a wild dive, I seized the Wincester rifle from Flicker's slackened grasp. By some accident of allied ignorance, I was also able to cock the weapon and bury its muzzle past the front sight in the hairy belly of Deputy Belcher. His face sickened.

"Gawd's sake, padry, don't shoot!" he gasped, skin the color of goat curd. "That thing's got a honed trigger."

As he said this, I heard Crench moving up behind me.

"Deputy Crench," I warned, "I believe it is merely

required that I crook finger rearward upon this trigger and—"

"Crench!" Belcher shouted. "Hold whar you be! You trying to get my innards blowed out? Here, padry," he pleaded. "See, I'm dropping the *escopeta*." He let fall his shotgun and said to Crench, "Come around hyar whar the padry can see you, you tallowbrain."

Crench slunk into view. At another curse from Belcher, he laid his shotgun atop that of the first deputy, then he blinked stupidly at both of us. "Now what?" he said.

It was Santiago Kifer who answered the question. None of us had seen the master scalper recover from the gut blow dealt him by Flicker. But we all saw him now, kneeling beside the black man, a knife to Flicker's throat.

"Unless you lay down that rifle, padre," Kifer rasped at me, "I'll bleed the bastard out clean as a market chicken."

Shaken, I obeyed. Crench and Belcher retrieved their shotguns, and Kifer strode over to face me. "Nigger's alive," he said, gesturing to the motionless Flicker. "They got heads like petrified Zunni gourds. You can't bust them open with anything less than a pickax."

"Thank God," I breathed, crossing myself. "But this priest of the people would feel better were the brave fellow to regain his senses and arise."

Incredibly, it was as if Flicker heard me. His lids stirred, fluttered wide. His vacant gaze found me.

"Ah, Father," he mumbled, seeing me cross myself again, "you've prayed me back to life, eh?" Focusing painfully, he said to Kifer, "Why didn't you kill me, scalper?"

Kifer rubbed his mummified ear. "I wasn't certain if you were a vital party to the hunt for the orange grove gold mine. If you were, you might know things we need to know to get there. *Comprende?*"

"For Gawd's sake, Kifer, get on with it," the hairy-bellied Belcher interrupted nervously. "We know the damn priest has got the map on him." The brute deputy shot a glance to the distant blufftop. "We got to get a move on, 'marshal.' Them hard-rock gophers back to

Tombstone are riled total. There's no bee as mad as one's been stung. They'll come after us."

Kifer laughed his senseless laugh. "Never mind those muckers," he sneered. "They'll not posse up on us again. The nigger cured them of that." He paused to turn to me, licking spittled lips. "All right, priest," he said. "We've come down to it; I want the map. Hand it over."

"Pardiez!" I delayed clumsily. "What map is that?"

Santiago Kifer was rubbing the mummified ear again, a bad sign. "Why," he said, "the one our new partners in the willow thicket yonder told us you had. Bring the ladies out, Crench," he ordered. "There's nothing like eyeball witnesses to jog a man's memory."

"New partners? Witnesses?" I croaked weakly. "I don't understand." But I was bearing false testimony. I knew all too well who those witnesses must be who were in that willow thicket. When Crench and Belcher dragged them forth a moment later, trussed up and gagged like prisoners in a tumbrel, they were of course Charra Baca and the Mescalero ancient, Young Grass.

The damnable Kifer now gloatingly recounted how he had come upon them that early morning as he and his rude companions had been making for the river in their escape from Tombstone. The three scalpers had cunningly portrayed honest men long enough to win from the frightened women—from Charra Baca of course—the story of their own flight.

Charra and the old Apache squaw had gone to see the people of Cochise, Kifer said, repeating what the girl had told them, but they had never arrived there. They were met on the trail to Apache Pass by Chiricahua fleeing from that place. The American troops were riding everywhere with harsh new orders to kill Apaches on sight. The Chiricahua, those who could, were trying to reach Mexico.

The girl and the old lady had turned around and gone with one small band of these refugees. But the luck of the trail had spoiled as bad meat in the sun.

A patrol of enlisted Apache scout cavalry, under famed government tracker, Tom Horn, had jumped the band just before daylight. All but Charra Baca and

Young Grass were killed. They escaped only because of the intercession of young Horn. "Let these last two go," Tom Horn told his San Carlos Apache scouts. "He among you who mentions their sparing will answer to Talking Boy."

Talking Boy was Horn's Apache name, taken from his skill as an interpreter of the Apache tongue. Some may challenge the accounting of this legendary fellow here. They will say Tom Horn was not then in that part of the Arizona Territory but mining near Gila Bend. *Pues, a mi que me importa?* What care I, Nunez, for such arguments? The truth remains: A young white scout was kind to a half-breed girl and an aged Mescalero woman. The San Carlos Apache troops serving under him would have murdered their own Indian sisters. This can be pondered. But forgive it, a preacher who will preach is nowhere welcome. The important fact was that the attack of the San Carlos patrol made the two women glad to travel in Kifer's protective custody. To be an Apache—or even half Apache—caught out of white company in that time and place was to risk death —or even worse: to be captured and sent to the far-off hell-prison of Florida.

Concluding his story with his empty laugh, Kifer boasted his true plan had been to sexually use Charra Baca and to knock in the old squaw's head with a rock, selling her ratty scalp lock for half price, twenty dollars Mexican, in Ciudad Chihuahua.

"Unloose the gags from the ladies," Kifer commanded his lurking deputies. "Let's see if either of them cares to correct my tale of their sorrows."

Released, Charra admitted that she had told Kifer about El Naranjal and the map to the mine of the orange grove. She had done so, she said, so that the scalpers would want to help them look for Father Nunez.

For her contribution, when her turn to speak followed that of the half-breed girl, Young Grass promised heatedly in Apache that, given first chance, she would pare out the living sphincters of the three white scalphunters and fry them for supper. Kifer, who understood her words, smashed her in the face and bid her mind her tongue, lest he rip it from her head and broil it for his own breakfast.

At this brutality, Charra began to weep.

"If you can only forgive me, father," she pleaded. "But I discovered I did not want to go to Cochise. I wanted to come back and be your daughter. It's all my fault."

"No," Young Grass said. "The people up there are no longer as they were. Cochise is five years dead and his Chiricahua have lost their power. Cochise had a tumor. It was big and putrid as a soured mare's bag. It killed him in a few weeks only. And more; did you know, Jorobado, that he accepted the White Eye's faith at the end? *Anh,* he told Agent Jeffords he believed they would meet again 'up there.' Cochise meant your black robe heaven. You see, Jorobado, your damned religion has made it so even an Apache is afraid to die."

I was of course indignant. "What?" I cried. "Do you say that Cochise was fearful to die because he spoke a belief in a life after death? Is that your *Indio* ignorance?"

"No, little broken-backed priest," Young Grass answered, "it was because he said he would see Jeffords where he was going."

"Well then?"

"Well then, the Apaches have no White Eyes where we go."

"For Christ's sake, Kifer," Belcher snarled into our discourse, "are we going to stand here Injun palavering all day? What the hell abouten the map?"

Santiago Kifer turned his disfigured face to his deputy, then to me. "The map, padre," was all he said.

For the final time I hesitated.

"Give it to him, if you have it," Flicker told me.

Charra Baca added her pleas.

Young Grass nodded curtly. "*Anh,* yes. What good is a damn piece of paper to die for?"

She had the best point.

I lifted flap to buckskin traveler's pouch. The vellum tube housing the map appeared in good repair. Removing map tube from pouch, I tendered it to Santiago Kifer. "You need only turn off the fitted cap," I instructed him, "to find the map rolled within." Kifer did as I told him. But when he then upended the tube to spill out the map, it was not the map that spilled out. It was some brackish water from the iron horse-trough of the Tombstone Jail. Intact as the tube had seemed, it had, alas, leaked grievously.

Kifer stood holding it upside down. He did not move. The last drops of horse-trough water seeped from the tube's dreary end. Only then did the scalper look up at me.

"If the map is spoiled, priest," he said, crazed orbs afire, "I will tie your hair to your horse's tail and whip him away from you."

I blanched with fear and could not speak.

Santiago Kifer felt carefully within the tube and extracted the sodden roll of the two-hundred-year-old map to the lost Naranjal mine. Cautiously, cautiously, he unfurled it. Then he held it up to the light of the new sun.

He studied it a long, nerve-bending time.

Then he lowered it to stare bleakly at me.

"There isn't a damned line left on it," he said. "It is plumb water-washed."

And, finally, with a fury of softness, "Bring up his horse, Crench."

19
THE MOVING FINGERS WRITE

Kifer crumpled the useless map and flung it to the sands of the bar, at water's edge. I was taken next instant by Deputy Belcher, a lank man who stood six and one-half feet in height and was surpassing powerful. No bantam rooster of my five feet and middle years would make sober issue with such a troglodyte. I suffered the deputy to retain his bruising hold.

Crench, meanwhile, was fetching over my horse. His master, Santiago Kifer, stood Winchester guard over black Flicker. Desperately, I searched mind for means to communicate with the Negro soldier. A matter of consuming importance to the dream for an Apache church had just been rolled into a ball and thrown away. A draft of air, the tiniest dust devil set awhirl across the light sands of the island bar, and the secret of the lost Naranjal mine would float away forever. The current cut in very stiffly here at the bend and was feeding thence into a high-banked gorge immediately below. *Espíritu Santo*, aid me now!

Did I say the water-soaked map was useless?

It was—to Santiago Kifer.

But to a priest of the company of Saint Francis, trained in the arcane skills of his order, that discarded waddage of ancient paper was yet priceless; there remained a secret method for restoring its every vital line.

Yet how to tell Flicker he must, if he lived, retrieve the seemingly ruined map. If I might only tell him why I wanted the gold, ah, Jesu! what an ally he could prove. But all that Jesus sent me in that moment of despair was the grunting Crench coming up with my horse.

"All right, cinch him on," Kifer ordered Belcher.

I saw brave Flicker move impulsively to aid me, but Kifer jabbed the muzzle of the Winchester rifle into him and I called over, also, that he should desist.

"You have another mission more important than my poor life," I shouted to the American deserter.

"If I have," Flicker responded with his unquenchable spirit, "you had best remind me of it pronto. Otherwise, *adieu mon pasteur. Jusqu'alors!*"

Santa María! By this fortuitous accident of a French farewell, a heroic comrade had unwittingly provided me with my method for speaking to him without alerting the scalphunters. *Zut alors!* why had I not remembered Flicker to be a highly educated man, an aborted graduate of the great United States Army university of West Point? *Quelle chance!*"

"*Mon lieutenant,*" I waved to my black Apache chief of soldiers, "*attendez vous. A brebis tondue Dieu mesure le vent,* God tempers the wind to the shorn lamb.

Here is that greater mission of which I spoke: *Sauvez vous la carte!"*

My words were broken off by the callused paws of Deputy Belcher seizing me bodily up. In a trice the hairy one had knotted into my long hair a stout tying-thong of rawhide. The free end of this he then bound tightly to the tail of my own horse, held by Crench, and the snorting beast would now drag me until my scalp's meat ripped from its boning.

"Croyance, courage!" Flicker shouted.

Kifer whipped him three times with the rifle's heavy barrel, the last blow felling the dauntless renegade once more.

"Flicker, *la carte!"* I shouted. *"Pour l'amour de Dieu, sauvez vous la carte! Qui peut-être restitué,* it is restorable!"

Of course, he did not hear me; in that dark instant, I did not imagine that even God heard me.

What I did manage then, however, in the very ultimate moment of Deputy Belcher tying me to the horse's tail, was a final blurred glance at the fallen Negro deserter.

Flicker had gone down nearly in the water of the current's set into the beach. His right arm was pinned beneath his body, the left arm outflung. And it was the hand of this left arm that now moved. Its black fingers inched like the sidelong crawling of some wounded crustacean to reach water's brim.

To reach it, yet not slide in.

No, rather to poise above and then enclose within the black retracting "legs" the sodden crumple of *la carte,* which lay at water's lap of Rio San Pedro.

Flicker had heard me; we had the map.

The lost Naranjal was still ours.

20
BEHIND THE WILD HORSE

My relief at Flicker saving the washed-out map knew the briefest of lives. Belcher, having finished tying my locks to the horse's tail, stepped back. He searched the nearby ground for a stick to whip the horse away from where we stood. From an eye-corner I saw Flicker try to rise up from where he lay at river's edge. But he slumped forward partly into the water and lay still once more. He had fainted surely. God grant that, face in the water as he now reposed, he would not drown.

Deputy Belcher, that evil *chupada*, that emaciated hairy snake of a man, had found his "whip." It was a driftwood cudgel, hard and polished as a bone. It would have served to brain the poor animal more easily than to urge it forward. But Belcher was a creature from the caves.

With a grunt, he swung the heavy club.

It struck the horse athwart the crouching haunch, and the animal squealed in surprised hurt. Its hesitation before leaping into a run was sufficient for my two hands—left free to permit me to prolong the dragging and hence the enjoyment of my torturers—to reach and seize the rawhide thong that bound me to the horse. Thus, when the poor thing did jump forward, I was able to ease the first shock of my body's careening course through rock and sand and jagged driftwood of the river bar.

I knew of course that death would come suddenly. The first direct contact of head with stone, the impalement into any vital organ of sharp driftwood snag—in a dozen ways my wild bouncing behind the terrified horse must end with my life destroyed. Whether or not my miserable hair parted from agonized skull prior to this death or following its grim fact did not interest me. As with any man, my only thought was for God to save me yet.

He answered me in a strange way.

Two figures, Apaches on foot, broke out of the heavy brush of the island of the lagoon. One of them ran toward the racing horse that bore me along. The other sped like a red wolf down upon the laughing Crench, where the gross buffoon roared his appreciation of the humor in dragging a mackerel snapper priest to death. Crench did not see the Indian coming for him, for the Apache broke from cover directly behind the hulking deputy.

Santiago Kifer, of course, did see the Indians break into the open. His rifle leaped to shoulder. But his finger never closed on trigger. The Apache had aimed his charge into the rear of simple Crench with typical cunning. If Kifer were to get off a shot at the Indian, that shot would have to pass through Deputy Crench. Kifer swung away from that shot to take the other Indian, the one running to cut off the horse that was dragging me. Here again the two Apaches had planned their rush with that animalistic instinct for the hunt that is theirs beyond any other race of man. As Crench blocked the first Indian from Kifer's rifle, so did the two women, Charra Baca and old Young Grass, now interfere with the scalper's line of sighting on the Apache coming to my succor.

I could plainly hear Kifer snarling like a kicked dog in his frustration. He ran zigzagging to get an open shot at one of the Indians, but in the time he did this the Apaches had achieved their own intentions.

The more muscular athlete of the two, the younger man, he who ran up behind Crench, now did a thing I had never seen. He leaped up into the air, five or six feet off the ground. Twisting his hurtling form, he projected his two feet into the very small of the back of the mighty Crench. It was as if the big deputy had been battered from behind by such a log as the Crusaders employed to break down the gates of some walled city of the infidels. He gave a single rupturing screech and collapsed on the sand in a jerking heap of flesh.

Before the yelling Santiago Kifer could then fire at the Apache, the Apache swept up the *escopeta* of Crench and fired one of its twin barrels in a reverberating crash of gunfire toward the scalper chief. I could literally see the leaves and twigs of the willows behind Kifer shred and fly from the bird shot of the heavy charge. Bawling like a throat-cut steer, Kifer threw both hands to his face. He dropped his Winchester rifle in a reflex of intense pain and great fright to do so and cried out repeatedly, as he did, *"My eyes! My eyes! I can't see! I can't see—!"*

He went to his knees in the sand, moaning his fear, crying out for God to help him in the bloodied sightless wounding of his face.

But God sent help to another instead.

Beyond Kifer I could see Robert Flicker's black body stir and rise up from water's edge, as from the dead. Being in the stream's cool wash had revived the fighting Negro, and he was now on his feet again, stumbling toward the discarded rifle of the scalper.

Now, too, God was hearing my own unspoken prayers.

The small dumpy Apache—who had run out of the willow copse to head off the horse that was killing me— proved swift as some human cannonball. Unbelievably, he guessed precisely the angle that the crazed animal would veer and gallop. The course passed the horse near an inclined up-pitch of driftwood log. The fat Apache ran up this log with the speed of a darting ground rat. As the horse galloped by, he leaped from log's end to the wildly bucking back of the animal, and he clung there.

Not alone did he stick to that horse, but he managed to find the flying reins of the bridle and to haul the brute to a sliding stop that was so abrupt as to end me up under the crupper of the animal.

If one can be grateful for being sat on by a thousand-pound horse, I was grateful.

The chubby Indian leaped to the ground, untied my hair from that of the horse's tail, bridle-led the animal up off my chest, and got it quieted down some safe distance from me. By this time, Flicker had Kifer's Win-

chester—and Kifer under guard of the weapon's muzzle—and the first Apache was using his knife to cut free
the two captive women. From the uproar of the insane
moments before, there came a sudden stillness on that
little beach. We stood looking at our rescuers, unable
to find tongue to speak our gratitude. Then, as by some
common signal, all commenced to laugh.

When enough of this relief had been taken, black
Flicker greeted the two Apaches. Of course they were
members of the raiding party of which he had been the
leader. They had their story to tell and would tell it.
But first Flicker directed the binding of the blinded
Santiago Kifer and of Deputy Crench, using the same
bonds as were employed to tie Young Grass and Charra
Baca. The missing Belcher remained a mystery for later solving. He had apparently seen how things were going against his cause and had faded into the river brush.
He was armed with shotgun and knife and must be considered extremely dangerous. A search to determine his
line of flight must be made, but not yet. First must
come a catching-up of other things.

Things such as what had come to pass with poor
Kaytennae. And such as what had become of the other
raiders, Lupe, Go-ta-chai, and Tule Moon. And then
lastly, what were we all to do, trapped here thus on
this small island in the middle of the Rio San Pedro,
in enemy Arizona.

Flicker waved his hand, deciding it.

"Earlier," he said to me, "you mentioned something
of a coffee fire and smoke wisping to suggest breakfast. I see the place past these willows. Let us go over
there and discover if these scalpers left us anything but
their three fine horses, eh?"

"All right," I replied. "Ladies," I said, with a gallant
sweep to bow, offering each an arm, "may I?"

Charra Baca laughed and took my arm, but the old
Mescalero harridan scowled at me and said all priests
were afflicted of their brain powers and she would walk
alone. The tough cherub of an Apache, whom I now
understood to be called Packrat, rescued my intent,
however.

With a grin he took my free arm.

"*Ugashe,* black robe," he said, in Apache, "let's go."
And, *por supuesto,* away we went.

There proved to be some food—tin of army hard-
tack, bundle of venison jerky, stale rind of rat cheese—
in Kifer's saddlebag. With coffee already simmering in
the smoke-charred pot, we began a fine breakfast. As
we ate, Flicker suggested to the other, younger Apache,
Chongo, that this would be the opportunity to bring
us the accounting of what had passed to bring Packrat
and himself to this lagoon of the old channel of Rio San
Pedro in just such an important time for our lives.

The handsome Chongo gulped his steaming coffee,
nodded his lip-smacking consent.

"It came to pass in such a manner," he said.

21
CHONGO'S STORY

As Apaches will when a thing lies recent to their eyes,
Chongo told his story as if he were reseeing it happen
to some other Indians, viewing it from a hidden distance.

. . . The five Mexican Apaches lay in their covert on
the scrub-grown higher sandbar of the San Pedro. Since
yesterday they had been there, bare miles only from
Fort Huachuca and the mean rifle fight. They had with
them the American Apache, their guide for the local
country, Kaytennae, adopted nephew of Chief Juh. The
young warrior was sore wounded. A head wound. None
of them knew how deep. But the American brother had
not stirred, except to moan softly in his hurt. Or to go
rough in his breathing. Or to shake in chill.

Such grievous injuries of the head the Mexican
Apaches understood to be exceeding dangerous.

They thought of it mournfully.

When a brother lay so long without his brain returning, *dah-eh-sah,* the Dark One, was hovering. Yet

they had not left Kaytennae and would not leave him. Indeed, the burden that he was to them had led to this need for going to earth under the very noses of the pursuing soldiers. Ysun, the Father, had blessed the risk. The cavalry had probed all around the sandbar but not come out to it. The reason lay in the opinion of the white scout who was with the soldier patrol that not even one Indian could hide in the brush on the midriver spit. To imagine that the bunch they were after, or any part of them, had crossed to that driftwooded bar was, in the words of the scout, "imbeciled nonsense."

The patrol had ridden on.

And the five Meixcan Apaches and their dying American brother had bellied deeper into the driftwood and debris of the spit, thanking Ysun for the lease of another day.

But now that day was breaking to the east.

They must go on. Kaytennae, in some miracle of great spirit, had come through the night. The blessing of that gift was arguable, although the obligation of it was undeniable. In the pure democracy of the Indian way, both views were freely heard.

"Goddamn," scowled Lupe, the second leader after black Flicker. "I say leave him here. He has water and shelter from both sun of midday and chill of midnight."

Lupe was a dangerous man. He was an Indian who had spent much time running back and forth across the border between Mexico and the United States, and he had served some time as a scout out of San Carlos. He had learned his profanity from the white troopers and, evidently, some little of their military morality, as well.

Chongo, on the other hand, was a brooding young man of utter seriousness. He was a half brother of the notorious Chato, fastest rising of all the young Mexican Apache raiders. Like Chato, Chongo was bright of mind. But he was unlike his fierce kinsman in spirit. Chongo understood the desperation of the Apache condition on both sides of the border. Yet he was not a *hesh-ke,* not a killer of the caste of Lupe and Chato.

"No," this sober young fighter answered Lupe. "Saying to leave him here is easy. But you know the law as well as any of us. He cannot be left behind except that he demand *nah-wehl-coht kah-el-keh*. Do you deny it?"

Nah-wehl-coht kah-el-keh was the Apache tribal law by which a mortally wounded person could request that he be left behind a retreating party to defend it from pursuit. In its applications, the term *mortal* had many interpretations. Warriors would claim the law who were scarcely scratched, or who could easily recover by running with the fleeing pack. It was thus always up to the leader of the raiders to say if *nah-wehl-coht kah-el-keh* were to be allowed in each case.

Now, with Flicker gone, that leader was Lupe.

Chongo knew that well. But Lupe had been much with White Eyes and was tainted in his thinking. He needed a hand on his hackamore, as the Apache said. But whoever offered that hand had better be prepared to have it bitten off. Lupe was a bad Indian.

"Chongo," Lupe demanded, "what do you think Kaytennae would ask for?"

"He would ask to be left behind."

"Where is our problem then?"

"He cannot speak."

"I am leader now; I speak for him. We leave him."

Lupe was tall for an Apache, shading six feet. He was strong of body and of will. He had killed more men than any of the raiders. Thirty-five Mexicans, alone.

The two men stared at one another. Their companions became very nervous. One of them thought of something.

"Say," he interjected, "I just remembered a factor here. Lucky that I did, too. It may be what we seek."

This fellow was called Packrat. He was a famous politician and "arranger" among his fellows. A rotund, merry-eyed small man, he was nonetheless tough in mind and had always an eye out for the major opportunity.

His two remaining comrades, Tule Moon and Gota-chai, were lean, fierce fellows who, like Lupe, had joined the expedition from the Bedonkohe band. These

were the people of another young fighter who was then
becoming a power among all the Chiricahua Four
Families. His name was Go-lithay, sometimes called
Gokliya. This was among the Apache. Among the
Pinda Likoyi, the hated White Eyes, he had another
name.

It was Geronimo.

So these last two of the raider band were rough men,
and their votes could swing the matter either direction.

Tule Moon leaned over and examined the still form
of Kaytennae.

"He is the color of a beached trout," he said. "He
cannot live."

"*Anh,* yes," his friend Go-ta-chai agreed, "he should
be dead already. He is *hombre duro.*"

"Well, Packrat, get on with your idea." It was Chongo speaking. "But only if it has to do with *nah-wehl-coht kah-el-keh.*"

"Yes," Lupe growled, "and it better have to do with
it. You hear me, *ratonito gordo?*"

Being addressed as "little fat rat" was nothing new
to the peacemaker. Packrat merely waved a chubby
hand and said, "I recall from my grandmother, who
was the noted Holy Woman Lozarita, that, in a condition where the warrior was unconscious, his comrades
could make a vote to say what the warrior would have
said were he able to speak. I say let us get out the voting sticks."

The sober Chongo could barely suppress an Apache
smile. There was never any such holy woman as this
Lozarita, nor any such sublaw to the rule of *nah-wehl-coht kah-el-keh.* But Packrat had once more done his
work. Now Chongo must do his. The morning light
was growing. This second day could not be spent on the
island. It must, rather, see them all traveling swiftly
and far down Rio San Pedro. That sunset must find
them safely home, in Mexico. Chongo well understood
these imperatives of their position. He took a final look
at the gray-faced Kaytennae.

"All right," he said. "Who is carrying the voting
sticks?"

Tule Moon had them, and he had brought them

forth. They had voted then, the five hidden Mexican Apaches, and the vote to abandon Kaytennae had gone three to two—against Chongo and Packrat. But, even so, Packrat and Chongo said, they would still remain with their fallen American brother.

At once, Lupe, Tule Moon, and Go-ta-chai had departed for the secret meadow where the party had hidden its horses before swimming the river to the island. It was not imagined that they would take more than their own three ponies; but Lupe was what he was: a Bedonkohe and a killer, a man who cared not for any rules, whether of the Apache or the Pinda Lickoyi.

When Packrat had shortly followed to the meadow to get the three ponies of himself, Chongo, and Kaytennae, the fat brave had found no ponies at all in the meadow. Lupe and his two comrades had stolen all six horses. *Quita!* What a foulness of luck. The damned traitors. Acting just like white men. Stealing the extra ponies to save their own red hides, to have thus a fresh mount for each of them to ride relay should the cavalry jump them again.

Well, it might make good Indian sense, Packrat admitted in reporting it to Chongo on his return to the brushy island in Rio San Pedro, but it sure as hell was not good Apache law. Nor very damned friendly, either.

Chongo had agreed.

A time would come when Lupe would pay for this treachery. The stealing of a man's horse in the country of the enemy was punishable by death. Tule Moon and Go-ta-chai might be found innocent. They would doubtless claim their fear of the wild-brained Lupe made them to do it. All right. Chongo would bring Lupe to account.

For the present, he and Packrat and Kaytennae could not remain on the island. But Chongo still refused to abandon Kaytennae. Although their wounded brother appeared *dah-eh-sah*, there was yet a heartpulse in the pale chest. So long as there should be, Chongo would carry Kaytennae on his own back, if need be. "What say you?" he asked Packrat.

"I will help you," answered the fat brave. "We can

fashion a sling from his horse blanket. It is insane, of
course. Kaytennae is already dead, and you and I will
both be shot by soldiers while carrying his cold body.
But, *ih!* yes, I will help you. I said it, didn't I?"

In this agreement, Chongo now concluded his story
to Flicker, he and Packrat had departed their island
bearing the body of Kaytennae between them. Down
the river not far they had come in sight of the black
robe being tied to a horse's tail. It had not seemed un-
fair to them that a priest be so dragged behind a saddled pony. They were just about to pass on southward
when they had noted the body of their black leader lying half in the shallows of the Rio San Pedro. It was
him they sometimes called Trasfuga, the Deserter. Or
Mirlo, Blackbird. Or Soldado Negro, Black Soldier.
But who was called by the Apache most commonly, as
by the White Eyes, merely Flicker.

Of vastly more import, the Apache called him friend.

"A priest is nothing, you see," Packrat broke in to
explain, "but a friend is beyond any other thing given to
an Apache. *Schicho,* friend. Damn to hell, you can't
permit such a one to lie bobbing in the water and to
drown."

"Certainly not," murmured the soft-spoken Chongo.

The handsome young Apache had been made uneasy
by his closer looking at these others he and Packrat had
saved. He had in particular fact just discovered Charra
Baca, who was looking him back in her way. It was a
way calculated to unsettle far bolder men than the
youthful Mexican-bred Chiricahua. Chongo attempted
to go around the issue.

"Who are these?" he demanded scowlingly of Flicker.

Charra Baca answered for herself, addressing Packrat
and Chongo, a wise thing which Flicker and I both remarked.

"My brothers," she said to the Apache pair, "my
own-mother was of the Chiricahua of Cochise. I will
always remember that you came to save our lives
when you might have stolen away." She was silent a
moment, the great wild eyes filling with tears. "The Cochise people are all running away now. None are left up

there." She pointed to the north. "If you will let me do it, brothers, I want to go home to Mexico with you."

Chongo and Packrat stared at her. Then Chongo turned to me. "What does she mean, priest? You behave to one another like father and daughter. Do you speak for her?"

"Yes. Her mother was Apache. Juh thinks she was of the Cochise or Warm Springs people. Mexican soldiers killed her. I reared this girl at my church, in Casas Grandes."

"You will let her go with us?"

"Yes."

"You bless it?"

"Yes, if it is what she wants."

"What of the rest of you?" Chongo asked, looking about our little circle. "Where will you go?"

Robert Flicker nodded, answering for me. "The black robe and I will also go home with you, Chongo," he said. "At least until we are out of this country. The soldiers are after me, and the citizens of the big new silver camp are chasing the black robe. When men will not run together, they will each be caught in a different trap."

He looked directly at the young Apache. Chongo looked him back.

"What of those two?" he asked, indicating the bound prisoners, Kifer and Crench. "I suggest a stone in their skulls. It's the quietest, and neat also."

Packrat nodded and arose. "I see a good rock over there," he said. "Let me hit the one-eared man; it would be a kindness, since he is now also blind."

As a priest, I could in no way countenance such a cold-blooded murdering, and I said so. It was decided that, Belcher being loose somewhere in the vicinity, we would simply leave the captives trussed on the island. That way they had a chance. It was all we could give them, and far more than they deserved.

If Belcher came back for them, fine.

If he did not, the high water of spring would bear two moldered skeletons down into the narrow gorge below Lagoon Island. Our Apaches accepted the solution, seeing its justice. They knew, or thought they did, the odds against the white man Belcher lingering near Mexican *broncos* who were wild from being shot at and run by soldiers.

"I guess that is the end of it, then," Flicker said.

"No," Chongo scowled. "You have forgotten one of us."

"What?" Flicker returned the scowl. *"No comprende."*

Chongo answered him softly, "You have forgotten the nephew of Juh. You have forgotten Kaytennae."

God forgive us, I thought, we all had done this grievous thing. It was the excitement, the confusion, the vast relief at living. But Flicker had it straighter.

"Schicho," he said in his deep voice, "are you saying he *isn't* dead? You let us believe that he was."

"He is alive," Chongo said. "Over there through the willow trees. Under a big cottonwood. We placed him there."

"Jesus Christ," Flicker said. "Come on!"

22
DOUBTERS OF THE DREAM

When we broke through the willows, a glad sight met our eyes. More than that, really. Kaytennae was sitting up. Another miracle, praise God.

The lad was weak, but his mind was sound and aware.

My hasty examination revealed no physical damage of importance. He should be ready to travel within the hour.

"Nephew!" I wept, gathering him to my breast. "Your god has guarded you, while mine has guided us to this spot to help you home."

"Gods?" objected Packrat. "What of Chongo, here, and, for that matter, old Packrat? Had we nothing to do with saving this Warm Springs warrior?"

"Everything, Ratoncito," Flicker interjected. "But

for you and Chongo, Kaytennae's shade would be riding under the ground." The reference was to the Apache belief that the dead live just below earth's surface. "Moreover, I suspect Padre Jorobado of being less than forthright here."

"Eh?" I frowned. "What nonsense is this, Flicker?"

The black rider extended and opened his hand. In it lay the crumpled treasure map of El Naranjal.

"This nonsense, padre," he told me.

I made as if I did not understand him. "What ever are you talking about?" I smiled.

"Talking about Kaytennae knowing the El Naranjal country," Flicker answered me, dark face watchful. "You said you could restore the map itself. That's all well and good. But I happen to have also lived with the Nednhi Apache and heard the full legend of this particular *carta*. It's a map of the mine itself only. It isn't worth a damn until somebody gets you into the El Naranjal country and up to the walls of the Ghost Canyon. For that," he concluded, "you need an Apache guide; a *particular* Apache guide."

"Pah!" I sputtered. "That is all common gossip. You know that."

"And you," Flicker nodded, "know that the Nednhi Apache of Juh are the keepers of the secret of the lost canyon of the orange grove. And you know Kaytennae was raised in Juh's own jacal. He ought to know the secret. He ought to make the perfect guide to lead you onward in your greediness to find the lost Franciscan gold, eh, Padre?"

Through the ensuing stillness, Kaytennae looked at me.

"Padre Jorobado, is this true?" he said at last.

"Is what true, *hijo?*" I delayed.

"That you would use me to betray the secrets of my people, and for your own greed of gold?"

The time, most unavoidably, was come.

"It is true," I said. "But the greed is not for myself, even though I have called it Nunez's dream. Will you hear me, all of you?"

The Apache, I knew, respected dreams, but even they were reluctant here, surprising me.

"I am not sure," Kaytennae replied for the others. "Do you claim courtesy rules for your story?"

"I must," I said. "Do you deny them?"

The young Warm Springs man studied the matter, consulting with Chongo, Packrat, and Young Grass. "No," he finally said. "Go ahead."

At this juncture, we all heard the moanings of pain from the injured Santiago Kifer, and I perforce, as sole physician, asked the moment's leave to attend the unfortunate. "Animal that he may be," I explained, "he deserves something; the man who has lost his sight has surrendered the most precious thing of his life." Even the Apaches agreeing, I departed.

There was naught to be done for the scalper chieftain.

Washing his face free of the blood upon it showed me no wound I might treat. Kifer would not, he said he could not, open his eyes to let me see their condition. "Blind," he kept repeating. "Oh, dear Christ Jesus, the red devil has blinded me." To this charge against young Chongo, I advised the suffering villain that he had blinded himself. Better than that, even. God had taken his eyes to punish him for all the lives of red men like Chongo whom his scalphunters had killed for their hair.

"They're not human, padre," Kifer groaned. "I vow before God, they're not." The sightless face turned up to me. "It doesn't seem rightful that a priest of the cloth could abandon the wounded," he said. "You're a minister of the faith; you daren't leave a man so."

He had tried to struggle upward, free of his bonds, and I put restraining hand to his heaving shoulder.

"Kifer," I said, "be at peace. I cannot help you, nor would my comrades permit me. But Crench is here with you, bound to the very next tree. Belcher is somewhere in the river brush, free and unharmed. You must pray that he will return for you. You have your life. Our Apaches wanted to crush your heads with rocks. I could only stay them by showing the cross, the black robes' 'medicine.' Be you thankful to your God, and ask only his forgiveness; amen."

"Belcher—!" Santiago Kifer screamed.

Only echoes down the river's gorge answered him,

and he turned to face blankly about and say in a frightened voice, "Crench?"

"Hyar, marshal," the simple one replied. "I'm lashed foot and paw to this hyar tree, just liken the padry vowed." I turned to go as Crench spoke to Kifer, and the great oaf called out cheerily in my wake, "So long, padry. You're a ugly little fart, but I kind of tooken a shine to you. I'm glad the horse didn't uproot your skull."

For answer I could but bob my head. The last I heard of the two desperadoes was Kifer bellowing for the fugitive Belcher to come back, to stand faithful with his captive friends, that vengeance would still be theirs. I thought to hear Crench inquire of his blinded chief how everything looked when you couldn't see it, but I am not certain. No reply that I detected came either from Santiago Kifer—or from the absent Deputy Belcher.

Returned to my friends at the breakfast fire, I resumed my accounting of Nunez's dream for an Apache church.

I left nothing out. My fall from the priesthood. The fact that I was in flight from black robe justice. The tender mercy of my Lord, by which he had sent me the map to the lost Naranjal mine, a true miracle. My fortunes since coming to the United States to outfit my search for the Franciscans' gold. My finding of Flicker —doomed to hang in Tombstone jail. His rescue of me from the angered citizens in good turn and time. And, lastly, our escape to this island bar in the middle of Rio San Pedro, in enemy Arizona. With the wondrous find, there, of Kaytennae, the one best Apache guide to the land of the Ghost Canyon of the mysterious River of the Oranges.

Here, I took natural pause. It was the perfect place to assess the friendly reaction of my listeners to my selfless vision for Apache salvation. Expecting a generous and grateful approval—after all, it is the primary business of a priest to sell dreams for realities—I received instead a full round of accusatory silence.

They were all staring at me, shaking heads and compressing lips. It was Chongo, in the end, who stated the case with Indian simplicity.

"Well," he said, "we are waiting. So far, priest, we don't believe you."

23
NUNEZ AND THE NEW FAITH

"*Schichobes,* old friends," I began, answering Chongo's statement of doubt and addressing the Apaches in especial, "I want to build a church for your people only. When the gold is found, I *will* use it to build this Apache sanctuary deep in Sierra Madre del Norte. No black robes' faith will be taught there. I shall teach the young in tongues and numbers and in writing. The aged and infirm I shall attend. There will be worship of your own gods. If any shall come to me and ask of my God, him I will answer but not persuade. Those who will keep to Ussen and the old ways may teach me. We will all pray together. Neither shall any priest come from Ciudad Chihuahua, nor any soldier from Ciudad Méjico, to arrest or harm one Indian.

"I have come to see, *schichobes,* that it is wrong to build a white man's or a Mexican's church for Indian people. Even I, Father Nunez, who am myself one-half the Indian blood, have no right to preach or tell the Apache what the Apache does not wish to hear.

"The church will be an Apache church and together we shall fill it with a new faith.

"Will you believe me, now, when I say this? When I promise it to you, both by Ussen and by *Dios?*

"Padre Jorobado cannot do this alone. He must have the gold to build a strong fortress for our faith, and to buy those things our black soldier-chief Flicker will require to defend this new freedom church. Here it is that only you may help.

"Go with your friend Nunez, the hunchback of Casas Grandes. He cannot find the canyon of the orange grove without that Kaytennae shall guide him. No black robe may go safely in Tepehuane country either, except that he goes with Indian comrades to secure the passage.

"It will be a long, long march, and exceeding dangerous.

"The way may lead to Durango and beyond to Sinaloa even. None of us truly knows that country, except to know that within it the savage Tepehuane Indians lie in wait for us.

"Those Indians were the slave miners of the black robes. They remember everything. They hate white man and Mexican more even than do the Apache. Nor do the Tepehuane people love the Apache overly. You know this. They are dangerous Indians. Yet to you they are still brothers, when to the black robes they are certain death; thus do I need you.

"Will you do it, friends? Will you go with Nunez to the land of the Tepehuanes?"

My Apache audience, restless and scowling at the outset, now ended listening intently. Surprising me, Chongo was the first of them to come forward for the new faith.

"Small humpbacked priest," he said, "you are bent in the mind as well as the spine. But I could feel the fever in your words just now, and, yes, I will go with you. Ussen, forgive me."

I thanked him, not failing to note that he looked not at the hunchbacked priest of Casas Grandes, but at the full-fronted daughter of the whore of Fronteras. I did not contest his inspirations, but turned to Packrat.

"Well," Packrat guessed, in response to my query of his interest, "you do seem *más loco, padrecito*. Crazy like hell, as the Americans say. But so am I. Always have been. Add me to your list of *idiotas*. Ussen be damned."

"Bless you, Little Rat," I said quickly, seeing the reproving look that Chongo gave him. "Your joking spirit will be good."

I eyed old Young Grass, third of my four Apache purebloods. "And you, mother; how say you?"

"Can you count, priest?" the Mescalero ancient asked. "If so, I will be *número tres* for you. *Ih!* Don't thank me. If I stay up here the White Eyes will shoot me on sight because I am an Apache. The Apaches have already turned me out because I am too old. The only decent treatment I remember since Cochise died is from that young white scout from San Carlos Agency. What was his name, Josana?" she asked of Charra Baca. "Tin Horn?"

"Tom Horn," Charra corrected. "Talking Boy."

"Ah, indeed, indeed——" The old Mescalero squaw lapsed away into her memories, and I turned my glance upon Kaytennae, last of my full bloods.

"Hijo mío, my son," I said to him, "what will you do? You are the most important of all of us. If you will not go, we cannot do so. Not and find the gold."

The handsome Warm Springs raider shook his head, frowning both with the pain this motion caused from the wound across his forehead and from his suffering of Indian doubts of my expedition's nature.

"Say this of it, *padre mío,*" he answered, at last. "I don't know if I will lead you to the country of the Tepehuane. I do know that I am still sick. I better go with you, if I dream to ride again. I cannot stay up here in Arizona any more than the old Mescalero woman can. They have shot me once, and I live. Who knows about the next time? Yes, bear me with you. I do not think this is my country anymore. I will go and live with Juh and the Nednhi once again. Mexico is the last place of freedom for us. May Ussen guard the way."

Finishing, he dropped his eyes as if in surrender to his fates. But he was not quick enough that Nunez did not see the eye-flick that he sent toward Charra Baca in the very process of giving in. Aha! A rival for Chongo? Two handsome young Apaches of the very best wild breeding warming in their manhoods for my hot-eyed foster daughter?

Well, *está bien! Bienvenidos, jóvenes;* most welcome to the company, young men. There is no glue like a little romance. If not to me, these dashing fellows would surely stick to Charra Baca. *Qué cosa maravilloso.*

I turned finally to the foster brother of the Apache.

"Well, Flicker," I said, "how votes my chief of soldiers, my black Apache?"

My coming to him surprised the Negro renegade. Indeed, I caught him also eyeing the remarkable breasts of Charra Baca. And he caught me, catching him. While Charra captured us both in the process.

She laughed first.

Then black Flicker.

And lastly I, the lively minded *cura* of Casas Grandes.

"*Loco, loco,*" our four Apaches cried out. But soon enough they joined us. Even poor Kaytennae, so weak he scarce could chuckle, had to hold his wounded head and laugh with us all. It was perhaps the thing most needed.

"*Vamos, vamos,*" everyone agreed. "Let us get away from here and go and find Padre Jorobado's gold."

24
A GIFT OF LOVE FROM LOAFER

Momento, por favor. Have I said everyone was ready in the little camp to depart for Mexico? That all were crying out *vamos!* and all prepared to leave the island? It was not so. Flicker and I had forgotten a noble comrade of the great retreat from Tombstone.

You are right; it was the trail companion of the tall bay horse, the old and lame dog of Santiago Kifer.

But for our pause of necessity upon finding Kaytennae and having to figure out how to transport him, we would surely have gone on without the gallant Loafer. As it was, the tottering brute nearly missed us anyway. This was out of loyalty and devotion to his former owner, a touching and sad playlet which, unhappily, I did not see.

Indeed, fat Packrat was the sole member of the company to witness the farewell. Perhaps it is as well. The last good-bye of a man and his fondest friend, his dog of many years and a thousand campfires, is best not pried on by too many cynical eyes. The view of a simple Apache warrior, a Mexican bronco of the wild tribes, may have been designed of *Dios* to tell us of the tribute.

"That is a dog of great feeling," Packrat remarked, pointing out Loafer, limping toward us from his detour to implement his adieu with Santiago. "He noted his old master the scalphunter tied to the tree and went at once over to him. He sniffed him good and then raised his leg upon him for five squirts. Then he turned around and scraped sand into his face with his hind feet and came on over here to you, Jorobado."

"*Enjuh!*" Flicker boomed, delighted. "Look out, padre, he might have something left for you." Then, with an uneasy, quick eye to the blufftop and all about us on the island, he concluded frowningly, "*Montad en vuestros caballos.* Mount up, and let's get out of here."

We got at once to our horses and turned them to leave, warned by Flicker's urgency, determined to obey its command. Yet one very last thing still delayed us. Even old Loafer was startled. Just as we spurred our mounts, having been careful to place Kaytennae with me on the tall bay horse that had won Flicker and me away from Tombstone, a great and bawdy shout arose to our rear.

Wincing, I bade Flicker stay the advance.

"*Mil perdónes*," I apologized, "but what may we do? That will be the foster-mother of the beautiful Josana."

It proved so to be, worse luck.

Next moment, astride a rat-tailed stolen mule, Zorra the whore rode out of the far-side willow trees. She splashed the animal across the stream, encouraging it continually with both lung and cudgel.

"Comrades," she shouted, dashing up, "onward to wherever we are bound. There is a fury of hell to be reckoned with back there in the new mining camp. The good wives of the town are grown overnight weary of being scorned by their husbands. They have arisen and cast out the women of the red-lantern tents."

Seeing my unhappy scowl at her coarse tirade, she at once broke into the yapping bark of her laugh.

"Here, now, Father Rat Turd," she cried, fetching me a terrible clap atwixt my shoulder blades, "you know how such things go. It becomes all the while more difficult for an honest Mexican whore to make a living off these Anglos. The Americans, *más especial,* are getting smart, the bastards. They want to pay you in pinto beans and red chilies, and their wives! *Santa,* let me tell you about those wives!"

"For God's sake, woman," Flicker said, "tell the rest of it to the padre on the run, will you? We've got to get shut of here."

"Isn't that what I just warned?" rasped the peppery Zorra. Then, taking second stock of the magnificent Negro, she cooed up at him, "Ah, now wait, hombre; I will talk to *you* as we run. To hell with Father Rat Turd."

"Hold," I requested the shameless one. "Who guided you to find us here? I find this disturbing, Flicker, that she could so easily come upon us."

"Well, woman," Flicker growled, "answer the padre."

"Don't worry about it," Zorra laughed. "It was a man of the posse that chased you here. He knew where you were, naturally. He told me of it when I told him you were friends of mine. This was when he came to warn me that the wives of the camp were in revolt, his own wife being the leader of their anger."

"Aha!" I accused her. "A satisfied customer of yours, you she-fox, you!"

"But of course. You know my wares, little priest. Men don't forget Zorra of Fronteras."

"Ai, Jesu!" I groaned. "Some of us would like to."

Flicker broke in to glare at me. "This is your doing, Nunez, damn you!" he snapped. "You had better take care of it. Now, everybody, by God, listen to me. *Vamos, muchachos,* goddamn it!"

With the blasphemy, he kicked his horse into a snorting lope. Away we all went with him. Zorra came last on her stiff-legged mule. She was shouting after Flicker, "Here, wait for me, *Entero Negro!* I won't charge you anything!"

The "black stallion," so addressed, made nothing of answer to the rude proposal. He only kicked his horse the harder. The sandbar and the island and the river fell away in the dust of our departure. Lost to sight also in that dust, hence lost to mind, were Santiago Kifer and his leering henchmen. We thought only of Durango and Sinaloa and of the waiting gold.

Thus at last and truly began the great adventure to find the lost mine of the Franciscans.

It seemed to me, as I urged my mount after the others, that already I could hear tolling faintly and from afar the mission bells that legend assured led onward to the gold of El Naranjal.

Follow the bells, always follow the bells, the legend said. Never mind it that these were the same bells that two hundred years of searchers had heard calling them on, calling them on, only to leave their bones bleaching beside the nameless, empty trails that led where the ghost bells whispered.

We were different.

The gold was God's, and I was his padre.

The bells would not betray us.

25
KAYTENNAE, APACHE GUIDE

On Rio San Pedro, at the sandbar island, we were eleven miles only from Tombstone silver camp. Our historic trek, then, is most easily reckoned by marking its outset as Tombstone. The island and its lagoon could be gone with each spring's high waters. Such a famous place, however, as Tombstone itself would not wash away in desert floodings. Neither would it otherwise vanish from the maps of vain mankind. And, akin to any minstrel of the past who labors to record his wanderings, Nunez yearned to be remembered. By this token, *y por favor, hombres,* let the long march begin.

Southward we went at first. The raven himself could

not have flown truer course; but there were questions.

We understood that we faced great and perilous distances. Eight hundred *kilómetros,* Flicker warned. Five hundred *millas,* even as drawn by a rule flatly over obstacles that would make the eagle weep. And this merely to reach the borders of the legend country, the land of the feared Tepehuane Indians. Also, as every desert mountain traveler must know, each mile gained straightaway is to be counted two miles up, down, and round about; so that the distances are in truth doubled. We faced in reality a thousand-mile journey. And every mile menaced by ambushed panther, stalking jaguar, howling wolf, and that *peligro más feroz de todos—Ursus horribilis,* the great grizzly bear.

Still, our essential problem was neither the length nor the difficulty of the way, nor the danger from wild beasts.

The submountain roughlands ahead of us were most noted for harboring human marauders. These parts were the chosen domain of Mexican Apache raiders, particularly Bedonkohe and Nednhi. Crossing this territory, we must encounter the intractable people who had twice reduced my mission at Casas Grandes. Even that was but the immediate option; a grimmer choice waited beyond the roving Apache.

Were we presently to continue our southward riding down into Sonora, skirting Fronteras and Nacozari to pass easterly over Rio Moctezuma and south again between that stream and Rio Bavispe, we must come in due and fearful time to the forks of Rio Yaqui, motherplace of the people of that name.

These Indians are impossible of accurate assessment. When one has declared the ferocity of the Apache, he must then add something yet of pagan cruelty to describe the Yaqui. Bear in mind that as we called the Apaches *los bárbaros,* the barbarians, so they in turn called the Yaquis the same name. And believe it in truth, amigos, any living people whom an Apache will consider and call "barbarians" must be avoided as the rotting plague.

Flicker was properly aware of this. It made for us a Satan's choice, he said. This, on the evening of our first camp south of Arizona, a lonely place called Contra-bandista Spring.

"How will you have it, Nunez?" he asked. "Apache frying pan or Yaqui bonfire?"

"That is the way you see it, hombre?"

"Yes. We can sizzle or get spit-roasted. Your call."

"You forgot something," I protested indignantly.

"Ah?"

"We can pray."

He studied me a moment, laughed softly.

"*You* forgot something, padre," he said. "Your license has been lifted. Your prayers aren't legal any-more."

"Nonsense, Flicker! I serve God."

"Your church says you don't."

"What do you say, Flicker?"

"I don't give a damn."

"Flicker."

"Yes."

"Why did you send for a priest in Tombstone jail?"

"I told you before: If those deputies brought back a padre, I was going to use him as a hostage under threat of knifing him. You can't run that bluff with a Protestant minister. People don't rate them half so high as priests."

"Flicker, were you baptized?"

"Yes, I was stream-dipped a Baptist."

"You are no atheist, then."

"I never said I was."

"But you defame your Lord."

"No, I just say he hasn't ever done anything for me but bad."

"You're alive. You might have been hung."

"I'm black, too, and I might have been white."

"But what does that matter?"

"It doesn't. Except to another white man."

"Flicker, you must come back to God."

"Father, face the facts. We're birds of the same stain, you and I. They took my commission away from me. They defrocked you. And I suspect for the very same reason. We didn't wash white enough."

"Absurdo! Qué pamplinada! You know better than that!"

"So do you, Nunez. You didn't lose your mission because you befriended the Apache. You lost it because you were half Indian yourself, and *then* you befriended the Apache."

"And you, Flicker?"

"Me, padre? I lost my lieutenancy because a white man raped his own sweetheart and said it was me. He even followed me west to make sure I was drummed out of the army, even as a sergeant in the ranks. He couldn't take the chance that I might yet prove him the criminal."

"But there was another raping, I remember," I told him. "And you fled from Texas."

"That was of *my* sweetheart," Flicker said in a low, cold voice. "And the same man raped her. The same officer who followed me west."

"She died," I said.

"She was killed," Flicker corrected. "By him."

"And they thought it was you?"

"Yes. I ran for Mexico."

"You went to live with the Apache of Juh?"

"Yes, the Nednhi. But you know all of this, Nunez. Why do you inquisite me over it again?"

"Because it bears on what I said of prayer."

"What?"

"Yes, Flicker; didn't you also have a dream, even as Nunez has, and indeed for the same wild people?"

The black soldier fell silent. I could see his mind traveling the years.

"I did," he answered at last, and softly. "It was to lift these poor damned savages into something important. To show them that being red did not make them less men than the White Eyes or the Mexicans. But God didn't see it my way. Look what is happening. This entire country we've been through today and will go through tomorrow is filled with American Apache fleeing American cavalry. The poor devils are getting shot, bayoneted, raped, shipped off to Florida, starved, poisoned, trapped, driven incessantly, lied to, cheated, robbed, betrayed, scalphunted, rounded up, made beggars of, and, in the end, destroyed as men. I didn't do this to them, Nunez. God did."

"Flicker, you blaspheme!"

"Don't be a fool, Nunez," he said, black face demonic in the fire's light. "It isn't blasphemy to call God a damned liar. How can God be truth, when he treats black man and Indian, even Mexican of too-brown skin, as dirt, while the white man wins it all, and every time. Answer me that, Father Alvar Nunez, Order of Franciscan Monks."

"I will not deign to answer it!" I said, pale lipped.

"You cannot," Flicker replied, low voiced. "I was winning with the Apache people, returning their pride and their power. I was doing good but I wasn't white, eh, Nunez? The Americans heard of my work and sent the U.S. Army down here to stop it, and to kill the black messiah, right, padre? But I just about killed the army, my Apaches and me, and would have but for that God of yours sending in the Texas Rangers. Nunez, you know this. It cost you your mission. That's your God, priest, always winning for the whites."

"Flicker, be sure," I said. "Think. Was it our God who lied to you? Wasn't it you who lied? Who deserted him? You who were praying to false gods, Flicker? To heathen images? To Apache gods who were not your gods? Weren't you the liar who was damned, Flicker?"

"Heathen images?" he said. "False Apache gods? Now who is lying, Nunez? Did I not hear you only this very morning telling these Indians of ours you would build them a church where their gods would be welcome?"

"But you are not an Apache, hombre!" I cried. "You were born in Christ, baptized in his holy name. I don't lie to you or to them. They can pray to their gods and I will listen with them. I said that. Where is my lie?"

"Let is pass," black Flicker scowled. "You saved my life. I can't forget that, or fight you longer here."

"God saved your life, Flicker."

"The hell!" he flared. "Was it God put me into that secret tunnel under your altar at Casas Grandes? Who sent me running through that tunnel when the rangers were inside the walls and would have riddled me with

Texas lead? If so, God is a little humpback Mexican half-breed."

"It was my God who told me to do it," I insisted.

"Ah, Jesus, padre," Flicker sighed, reaching to place his hand on my shoulder. "There is no hope in your faith for me. My Apache dream is done, and so is yours."

"No, Flicker! Together, we can make another dream. We will share this one. You, the Apaches, Alvar Nunez."

Slowly, Flicker shook his head. I could see that he had for that hesitating moment considered the salvation I had offered him. But the moment was gone. In the black soldier's face was only his old sardonic distrust.

"I will tell you what I'll do with you, Nunez," he said. "You said that by prayer we could seek solution of a way through the bad going that lies ahead. All right, I'll pray with you, providing one thing—that you can arrange a miracle for us."

"Name it," I said, jutting priestly chin.

"Send us the answer to this question: What trail shall we take, Mr. White Eye God, to get us past both Apache and Yaqui. That's a tough one, padre. I'll wait."

He said it without meanly ill humor but decidedly in that derisive manner he had whereby he held the entire world at black bay. In the ordinary case, too, he would have been the easy victor over me. God is always hard put to vanquish doubters of the exceptional talents of Robert E. Lee Flicker. But this was a Roman night.

I later thought it a grand touch that, through an Apache pagan, the Holy Father answered Flicker's little faith.

Of course it was slim Kaytennae who stepped forth from the shadows behind us. He was apologetic. He had overheard too much of our talk before we were aware of his Indian approach. Yet he could not help but understand our dilemma and be brought, therefore, to speak out.

"There is a way to follow from this fire," he said, "that will spare us from Apache as well as Yaqui bad ones. Its secret has been given to a few of my people; I am one of them. If you want me to, I will show you this way."

I crossed myself and turned to Flicker.

"Did you hear that?" I asked, and he nodded.

I quickly put to Kaytennae our gratitude for his coming forward, bade him suffer no embarrassment at overhearing our troubled talk, accepted his offer with alacrity but of course dignity. He was pleased. Both black Flicker and humpenbacked Nunez sat wordless, while the young Warm Springs warrior melted back into the night that had brought him to our fire at Contrabandista Spring, in Sonora state, that long-ago night.

When he was gone, I asked of Flicker, without looking at him, what he would call Kaytennae, what would be his name for what had just walked away into the darkness.

"Was that an Apache?" I said.

"No, that was a miracle," Flicker answered.

And so we had our guide, and our agreement, for the dangerous way ahead.

"Flicker," I said in gratitude and thinking to remind him of his promise to pray with me should I produce a suitable *milagro,* "let us give our thanks to the Lord."

I bowed my head, crossed myself, commenced to mutter some applicable litany or other. Not hearing answering recitation from my black comrade, I unbowed head sufficiently to steal a side-glance at him. His head was unlowered, his lips motionless. He was staring past me into the night and the silences that crowded in upon our little camp at Contrabandista Spring.

There was such a look on his face as would bring foreboding to a senseless stone. A priest feels these things. It came to me that Flicker was seeing not the future but the past. Not our problems of tomorrow but his own sorrows of yesterday. He was seeing his life as *hombre negro.* As a black man with no home among brown Mexican, Anglo white, or bronze-skinned Apache. No true place with any color of fellowman, saving for his own race. And that race knowing a despair of past, present, and future to break the human heart.

I had been about to accuse him that he was not praying. That he had broken our small bargain.

I did not do so. Not that night and not ever.

For the first time in my lifetime of devotion to God, I knew a doubt of the Holy Trinity, of the Father and the Son and the Holy Ghost—of my dear God himself.

If there were not, as black Flicker had insisted, a God for all men of whatever skin color, then there was no God for any man of any color.

The idea—its sheer possibility—was frightful.

It was heresy.

And I was thinking it.

26
HAY MUCHO TRABAJO

I sat on with Flicker seeking to counter his despairful mood. The expedition, I recited for him, was assuming the nature of a full and proper company. Did this not cheer him? We had the three good horses of Kifer and his deputies, plus the tall bay, the two mounts of the Tombstone possemen, and Zorra's ragged mule. Our armament was bristling with the addition of Kifer's Winchester and Crench's shotgun, together with the revolvers, or belt guns, of both. We had also secured a supply of rifle and revolver ammunition in the cartridge bandoliers of the scalpers. Numbering these items with the very latest Winchester lever guns of Kaytennae and our Mexican Apaches, and adding in the sundry blades carried by the Apaches and taken from Crench and Kifer, we were in reasonable armor for the moment. "As well," I finished, totting up for Flicker, "I have found my chief of soldiers, my Apache guide, my good watchdog for the camp, and, barring but my mining expert, it would appear my little company has been blessed by God."

Flicker looked at me, dark lips pursed, the sardonic smile lifting to show the least gleam of white teeth.

(cont'd from other side)

of the Horses.

The Hash Knife Outfit. The softest among them lived only to kill. What hope for their pretty hostage—or the riders trying to save her?

These handsome, hardbound books are clothed in sunset red, desert tan and cavalry blue, with tinted page tops and golden stamping. They're the first of what could be a library of Western classics you'll be proud to own.

That's why we offer you four Zane Grey books (which are regularly $17.56) for only $1.

We think you'll be impressed. And that you'll want to own others in the series as they become available.

The Hash Kn...

Riders of the Purple Sage

The Thun- dering Herd

Wild Horse Mesa

...s large quantities, and ... e can offer

"I will name you some other gifts of your God, Nunez," he said. "Back there at the island we have Crench and the blind Kifer. Somewhere in their vicinity Belcher lingers. He will surely free them and, even if the scalper is sightless, I cannot rest easy with Kifer to my rear." He paused, swinging handsome face to peer into the night, southward, were we would go tomorrow.

"And out there ahead of us somewhere," he continued, "are Lupe and those two Bedonkohe *hesh-kes* of his. Three bad Apaches, well armed, well mounted, and knowing that Chongo will be thinking of them and of what they did to him and Packrat. That will make them nervous, and when an Apache gets nervous, clear out of the vicinity. When three of them do it all at the same time, sleep light and on your rifle. Now, you want more, padre?"

I assured him it mattered not if I did, there was no more of bad news that he might dredge up that night.

"Ah," he nodded. "Let me try."

I saw he was still smiling his Beelzebub smile, and I nodded back for him to go ahead, to have his try.

"We are carrying an old Mescalero lady who has to get down from her horse every half hour to make water," he said. "We have also two other women who will be worse than useless on the trail or in a fight. Indeed, they present a real danger to us. There is simply no way that a Mexican whore with good teeth and a chestnut-maned she-child like that daughter of hers can be anything but scary news to the men they're with. I just hope to Christ we don't meet up with Loco or Geronimo, let alone those devils down along the Rio Yaqui.

"Also, that damned guard dog of yours can't even keep pace with the whore's lame mule, and I will have to shoot him yet. I won't be held down by an old, sick dog."

At this juncture, I found my feet like an Indian orator, letting Flicker know I meant business.

"See here," I scolded him, "please don't call that whore a whore. Her name is Zorra and you will find she carries her own weight in any fight. As for the girl, I realize the problems posed by the jiggling of those noble mammaries and the fine bounce of buttock that is hers. However, I shall instruct her to loosen her garments to ameliorate the temptation, and I will personally see that her mane is braided and put up on her head so that a good sombrero will cover it. Now——"

I suspended my lecture to probe his muscled chest with threatening forefinger. It was like tapping a cabinet of teakwood, but I did not flinch.

"As to the dog and any posture that means harm to him, you will have to kill Nunez before the dog may be shot. Do you hear, you black scoundrel?"

Flicker did not laugh.

He scowled, rather, and pushed away my finger and said in the soft, dangerous way he had when aroused, "It could come to that, Nunez. Don't get between me and anything I need to do from this camp forward. We are just over the line into Sonora. There is no safety yet, nor none until we have come out of the country of the Apache on this side of the Sierra and managed to successfully outmarch the Yaqui the next two hundred miles. By then we will be damned near into the Tepehuane country and, as you well know, the Tepehuanes are the Indian guards of El Naranjal. 'The bronze guards of the orange grove,' the legend calls them. So it will be our ass wherever we go and by whatever trail Kaytennae may think he knows."

Flicker scowled the harder, concluding, "Now how do you like the lie of those horse apples that your God has mixed into the roadway of our grand luck so far, friend priest?"

I refused to dignify the question with an answer.

At the moment, saving me further embarrassment, Packrat came over to the fire from the picket line, where our people were sleeping near the horses. He seemed happy about something.

"Kaytennae is saying that you are well pleased, Jorobado, with our little party, but that you wish aloud for a mining expert, one who knows of gold, especially."

"Why, that is so," I said, puzzled. "Are you saying you know of such a one?"

"No, damn it, priest; I am such a one."

"You, a mining expert?"

"Ask me some questions," said the pudgy brave. "Let Flicker there do so. He knows of mines and yellow metal."

"I also know of little fat rats," Flicker said. "But I never heard before that you were a prospecting rat, as well. Where did you learn?"

"From two masters," Packrat said. "One a student like yourself, one just a plain white man, but very smart."

"First one?" Flicker said.

"You ever hear of Mackenna, Filcker?"

"The man who found the lost Adams Diggings?"

"The same one. I was his packer and guide for seven years before he found that Adams map. He taught me much about gold, where it might lie, and where not."

"And the other, your second man?" Flicker queried.

"You will know him, too," Packrat said. "It was Old Mad. You know—Seebie."

"Sieber?" Flicker asked, unbelieving. "Al Sieber?"

"He was the only Sieber," Packrat shrugged.

"He was indeed," Flicker whistled softly. "How did you come by him, or more likely him by you?"

"He saved me from some bad Indians—Yaquis."

"With Yaquis, there is no other kind."

"Yo lo creo, hombre; I believe it. *Animales, todos."*

"Were they from the high Rio Yaqui country, where we must pass? Above the big forks? Above Soyopa?"

"Yes, they were of Monkey Woman's band."

"My God, no. Not Simialita? Kifer's mother?"

"The same," shrugged Packrat, but his laconic reply to Flicker's startlement only struck into my own memory like the shaft of an arrow of curare. *Nombre Dios—Simialita?*

Here, *amigos míos,* a man must take you back. While brave black Flicker shakes his head to Packrat's innocent creation of a nightmare by day, Nunez must tell you of what the dread name meant. It begins with the father of Santiago Kifer, and in this wise:

The original Dutch John Kifer, sire of Santiago, was an American scalphunter operating through northern

Mexico in the decade of the 1840s. Unquestionably, one of the most gruesome mass murderers of human history, the senior Kifer was still the product of his era and its environment of Indian hatred by both Anglo and *Mejicano*. Scalphunting was neither an invention of Dutch John's nor an exclusive viciousness. Men of his time did stalk and kill other men simply for the bounty paid upon the hair of their heads. If Dutch John Kifer in an average season murdered more than two hundred Indians, was his the primary crime? What of the government in Ciudad Chihuahua that paid each year, for many years, a price of one to two hundred American dollars for every Indian scalp lock delivered to it?

It is said that in one particular season Kifer earned a hundred thousand dollars selling human hair.

Quita! as the Mexicans said, God forbid it.

Could another man ever equal this accounting of horrors? Did another man live, in fact, who might even approach it?

The answer was yes.

Such another man did live.

Santiago Kifer was the offspring of Dutch John in fornication with the mentally deficient Yaqui squaw, Simialita—Monkey Woman, or Little Monkey—herself a murderess and pariah of the outlands. It was she indeed who, outliving the elder Kifer, ran in pack with her notorious son Santiago—who carried none of the half-breed look and seemed a white man to all who saw him—and she served her son as Judas goat to entice her Indian kinsmen within the various inhuman traps laid by Santiago Kifer and his Texas scalpers.

It is said that the evil men do lives after them, while the good is too oft interred with the bones.

No man knows where rest the bones of Dutch John Kifer. Or what single sand's grain of good might lay in the crypt with those bones. But all men living in his time and after him knew the evil that Dutch John left to murder for him beyond his grave.

Its name was Santiago Kifer.

Santiago, the One Eared. Santiago, the Mad. Santiago the Cruel. Santiago, the Shame of God. He had a dozen names, each more fearful than the last, and more

monstrous. This was the man we had blinded at Sandbar Island and, God be praised, left there all safely behind us. This was the son of Simialita, the Yaqui Monkey Woman, whose name had only this moment past
caused even the ebony face of Robert Flicker to go
gray.

Indeed, the brave Flicker was just then recovering.

"Excuse it, Ratoncito," he apologized for the long
pause to Packrat. "Now, then, aside from being saved
from the Yaquis, what did you learn from Al Sieber
that you did not from Glen Mackenna?"

"All about silver," explained Packrat. "How to guess
it apart from gold in its ways of hiding in the earth. I
worked like a white man for Seebie, like a dog.
Apaches don't work like that with shovels and
wheeling barrows and long iron drills and jackhammers.
We called the drills bull penises."

"That's close," Flicker grinned. "Try bull prods."

They continued, and shortly Flicker turned to me
and said that Packrat actually did know a great deal
more than he, Flicker, about locating precious mineral. "You've got your mining expert, padre. And na-
tive-grown, at that."

He paused, shaking black, fierce head.

"An *Apache* prospector," he said, entirely unto himself. "For Christ's sake, what next?"

Packrat had a reply for that, too.

He brightened visibly.

"Chongo is next," he informed the black deserter.
"See, there he comes. *Hola,* Chongo. *Qué pasa?*"

Chongo did not answer his Indian brother but came
straightaway around the fire, to Flicker.

"Send the others away, *jefe,*" he scowled. "We must
talk alone. *Hay mucho trabajo. Comprende?*"

Flicker and I exchanged glances, and the black leader motioned me with his head to go on, to move away.
Packrat was already leaving. I went with him, looking
back uneasily. Chongo had said that there was trouble,
much trouble, and the manner in which he had made
the statement left no room for interpretation or nuances
of meaning.

When a wild bronco Apache from the Mexican Sierra Madre del Norte informs you there is trouble, *de ahí!*

Do not linger in its presence.

When I came over to the blanket-place of the women, I imagined they were all asleep. The horses nickered me a soft greeting, and the old dog Loafer stirred his tail to thump the dirt where he lay curled up by Charra Baca.

"Father," the girl whispered, unexpectedly, "what is Chongo saying? What has he found?"

"Found?" I whispered back. "I did not even know he had been looking for something. What do you mean, *chica?*"

"I mean," Charra told me, "that Chongo has been gone since sundown. He just now returned. Didn't you miss him?"

"No, I'm no Apache like you."

"Father, you better learn to be. There is trouble. I could smell it. It rode back into this camp with Chongo."

"Ussen's name!" a familiar graveled voice complained. "When can a person expect to sleep in this damnable company of braying jacks and half-breed jennies? What time of the night is it, anyway?" Young Grass sat up, digging at her rheumy eyes. "Josana," she said to Charra, "you will never make a good Apache. You talk all the time."

"Jesus protect us," objected the third female voice. "This camp is busier than Tombstone. I might as well get up and go and look for a customer."

Zorra made as to go over and stir the fire, preparing to reheat the supper's coffee. But an instant reprimand came from Flicker. "Go back and gather up the others; get the horses and your mule ready. And send the priest to me," he ordered the Mexican harlot. *"Más aprisa!"*

"He wants you over there," Zorra grumbled to me, returning. "Damn it, I don't like to be commanded about by a *negro*. But, then, ah! such a *negro*. I will sell him something before this journey is out."

"Baggage!" I cried. "Away with you!"

"Nevertheless, we shall do business," Zorra insisted.

"Pah!" I snorted. "Do you imagine that such noble fellows as Flicker will pay for what is offered free?"

"Aha!" the shameless one gloated. "Just like a priest, eh? Why, you scoundrel, Jorobado. I ought to tell—"

"Hush," I said. "Do not alarm the others. Do as Flicker has told you; ready the riding stock. Charra, you and young Grass do as Zorra directs."

"Since when has a settlement Mexican told a Mecalero Apache how to get ready for trouble?" Young Grass demanded querulously. "I won't obey a thing she suggests." •

"Don't then," I snapped. "Stay here by yourself and wait for whatever trouble it is that Chongo has found."

I scuttled over to join Flicker at the fire, noting by a covert glance behind me that Young Grass was working harder than either Charra or Zorra to get ready. Like her half-Apache neophyte, Josana, the old woman could "smell" that *trabajo* moving ever nearer through the night.

As I came up to Flicker, the nature of our difficulty was swiftly sketched for me.

Chongo had scouted both backtrail and foretrail on direction from Flicker. Neither jaunting had been wasted. Behind us came Kifer and Crench and Belcher. They had stolen some horses from a ranch along the way. Kifer had his eyes bandaged, and his horse followed on a lead rope after those of his deputies. It made their going somewhat slow but did not promise us, with our weary stock, any safe lead. The one thing that was certain about the scalpers was that they were following *our* trackline. They hadn't stolen horses merely to put miles between themselves and the angry men and wives of Tombstone, Arizona.

"But do not imagine," Flicker warned me in ominous tone, "that these are the worst of our followers."

Ahead of us, Chongo had found the hoofmarks of Lupe and the two Bedonkohes. Those marks were bending in a wide circle to come back toward us. Lupe had discovered our band and was "getting nervous." He and his henchmen would likely be camped now, but first light would see them moving to do something about Kaytennae, Chongo, and Packrat, whose story of their treachery to Apache comrades in a war situation could mean a tribal vote of death. Not even Geronimo would dare flout the war rules of the Apache to pardon Lupe, Tule Moon, and Go-ta-chai. So it was, Flicker concluded, that we were in the middle of bad trouble.

"Will we then leave camp now?" I asked anxiously.

"It would be less a gamble to stay," Flicker answered, "but I am trusting you to have the camp ready when we return."

"We? Return? What is this, Flicker?"

"What it is," Flicker explained, "is that Chongo and I are going to take the fight to these two sets of beauties who are trailing us."

"But, God's name, Flicker, I can't run a war camp."

"You will have Packrat to help you."

"He's unreliable," I complained. "You can't believe a word he says."

"That ought to be a familiar thing for you," Flicker grinned. "A priest and a pack rat trading lies."

"Be gone!" I said. Then, courage vanished. "But where to, Flicker? *Santa,* you may never come back." I peered to the north, toward our rear. "Those devils, that Kifer and his twain of foolish deputies, beware of them, Flicker!"

"Advise Chongo of that," the big Negro told me. "He is taking them. I am going after Lupe."

"You! *You* trailing the Bedonkohes? Why is that when we have Chongo, their Apache cousin, to do it?"

"Because, good priest," Flicker told me, "I am the superior horse thief to Chongo."

"What?"

"They have six good horses, and it is good horses we must have to make it away from any enemy. That applies to Kifer, or Lupe, or those Arizona ranchers stirred up by the scalpers stealing their horses, or anyone else who may come after us. We will not get far, padre, with our poor and few mounts."

"But the risk, Flicker. The gamble!"

"Only life or death, Nunez. Come along. I want you to tell that tall bay horse of ours that it is all right for me to ride him. He seems to have attached himself to you. Just like that scrofulous dog."

"Merely a matter of life and death, Flicker," I returned his hard saying. "I owe the dog my life and the horse owes his life to me."

"Spoken like a true slave of the faith," Flicker grunted. "An answer for everything but never a solution. Talk to the horse for me; I'm in a hurry."

Five minutes later, Flicker was gone, riding the tall bay *más aprisa,* very swiftly, and as if he knew precisely where to guide the animal. Chongo was already departed, taking Zorra's ratty mule, "surer of foot for short night-riding." There was nothing the others of us might do then, but wait. Wait and be ready.

But there are some things we are never ready for.

27
SANTIAGO'S MESSENGER

It was about 8:00 P.M. when Flicker and Chongo left camp for their night scoutings. My instructions were to take a daylight departure should they fail to return. Accordingly, when the sun came pink and gold through the dawning mists and neither Flicker nor Chongo had returned, I consigned our souls to God and ordered the march resumed. Some bickering at leaving their warm blankets arose among my female marchers. But none of them wished to be "walked in on" by Lupe and his *hesh-kes* or by Kifer and his scabrous deputies. And of course failure of our scouts to come back could mean but one thing, Flicker and Chongo had been killed. The way was clear for both the Apaches and the white scalpers to strike our camp.

"Más aprisa!" called old Young Grass to Charra Baca and Zorra the whore. "Santiago Kifer has already promised to sell my hair for half price in Ciudad Chihuahua. Imagine what he will get for yours. That is, after he has taken what else he wants of both of you. Aha!

Now you scuttle to your horses, eh? *Vamos, vamos,* you cow-breasted cowards!"

From this point, Packrat took command of the decampment. Kaytennae, able now to ride alone, was sent out to scout the trail for us. We all pushed our horses hard after him, anxious to be clear of Contrabandista Spring. Nevertheless, we had gone but a quarter mile when we heard behind us an outrageous braying.

"My God," Zorra said, "that is my mule. Chongo must be all right, after all."

"Thank God for that," I added.

But Packrat was peering into the sun back toward the spring, and he said, in guttural Apache, "Don't thank your god too much. The mule is alone. There is no rider on him, only a sack tied to the horn of his saddle. Get into this brush here, all of you. Be still. I don't care for the smell of this business."

We pushed into the nearby growth of paloverde and desert mesquite. But a mule's eyesight is nigh unto as keen as an antelope's. The long-eared devil had seen us. Braying to us to wait for him, he broke into a jarring lope straight toward our hiding place.

I took the minute of his advance to do some hard praying. It was not enough.

In the bag that jounced and banged soddenly from the horn of the animal's saddle was a gruesome burden. When Packrat went out to the mule to look at the sack, all of us could see the blood soaking through it from its interior. Without a word or look to any of us, Packrat untied the sack from the saddle's horn and upended its contents on the ground.

The object that fell out to bounce one time and then lie still between two rocks of the trail, its sightless eyes staring squarely into our horrified faces, was a human head. A naked human head. There was no hair on it but for the eyebrows, and the scalping had been to the skullbones from forehead to base of brainpan.

Packrat looked at the head, then at our huddled company.

I made the sign of the crucifix against Lucifer.

Charra Baca, only one-half Apache, uttered a rending sob and began to weep brokenly.

I could hear the whore of Fronteras shakenly praying.

In the terrible pause, the old dog Loafer went over and sniffed the head where it lay. He backed away from it, every individual hair of his roach erected.

Gathering every force of will, I walked out to Pack-rat. We began to talk in his tongue. It was soon evident that Packrat knew well the codes of this grim business. The head and its loathsome sack must be left in the trail as a danger sign to Flicker, he said. This was in case the black rider might still be alive and coming on. There was no choice so long as there was any chance that Flicker lived; to not leave the terrible article would be to deprive a fellow raider of his due warnings of peril all around.

It was agreed swiftly. We went back to our comrades and gave them the orders to mount up and move out. The fear and dread of the place lent Apache wings to our flight. Not one of us looked back, but I breathed a prayer as we fled.

Requiescat in pace, Chongo, our brave friend.

28
SHUT UP AND RIDE FAST

With our underrested horses and Kaytennae's exceeding caution as guide, we made poor progress. At noonhalt we were but fifteen miles south of our start, out upon the open *monte* north and east of Cananea. A few miles on to the south lay Fronteras. Off to our left sprawled the Sierra de la Madera, a subrange of Mexico's great Sierra Madre del Norte, the mother mountains of the Apache people.

The presence of these wild ones could be felt.

The country about us held silent as some rocky sunlit tomb. Nothing in it seemed to move. I could not hear even the song of a bird. No lizard's tail rustled the drifted sand. The Sonoran desert was waiting for something.

Soon enough we saw what it was.

A cloud of the yellow dust of the country rose into the windless skies behind us. Horses. Horses on the full-out run. Coming, as we had come, from Contrabandista Spring. We were being followed, and at furious pace.

"Kifer!" I cried out instinctively. "My God, he is after us!"

But Packrat and Kaytennae shook Apache heads.

No. This was light dust. It was not made by heavy pounding of burdened animals. These horses were running free. Or perhaps being driven *en caballada,* bunched.

Again, we saw soon enough which it was.

Even as Packrat was disposing our meager forces for defense within the straggle of sahuaro cacti that shaded our rest, Kaytennae, watching the dustboil come, let out a thin Apache wolf yelp. The cry was answered in kind from within the rolling dust of the running horses. Next moment the animals slowed, the dust of their galloping thinned off and fell away. They gladly came in to share our sahuaro grove, wet and panting with their run. From behind their lathered number a tall bay horse emerged bearing a rider with the muscles of Adonis and a complete armor of yellow white Sonoran dust cake to camouflage his ebon underskin.

"*Buenas tardes,*" said Robert E. Lee Flicker, stepping down from the tall bay horse. "Is there coffee for a hardworking horse thief?"

We gave him the last cup in our tin of noonhalt brewing. He gulped it down, then ordered the company at once back on the march. To this point he had said no word of his adventures since leaving us. But he came to ride with me after the start, telling the story for my ears alone.

He had come in the blackness of night to the fireless camp of the *hesh-ke* Apaches. He had found it with his nose, smelling the Indian horses. Leaving his own mount tied downwind, he went forward. Luck befell him. The Indian horses were all on hobble grazing, none tethered near its owner. It was but the work of moments for Flicker to slip among them, cut the hobbles, free the horses, and glide on into the bedding spot of the Apache "cold" camp, all unknown to its blanketed sleepers. Now there was a decision, a choosing:

Ought he to kill all three in their slumbers, either by knife or skulling rock? Or should he awaken and permit to flee on foot the two dupes of Lupe, slaying only the guilty subchief? Or ought he to slay none of them but merely take the horses and so set them afoot in dangerous land where Mexican cavalry roamed? Well, Flicker knew the best thing.

He found his killing rock in the darkness and crept with it upraised to the side of Tule Moon. But he could not do it. He could never be what the United States Army had said he was. What they had banished him for with a death-price on his head—murderer. No, Flicker would take the greatest risk of all: He would awaken all three Apaches and claim the Vengeance Rule against Lupe.

This was the Chiricahua code that held that a man cannot go against his chosen leader in the field on a raiding expedition except that he might do so to save his own life—*if* the leader and all the others were inescapably trapped. This had certainly not been the case when Lupe stole the horses of his brother Apaches and tried to get away thereby. Flicker, as raiding party head, had explicitly forbidden any splitting up of his men under duress of pursuit. In this, he flew directly in the face of Apache tradition. But he was Soldado Negro, the Black Soldier, and his fighting methods were a mixture of the Indian and Anglo warfare tactics. He was also, by the use of these same hybrid tactical strategies, the most successful of all Mexican Apache raiders.

Lupe had known all of this, of course.

It was why he had turned back to finish off Chongo and Packrat, who might bear witness against him for his treachery in the field after the loss of Flicker.

What Lupe had not figured on was finding that he still had the same black Flicker to account to, rather than merely Packrat and Chongo. Flicker was counting now on the surprise of this discovery. Awakening to see his black war leader alive and standing over him

must make Lupe *muy chaveta,* very rattled. Flicker
hoped!

He moved away from Tule Moon and Go-ta-chai to
the side of Lupe. Bending, he seized the long hair of
the sleeping Apache and jerked Lupe completely free
of the ground. His forearm barred the throat of the
struggling Indian. The life of Lupe was shut off. The
life and the voice. It was Flicker's voice that now
shouted to the arousing Tule Moon and Go-ta-chai.
They were not to reach for their *besh-e-gar,* their rifles.
Lupe's death would be the price of the first movement
from either of them.

Uncertainly, the two warriors agreed to the warning.

Flicker eased his stranglehold on Lupe. Lupe went
to his knees, sucking for the breath of life. Flicker at
once planted his Colt's revolver behind the ear of the
gasping Apache. Lupe was not that far gone that he
did not understand how near to him in that moment
was *dah-eh-sah.*

Flicker, however, took no chances with that understanding. There were only three of them, he reminded
the Apaches, and he had six bullets. Were they going
to argue with that kind of war trail arithmetic? Or were
they of a wisdom sufficient to stand very still and listen?

Lupe was still troubled to breathe, and he did not
answer.

Go-ta-chai and Tule Moon had a mixture of feelings.

They would not move against Flicker, they said, but
why had he scattered their ponies? This was no good
country to be afoot in. Too much Mexican cavalry
about.

Flicker accepted that, but he said that neither was
Arizona a good country to be afoot in. And the three
of them had put Chongo, Packrat, and Kaytennae afoot
up there, with too much American cavalry about.
Wasn't that a true thing?

It was, Tule Moon had admitted. And they were
sorry for it, he and Go-ta-chai. It had been Lupe's idea.

Flicker knew that, he said. But their only chance to
gain tribal clemency for themselves lay in their willing-

ness to now serve as witnesses in a Vengeance Rule fight between Flicker and Lupe—a fight then and there. Such witnessing would show Geronimo and the people that Tule Moon and Go-ta-chai had repented and were repudiating Lupe. What had they to say to that?

Go-ta-chai had a question to that question: How was Flicker to trust them, once the fight started?

Flicker had answered that he knew precisely how to trust them, and it would be in this way: He would have Lupe tie them both to sahuaro trees before the fight, so guaranteeing their honesty during that contest.

Now, for the last time, what did they say?

"There was one hell of a pause, then," Flicker said. "But finally they accepted their roles as witnesses. I made Lupe tie them to a couple of sahuaros, and he and I stripped and took our knives and went at it.

"He damned near got me, padre. He sliced within a quarter inch of my life too many times. That Lupe was the best with a blade I ever saw. Finally, I had to take him with my hands."

"Eh, you threw away your knife, Flicker?"

"It was that, or my life, padre."

"Then?"

"Then it went fast. You've forgotten what I told you so many years ago—I was military academy champion in fighting with the fists."

"I remember it now, yes."

I moved my mount a bit away from that of the black man, the better to admire him. "You beat Lupe senseless. You took away his blade but spared him. Flicker, I salute you. What a brave and exceeding merciful thing to do."

"It wasn't as you think," Flicker said. "When I had him down and out, I wanted to kill the son of a bitch, but I couldn't do it."

"Of course, Flicker! You—kill a helpless man? In cold blood? Never, hombre."

"You still don't know me, do you, padre," he said. "I would have as soon killed him as spit on him. But something stopped my hand. I actually reached for the rock."

"Hah!" I cried. *"Something,* eh, Flicker? Don't you know the power yet? It was him, the Lord your God."

"No, padre," Flicker said. "It was the devil."

He stopped to gaze off over the desert. There was trouble in the dark face. And an unspent anger, also.

"The devil was saving Lupe for something worse than the skulling rock," he continued. "I untied Tule Moon and Go-ta-chai and had them tie Lupe on his pony, still unconscious. It was in my mind to take him back with me and turn him over to the mercy of Chongo. That was what had stopped me from killing him, you see. I knew that Chongo's justice would not be so simple, so quick."

Again, the black rider looked away, and the look was not good to see.

"I let Tule Moon and Go-ta-chai go free on foot, advising them to tell the Bedonkohe that Flicker had returned from the dead to punish Lupe, but had declared them innocent. It was a good story and it convinced them. They took off like scalded cats. I then got a lead rope on Lupe's pony, put the horses on drive, and headed back for Contrabandista Spring. But when I got there, the spring had been occupied."

"Kifer!" I interrupted. "Do not say it!"

"Yes, and both Crench and Belcher with him. Plus they had their fresh stolen horses, guns, grub, blankets, everything. I couldn't do anything but circle them wide and cut for your trail. Which I did, but I hadn't run it a quarter minute when I came up on some heavy-bellied buzzards in the trail. They waddled off and I saw a human head there. They had been at it pretty bad, but one side of the face and one ear were left—the ear that Chongo wore that turquoise ring in. I cursed low from my guts and the devil brought Lupe back to consciousness just then, and the Apache bastard saw the head and the earring and let out a whoop of laughter and began to howl like a loafer wolf.

"The killing blood got in my eyes, padre. I recall running at him with my knife and cutting him free of the pony. Then I threw the knife as far as I could, and

we both ran for it. It was a tie and we fought like
panthers for the blade, and I got it and sliced Lupe
above the eyes and around over the ears, each side. I
had him throat-barred with the left arm when I cut him.
I then seized the skin of his head and ripped it free
with every ounce of hate I had in me."

For the last time, Flicker broke his narrative to let
his dark eyes run the distances of the Sonoran *monte*.

"The scalp came away in my hand," he finally said,
"like peeling a cooked calf's head. I took it and put it
on Chongo's bare skull, where his own hair was gone.
It was madness."

"God's name, Flicker; you scalped Lupe *alive?*"

"I told you, padre. The devil knew where he wanted
Lupe to end. And how. Last I saw of him, he was
walking around in circles feeling his head and laughing. He had his chance at the knife. That's why I threw
it in the Apache way. Neither of us ran until it hit the
ground."

I reached to touch Flicker's great arm.

"Your mind was sick for that minute," I said. "God
will forgive you. You are all right now?"

"Yes. But Kifer saw me. He was alerted by Lupe's
wolf howls and wild laughing. You see that dust moving back there, padre? That's Kifer and his deputies.
But it isn't all that simple that they're just following
us. Because, by God, they're not."

"What?" I rasped. "You say they no longer trail us?"

"I don't know. Their line is easterly of ours now.
They're going around inside us and driving hard to
pass us. Question is, why?" Flicker was frowning now.
"If they hold to that course, they will wind up past
Nacozari, into the forks of the Yaqui. You've heard
about the Yaqui, padre."

"The people, you mean?" I said uneasily.

"I'm not talking about the river, Nunez."

"My God," I breathed. "I've just thought of a thing
that pales the gills. Maybe Kifer is going home."

"Home?" Flicker scowled.

"Yes," I said. "Don't you remember?"

"Remember what, padre?"

"His mother, Flicker; she's a Yaqui."

"Jesus," said Flicker, long and slow. "You're right."

He spurred his horse out of line and rode up to join Kaytennae and Packrat at column's head. There was an exchange of grunting Apache, and Kaytennae kicked his horse into a lope, waving our comrades to do likewise. They all responded. We made quite a dust, being now a dozen horses, one mule, and an old lame camp dog. Flicker dropped back in moments to rejoin me.

"I still don't know why Santiago's so set to beat us to the Yaqui country," he said. "Only that he is."

"One thing we can be certain on," I said. "His reason is evil. The brain of Santiago Kifer never rests."

"He wants the gold," Flicker frowned. "So why does he leave our trackline?"

"Remember, he is blind," I said. "Perhaps it is that fear outreaches the wickedness within him. He may want only to be where Yaqui eyes can see for him."

"Yes," Flicker nodded. "Or Yaqui rifles stare us down where he can't."

"What will we do?" I asked, seeing the dust of Santiago Kifer and his henchmen fade farther yet to our inside and gaining still around us. "A prayer, perhaps, Flicker."

"A letter would be better, Nunez," the black rider suggested. "I will compose one; take it down:

" *'Dear Monkey Woman, we are sorry that one of our redskin Indians shot out the eyes of your boy, Santiago. But you know how it is. Accidents will happen. We know you won't hold it against us and will order your peaceable tribe to let us pass to go steal the gold of the orange grove, down in the Tepehuane country.*

" *'Of course the gold belongs to you Indians but wouldn't you rather that some good old niggers and half-breed priests and Mexican whores got it than some Yori sons of bitches, some damned white men?*

" *'I remain, your favorite Chihuahua black robe,*

                        Father Alvar Nunez, O.F.M.

" *'P.S. The Indian that shot Santiago can't see anymore either; Santiago chopped off his head. Ha, ha. Your boy is certainly some funner. Chock full of laughs, isn't he? Oh, you Yaquis—!' "*

"Flicker!" I shouted, exasperated at last. "Enough!"

"More than plenty, padre," he agreed. "Lick it shut and mail it at the first post office we come to. Meanwhile, kick your horse in the ass, and shut up."

29
JUST NORTH OF BACOACHI

Late that afternoon, Kaytennae brought us to an Apache water hole in roughening *monte*. Now the ranges were running higher on either side of us. And were closing in on us. The country ahead seemed impenetrable. Kaytennae said it was not, but only more dangerous. He said we were now in the headwaters of Rio Moctezuma, westernmost of the Rio Yaqui's two main forks. We could see no headwaters nor any water of any kind except that to which the Mexican Apache-raised youth had led us. Packrat, who had spent a great deal of time in Mexico, thought we were lost. So did black Flicker, who had ridden with the Mexican Apache people the past ten years. Kaytennae only shook his head.

If such as Packrat and Flicker knew of the secret way down into Yaqui land, then every Apache would know it.

Either they trusted Kaytennae to know where he was and how the legendary trail to El Naranjal lay, or Kaytennae would gladly turn over the guiding to any one of us who might feel he was being tricked or misled.

Of course there were no candidates for this duty, and Flicker smoothed over the matter by telling Kaytennae that we had already put our lives in his keeping. What we voiced now were merely uneasinesses. He, Flicker, knew, for example, that truly we were not yet in the headwaters country of Rio Moctezuma. And would not be until we reached the settlement of Bacoachi, perhaps tomorrow, with luck and a long ride. But, meanwhile, we all understood our guide to mean only that we were hard upon Rio Moctezuma and that this stream was indeed the big western fork of the main Yaqui.

This was *not* what Kaytennae had said, in fact.

But the Apache nodded to Flicker's words and all was well. One must know Indians. They speak in sweeping ways. The same way as they think. The red man is not restricted of imagination. Nor of expression.

Neither will he tolerate being cornered.

I gave Flicker high marks for his astute intervention; it was only later that he told me the idea wasn't his, at all, but had been given him by Packrat, who believed that Kaytennae would respond more happily to balm from Soldado Negro than from Ratoncito. It was in this same later confession to me that Soldado Negro advised me that Packrat was not a Mexican Apache but an American Indian—of the same band, and once closest friend to, the notorious bronco, Apache Kid. But this is another digression. Forgive it.

A true story such as this one of mine never comes all of a piece and flowing in order. One must tell it in the same fashion as it happened, by episodes, accidents, oversights, rememberings, and, betimes, happy invention.

After all, where memory fails, fabrication will do as well. Ofttimes better. The heart of the matter is that one bear sternly to the real trail where he may. And the way Kaytennae now led us, from that water hole of mountain quail and kit foxes just north of Bacoachi, through the land of the Yaqui and beyond, to the country of the fierce Tepehuane, even to the very towering brink of Ghost Canyon above River of the Oranges, was the true trail. If it must be shortened here, do not believe that Nunez has also shrunk its truth. We faced the real death in a dozen places. Of these, I give but the most central to our dangerous track. Where the way lay but frightening and awesome for its heat; its dizzying

heights and fearsome deeps; its lack of water, of game
to eat, of fuel for fire, of shelter from raging mountain
winds and rains and bolts of rivening electric fire from
the skies, the listener will be spared his fellow suffering.
What follows now is the meat and bone of the soup. No
broth is included. Nunez thinks that the deadlinesses of
people unto other people is the stuff that excites man.
The hells of nature are too large, too overpowering, and
moreover too well known to all travelers of the wild
places.

But man—ah, may one ever say it better than the
Bard, not of the Yaqui but of the Avon, said it these
two and one-half centuries gone? *Oigan Uds:*

> . . . but man, proud man,
> Drest in a little brief authority,
> Most ignorant of what he's most assur'd,
> His glassy essence, like an angry ape,
> Plays such fantastic tricks before high heaven,
> As make the angels weep.

Our little company was to play its own fantastic
tricks before the angry apes and the mountain mirrors
of Sonora. Our glassy essences were in fact to make the
angels—and our poor Apaches—weep. But two proud
men, Flicker and Nunez, dressed in their tiniest of least
authorities, were indeed most stupid where they should
have been the brightest. And disaster followed.

30
INTO THE DESERT OF DAH-EH-SAH

Next day, the country opened out. We came from the
narrow darks of the previous night's camp into a land of
sere yellow bluffs and thinly grassed savannas. A pock-
ing of trees and scrub growth marked a few of the dry
watercourses. Some small desert quail scurried ahead of
us. A red hawk floated above our cavalcade, seemingly

glad for any company in that empty place. During the march we saw several bands of mustangs far off. Just before noon, Flicker shot a wild burro. Packrat prepared it in the Apache manner, throwing away everything but the loins and the intestines. At noonhalt, we ate the loins broiled over mesquite coals. Young Grass took the large intestine to clean and tie off and so fashion into an Indian water bag. We had no coffee, bread, flour, salt, beans, or other decent provision. Wiping his hands on his thighs after the last mouthful of smoking burro loin, Flicker announced that we must seek supplies, and soon. Our animals, being desert-bred, could survive in passage of the unfriendly land. But we humans could not. Not we half-breed priests and adopted Negro Apaches, at least. And not the sultry white-sired Charra Baca. Probably even the aged Young Grass, Apache or not, would also die unless the expedition were speedily outfitted.

I did not care for the idea that Kaytennae and Packrat could make it through without our company.

Somehow that thought preyed upon our trust of them.

Why ought either to be loyal to our deaths in their leading of our chanceful mission to find the gold of El Naranjal? What was in it for them as pureblood Apaches?

Then Flicker reminded me.

They were members of his raiding party. It was Apache law that they should cleave to the very end to his direction. They might leave us only when and if our lives were doomed, while theirs were not. Such a condition could arise momentarily, of course. The while, Flicker chided me, I should do well to show a more confident face.

After all, it was my dream that we pursued.

Restored of some strength by the burro meat, we went on. Skirting the settlement of Bacoachi that afternoon, we traveled until well after twilight. Kaytennae wanted to be safely around the Mexican town. Also, the water he had expected to find just east of Bacoachi had dried up. The next Apache well was many miles on, but we had to reach it. Even our Indian comrades were worn to exhaustion by the time our guide said softly, "Here it is, this is the place," and we all literally fell from footsore mounts.

The water was almost but not quite bad.

By sitting up all night skimming and straining its slow seepage, Young Grass was able to fill our solitary burro-gut canteen. It was as well. Next day's journey on into the real headwaters of Rio Moctezuma was even longer. But it was broken by a gift of God.

Shortly before nooning, Flicker saw smoke to our left. It was where no settlement was and no rancheria familiar to him, Kaytennae, or Packrat. The column halted in shade, another offering of *Dios*. It was a sycamore grove, an oasis in the desert of gray and thorny scrub. These lovely white- and brown-barked trees meant groundwater always. Flicker commanded Packrat to instruct the women in digging for this precious find so as to replace the poor water in our burro bag with sweet fresh water from the sycamore sands. Also the trees would hide us, no idle advantage with strange smoke showing.

"What do you make of it?" Flicker asked Kaytennae.

The two had drawn off a bit to be away from the women, and I had come over to stand with them.

"*Yo no sé*," shrugged the Apache. "Not Indians maybe."

"You got a better idea than Indians?" Flicker said.

"Mexicans maybe," Kaytennae answered. "*Una recua de mulas*. That's the old trail over there."

"Hmmm," Flicker nodded. "From Nacozari up to Agua Prieta, eh? I'd forgotten that old road." He paused. "A mule train, you say. At noonhalt, likely." The Negro tilted his nostrils to meet the light breeze working our way. "They're cooking something. I smell meat burning."

Kaytennae sampled the air in his turn and nodded. "Bad meat," he said. "We'd better go over there."

Flicker hesitated. "How bad?" he said.

"I've smelled it only once before," the slender Apache replied.

"Where?" said Flicker, dark eyes narrowing.

"In a Yaqui camp," Kaytennae said. "Get the horses."

"Hold on," Flicker scowled. "You saying it's Yaquis over there bushwhacked a Mex mule train? *De ahí, amigo!* You don't massacre a mule train without firing a shot, and we didn't hear a pistol pop, nor a musket boom."

"You talk empty," Kaytennae grimaced. "I'm going; I smell bad meat. Stay here with the women, if you are afraid. I won't blame you. It might be Yaquis, still."

"Make up your mind," Flicker complained. "You said it wasn't Indians, first off. Now you keep saying Yaquis."

"They're not Indians, they're *bárbaros,*" Kaytennae said.

"Jesus Christ," Flicker growled. "Padre, you want to come over here and go along with your foster son and your soldier-chief? I'm going to need an interpreter for this Apache guide of ours. He's harder to follow than a white bee in a ˌ ˌowstorm."

"Follow?" I queried, feeling my stomach shrink. "Where to?"

"To Banbury Cross to ride a cockhorse," Flicker replied cynically. "What the hell you think, padre? We have to know who's cooking what, yonder. Or haven't you savvied the idea yet that we're getting close to Monkey Woman's country?"

"I thought Yaqui land did not begin until we were beyond Nacozari?" I argued hopefully.

"Well, if we run into any Yaquis, yonder, we will tell them they are out-of-bounds," the black rider answered. "Come on, I want you along. It's past time that you got some war trail experience. It's not safe working for a man that doesn't know mule-pack smoke from peaceful cookfire sign. Packrat can watch out here while the women dig for good water."

I found my horse and clambered aboard the resentful brute, which had just found some green grass growing by subirrigation of the sycamore water. Kicking him around, I brought him to where Flicker and Kaytennae waited.

"First war lesson," the black rider greeted me, pointing toward the distant, thin smoke. "Never argue with
your pureblood Chiricahuas. You *can* massacre a mule
train without firing a shot; *mira*."

He pointed again, above the smoke this time, and I
saw the ominous dark birds at circle there.

"*Buharros!*" I cried. "God help the poor souls."

"Maybe it's only the dead mules," Flicker offered.
"Buzzards aren't particular."

"True," Kaytennae said, unsmiling. "They will even
eat Mexicans—just as the Yaquis will."

"*Vamos, amigos*," I said, suddenly afraid.

And away we went to see what lay dead, man or
mule, beneath the white smoke and the black bare-
necked birds.

And to find, God forbid, what strange meat cooked
there, where *el buharro* circled.

31
THE KING AT KILL

We lay on our bellies just at the crest of the rise.

Ahead was the place of the smoke. In the pellucid
air of the desert we could plainly see each detail of the
uniforms of the native *rurale* troops who were the patent murderers of the Mexicans for whom the buzzards
circled.

The mules were all yet standing, all yet under pack,
in the spider line of the ancient trailway. There had
been *tres arrastreros*, three drivers, and a woman as
well. The men were dead, the woman wishing she were,
and we three behind the rise raging in our hearts to see
her as she was.

Well, two of us were.

Kaytennae's slitted Apache orbs studied the scene of
rapine and death without blinking. If he had any
emotion whatever, let alone of empathy for the captive
woman, it did not show on his narrow dark face.

Coming to that, Flicker's black features did not twist in the same fury of helplessness as did Nunez's. That was a white woman out there. Did my Negro chief of soldiers see her as my Apache guide did? Were they gazing upon the poor bloodied creature as a white man might study, in reverse wise, a black or Indian woman broken thus by brute captors? Although my own white blood was minimal, I did not think so. The Anglos have a compassion for suffering things, fearsome as they are in their other cruelties. They have never achieved the stony emotion of the Apache, nor the entire savageness of the African. They are—for that very reason— less adapted for survival in any land such as that within which we lay beneath the fierce sun and watched to see what the brutes below us would now do.

Kaytennae looked finally at me. "The woman is Yori," he said, using the Yaqui word for white people. "I don't think she will die. A lot of blood there, but she seems active enough. Just badly beaten."

"I saw she was white," I answered him. "Why are we waiting? Why don't you and Flicker kill them?"

Both had their Winchester rifles, yet neither had made a move to use the weapons. At this range, of course, they could not be sighted closely enough for certain kills. But that was not the answer and I knew so.

"Get up closer where you can shoot these *cimar-rones*, these outlaws," I whispered fiercely. "Someone must reach the woman before she bleeds to death lying there."

"You heard Kaytennae," Flicker grunted. "He says she won't bleed out. Now, *calla*, padre. Let me think."

He had told me to hush up, and I did so.

Flicker let the wind blow another soft-whistled time of silence, then said to Kaytennae, "You thinking what I'm thinking about those noble *soldados, schichobe?*"

"Do you mean that they are not noble *soldados?*"

"*Anh, schichobe.* If those *ladrónes* are genuine *rurale* troops, I'm a *teniente* of the Mexican Cavalry. *No es verdad?*"

"Yes, true," Kaytennae nodded. "Let us kill them."

"No shooting," said Flicker. *"Ojo por ojo, diente por diente. Bueno, hombre?"*

"Si, bueno," said the Apache. *"Ugashe,* let's go."

"Stay!" I gestured desperately. "What is this Hebrew vengeance of Moses, in this pagan hell? Eye for eye, tooth for tooth? Have you mislaid your senses, Flicker?"

"Long ago," nodded the muscular Negro. "All we are saying here, Nunez, is that we think it fit that those red-ass Indian *rurales* yonder die as they killed the Mexican *muleros*—by ambush and blade; no easy shootings."

"Idiotas, no!" I pleaded. "You must use the rifles."

"Calla, padre, por favor," Kaytennae cautioned. "You talk too loud, and the wind is falling. We had best go, Mirlo."

Kaytennae was one of the Apache who called Flicker "Blackbird." Flicker seemed to like the name, for he grinned now and said, "All right, Kite. Lead off. Padre," he turned to me, "you get back to that mesquite draw and make sure the horses don't get tangled in their tie-reins. Keep them happy. We won't be long. Providing."

"Providing what?" I hissed at him.

"Why, that our approach to the problem proves efficacious, father."

"Which is to say what, Blackbird?" I asked caustically.

"That Kite and I can get in there and salt the tails of those birds without gunfire."

"Sweet Mary!" I blurted underbreath. "There are six of them."

"Yes, well, almost. You missed one. Look near the base of the paloverde to our right. Close to where the woman bleeds."

"Another. And stark naked. Seven of them!"

"He's the one tried the woman, then beat her," said Flicker, and for the first time I saw the muscles move to grow hard in his jaw. "We'll save him for later."

I called some other queries after them, but they were gone now, snaking off, one each way, to come down upon the massacre-place in the mule path from Nacozari to old Agua Prieta. The fascination of the playlet of death held me in trance. I did not go back to the horses as commanded but lay where I was, witness thus to one of the most appalling stalks of men by other men in the folklore of North Sonora.

All the while that Flicker and Kaytennae went forward, creeping bent over double, or on hands and knees, or even running where hard rock gave guarantee of no dust sign arising to betray them, I could see them clearly as flies on a sheeted corpse. Yet the *rurale* soldiers at the noonhalt fire had no least warning glimpse of them. Thus utter were the war talents of my two *bravos* and so unbelievably swift was the little time of their closing in on the unwary feasters.

The first sign that came to my worried vantage at the last of it—Flicker and Kaytennae had by then disappeared from my sight—was the reappearance of the black warrior. He stood, as I saw him, within five feet of the naked brute who dozed by the captive woman. I could even see him bend to pick up something. Then, unpausing, he came over the drowsing one and struck him with the skulling stone. The creature arched his back like a snake that has been run over, quivered there, and collapsed.

Flicker stepped over his still form, and I saw him reach a hand to the woman's shoulder and touch her in warning to be silent. I saw her respond. Then he was gone again on the instant.

Next heartbeat, he reappeared behind and beyond the line of pack animals dozing in the trail. Taking cover of the halted train, he slipped from mule to mule, directly toward the fire about which the remaining half dozen *cimarrones* were feeding. Before these outlaws might know an enemy was within day's march, my black fighter knifed two of them in their backs. Then, as the survivors *did* spring to foot, Kaytennae rose up from behind the bodies of the dead Mexican drivers. His Apache blade went into the backs of two more of the brutes as they all whirled to face Flicker's presence.

Two of the murderers of the Mexican *muleros* remained alive, all within my one held breath of watching. And those two wished to stay alive. They took wild flight.

It was then I witnessed *la cosa más increíble de todo mi vida:* It was Flicker at the kill.

Now all Indians of the desert can run. It is a part of their life from birth. Apaches can run down horses. What these strange *broncos* of Río Móctezuma might do, I could not know; they seemed swift as darting birds to me, utterly uncatchable. But I had never seen Flicker at full race. *Espíritu Santo,* it chilled the spine.

The great black body launched itself after the fleeing *cimarrone* killers like some dark arrow from the bow of an alien god. The muscled legs exploded. The lean torso whipped and strained. The sinewed arms arose and thrust like black and living pistons. Yet with all the vast power of his springing drive, the remaining effect of his gait was of fluidity and grace. It was compelling and yet beautiful to watch him run down and kill the first prey, and then the second. I could not believe it. That was no ordinary man yonder. It was a black lion of the desert of another and far-off land. Africa was that land and Flicker the lion that killed like the king-beast he was.

He was back at the mule trail before I could even go and get the horses and ride them on the gallop over to the grim site. He smiled to see my reddened and perspiring face, gave me a kindly pat on the knee for reassurance, then told me to please take the lead rope of the first mule and guide the halted train back to our women at the camp of the sycamore water. He and Kaytennae would do what must be done here, then follow on.

I did as he told me. With the mules under way behind me, I looked back. Flicker and Kaytennae were coming on. The Apache had the unconscious rapist over his horse's withers, carrying him "sacked" as the Anglo and Tejano expression put it. In his turn, Flicker came proudly straight, bearing in his great black arms the limp form—with its fall of long, blood-caked hair—of the battered white woman. In the Apache way, he guided his horse with his knees. I could not discern, from the slack hang of the woman's body, if she were now quick or dead.

Tending my string of purloined packmules on toward the sycamores of our camp, I prayed that the woman did live. And that, as well, our way through that fierce land would continue to be guarded, as on this day, by His hand. And, ah! how generous He had been.

It required no practiced eye to see why the attackers had stalked this particular small train. Those half dozen good mules each bore a double pack abulge with desert treasure. One could smell the fat provisions of food. And see the trade goods, the pots, pans, cutlery, tools, all things needed for survival in outland Sonora state. *Gracias a Dios. Y a Jesús y María, también.* What some worthy merchant of Nacozari would now never receive from his agent of trade in old Agua Prieta would instead supply our long march to Durango and Sinaloa.

Flicker had found his commissary.

With six stout mules to transport it.

I could scarce wait to demand of him what he might now say in denial of our God's hand in this unprecedented luck of the desert.

32
SISTER OF THE PISTOLERO

What a dunce and *simplon,* I; of course Flicker did not care to speak of Divine intercession immediately upon such a chase and blooding as his Yaqui killing had been. He was much too wrought yet.

"Here, damn you, Nunez," he growled at me. "Never mind God. Help me with this lamb He damn near let her get shorn yonder. I don't know if she's going to make it."

Humbled, I fell to the work, beside him, of reviving the woman. The first moments were anxious ones. Then her breathing steadied and she opened her eyes. After another few moments, and although still in some shock, she commenced to glance about and to show other signs of a returning normal curiosity. Much relieved, I sat back and pronounced her safe.

At this, Flicker forgot himself enough to mutter, "Thank God," and I said soberly to him, "That's a beginning, Flicker," and he laughed and patted me on the head and said, "Amen, Nunez," and the woman, hearing us, smiled fleetingly.

Further efforts to encourage her failed however.

After some particularly futile tryings to get her to speak or even to nod in response, I gave up and went off to examine the captive *rurale*. Flicker stayed on with the woman, I noted. That was interesting, but I found the *rurale* prisoner compulsively more so.

Our Apaches had spread-eagled him against the gnarl of a sycamore stump. They had tied him standing upright and left him naked as a new-fledged bird, private parts adangle. His sole adornment was the gag they had stuffed in his mouth to garrot his snarlings while he thrust and strained to be free of the pack-ropes with which they had lashed him to the ancient snag. As well, I suspected, they hoped the gag would strangle more than the *rurale*'s animal growls. But that was the Apache of it. For centuries they had feared these squat wild men of the western slope. One dared not now instruct them in Roman charity to the helpless foe.

Moreover, the fellow's behavior appeared to demand some overcruelty of restraint. He was glaring all about and slobbering in the manner of a rabid wolf. Plainly, he was a most dangerous guest in our little camp. Flicker had made me to see this even as we labored over the rescued white woman. His words were tight with warning.

These seeming *rurales*, in their baggy uniforms so common to north Mexico of the time, were a fraud and deception. The leader and his half dozen dead comrades were in fact renegade Yaqui Indians. They had little doubt gotten their uniforms the same way they had the packmules of the murdered Mexicans. What the band of dissident Yaquis were doing this far north of their usual haunts in the main forks of the River Yaqui, Flicker could not guess. Like their Apache cousins, they ranged far and near. But it was forever worrisome to find them farther from home than nearer it. For this very reason, we must work hard at discovering this group's true purpose.

To accomplish this discovery, however, the big Negro admonished me, I, Nunez, must be brought to understand more of the Yaqui as a whole people. We must not judge them by these misfits masquerading as *rurales,* nor by Apache opinion.

The Yaqui were the largest of all Indian populations in Sonora, outnumbering the Apache of all bands by five to one. As well, the Yaqui spread over nearly the whole of Sonora, where the Apache, chiefly Chiricahua, ranged only the northernmost border—convenient to their American cousins and the conjoint raidings into Arizona and New Mexico. The Yaqui, on the other hand, had no second base in *Estados Unidos,* hence made no war on the Anglos there.

As to their fearsome Mexican reputation, Flicker concluded, this was also fearsomely exaggerated. The Yaqui, historically, could not begin to match murderings, Mexican and American, with the Apache. The good Yaqui were no more represented by such killers as our prisoner and his men than were the good Apache by wild ones of the breed of Chato, old Nana, Chihuahua, Geronimo, or Delgado. Tribally, the Yaqui of Sonora were an intelligent people, notably more industrious than the Apache, say, of Chihuahua state. Like most dwellers in the desert and the main of arid-mountain peoples, the Yaqui were possessed of keen senses both of humor and harsh reality.

A dangerous people—in that time and that empty, brooding *monte* that was their *querencia,* their place —yes.

But depraved and vicious as an entire people, *ridículo!*

Flicker, the lecture completed, returned his frowns and scowls to the subject of determining what the outlaw Yaqui *rurales* had been about, so far from Rio Yaqui and so near to old Nacozari. As to this, he had one immediate concern.

We must remember, he said, that Santiago Kifer had passed us and gone ahead of us into the land of his mother, Monkey Woman. It was not impossible, from this, that the prisoner and his men had been looking for us when they happened upon the Mexican *muleros* and their rich train. It was not, at the same time, highly likely that such was the case. He had not wished to alarm me, Flicker stressed. Only to caution me against disturbing the prisoner, either to comfort or to converse with him.

"Leave him to me," the big Negro had said. "He's mine."

But the captive fascinated me, the while.

It was like exhuming some live man of the caves from his limicolous pit of mud, a million years later.

His head was enormous. It was far too large for the gross, square body. The great skull appeared to grow directly, like some loathsome tumor, from the shoulders. There could have been no more than two fingers of neck. The hair, harsh and straight as wire, grew in a black shock down over the eyes. The effect of the simian orbs, thus buried and set close as those of a ferret to the flattened, big-nostriled nose, was startlingly prehistoric. Unlike most Indians, this creature had the hard-carven muscles of an Anglo or African. The thick torso was borne on short hairy legs so grotesquely bowed that the knees bent several inches outward of the ankles. The horn-soled feet turned inward so they well-nigh trod upon one another. Erect, the knuckles of the dangling orangutan arms came nearly abrush of the desert sand. The man was, withal, a creature from another time.

What there was, or might be, of a mind behind the wild and hating eyes, we were yet to determine.

No least hint had thus far been shown of a rational intelligence.

Turning to be back with Flicker and the woman, I made toward the creature, and by habit, the sign of the cross and of the benediction. For the first time the man ceased struggling to peer at me. It was the look of a lobo or a mountain puma pinioned in the steel of the jawed trap. Release me, it cried. As God is your conscience and Saint Francis the patron of my kind, let me go free. "I cannot," I said aloud to the creature. "I cannot do it." And went on away from there, shaken that the thought had reached me and that I had considered obeying its plea.

Crossing the camp, I saw that my people were busy. Zorra and Charra Baca had a fire lit, and the smell of bacon, asizzle in one of our grand new skillets, was in the air. There was also, where Packrat squatted to ably help them, the odor *más magnífico de todo* of Apache bread baking in a greased pan, being "fried," in their description. Kaytennae stood nearby, watching them.

Yonder, past the fire, Young Grass tended our new and old stock, getting them all under "Comanche picket," a method of loose-roping trailstock together borrowed by the Apache from their Staked Plains cousins.

The scene warmed me. It gave me confidence in our small company. It made Nunez's dream grow more real, more possible, more urgently beckoning than ever.

"Praise His name," I said, and made a *cruz*.

Flicker heard me and glanced up as I approached. His quick eye saw my motion of the cross.

"Save it for the white sister," he said to me. "She's slipped away again. They must have used her more than seemed likely. Have a look."

I bent down and saw that the woman had indeed lost ground. It was not that actual suffering from the attempted rape yet pained her, except in the contusions of the beating, but her inner spirit had withdrawn. Now not only would she not talk to us, she would not look at us.

"What do you figure, padre?" Flicker said.

"You know what it is," I answered, and he nodded.

Both the Negro American deserter and myself had seen other white women long held captive by bronco tribes, whether Apache, Comanche, or mixed-blood bands of wild nomads. This woman was suffering from and showed harsh evidence of just such prolonged captivity. Perhaps—no, almost surely—she had been many times traded. Sold in some cases as a woman, some as a pack animal, some as a slave to the Apache or Co-

manche squaws, cruelest fate of all. This poor thing
had not seen the inside of a white or a *mestizo* house,
or even a lowly jacal of the *monte*, for more winters
than she would remember or want to remember. Her
hands and feet were thickened with calluses and scar
tissues. Her skin was burned by wind and sun to a
cordovan brown. In places, as beneath the eyes and
around the mouth, the burn was nearly black. Yet the
long hair bleached nearly colorless and the remarkable
paleness of the eyes named her race as Anglo. There
could be no question here; this *had been* a white woman.

And more.

There was that about her that stirred the memory.
Something in the rawboned defiance of wasted figure. In
the unbroken bearing of great pain. The angular boning
of the narrow face. And, above all, in the slanted set
of the brilliantly light gray eyes.

Somewhere I had known this woman.

Or known someone enough like her to make of our
gaunt, lost sister an eerie reminder of my own past.

Who was she?

And why could she not, or would she not, tell us?

We continued to wash her wounds with cool water
brought from the sand-well dug by our women. We did
not give up. Especially did black Flicker labor to restore this blistered, bleeding, pathetically desexualized
woman. His dark eyes never left the bruised and swollen face. He laved it constantly with both the water and
the touch of his hands. All the while, he gentle-talked
her and kept the others of the company back from her,
protecting her.

I did not understand it then. Since, it has become
clear to me, and it ought to have been obvious at the
time. I thought it was the common bondage of their
backgrounds—both had been enslaved, both robbed of
an identity of self in an alien society of other skin colors
—that kept the black man at the side of the exhausted
white woman, and kept her mind from breaking that
day at Sycamore Water. Or so Nunez pompously assumed.

And, ah, how ever far from the truth I was.

But that will wait its time of blossoming. It will bear its proper fruit before this tale is done.

For then, for that hour of that day, Flicker won his battle to bring the woman back. Miraculously, her color and strength returned. The gray eyes opened again, and this time clear of all cloud, of all staring blankness. Flicker and I knew the victory when, in sudden unexpected response to a lingering touch of his, she reached forth in return to take the black man's hand.

Flicker put his other hand atop the woman's hand and held it thus, and he asked her softly who she was.

She spoke with difficulty but with no disarray of mind.

"My name is Stella," she said. "Stella Allison. I have been with the Indians nineteen years."

The name leaped my memory ten years back in a great heart-bumping tug. Wonder of God, was this the sister of the famed Texas *pistolero?* Would my words now bear the miracle to her that she had been found?

"You are the sister of Ben Allison," I said, and she answered with tears and a low moaning cry of weeping affirmation that outspoke a dozen clearly worded answers.

Flicker put his great black arm about her whipmarked shoulders, his deep voice soft as east wind.

"You're home, white sister," he said.

And then she slept.

33
STELLA'S STORY

The noon meal was done. All had fed well. After some debate with Kaytennae, Flicker had decided to rest here at Sycamore Water the remainder of the day. The Apache had thought such delay dangerous. He did not like the presence of the Yaqui band outside their usual range. But he had scouted a circle entirely around the sycamore oasis and found no track of other Yaqui than those he and Flicker had killed. As none of these had escaped to bear warning to the main tribe or to the unknown camp of Monkey Woman, the Apache grudgingly agreed. As Indians forever will, he had a defense for his surrender. The flow of the well our women had dug was so little that it would require all the afternoon to let the stock drink. This they must do, also, having had no water the previous night at Burro Meat camp.

Flicker was gracious in the victory.

"*Anh,* yes," he grunted to Kaytennae. "Thanks, warrior; I had not thought of that."

The truth was that Flicker knew more of stock and of slow wells and water than Kaytennae did. But he had been ten years with the Apache. And was himself a Negro. He knew you trap more ants with molasses than with mustard seed.

To me he said, aside, "Be easy, Nunez. It's time we powwowed. For openers, I want you to help me get her story out of the Allison woman. The hunch is gnawing me that she's holding cards we've got to read. Come on."

I delayed, mentioning my sharing of Kaytennae's fear that somehow the Yaqui would learn of the massacre of their comrades and seek us out in whelming numbers there at Sycamore Water.

"Look, father," Flicker said impatiently, "there was one survivor of our fight with the sons of bitches, and we have got him diamond-hitched to a stump that all our mules and three sticks of giant powder could not uproot. Now, come on. The woman's awake and feeling better. I think she wants to talk. And I *know* I want her to."

He was right, as nearly ever he was.

Stella Allison, after some little awkwardnesses to use the English tongue she had not spoken in nineteen years, of a sudden broke wide the dam of memory and of nightmare. The story spilled in a rush from her bruised lips. We sat spellbound to its dark flow.

In 1859, when she was twenty years of age, she had been at a boarding school in Brownsville, Texas, learning, her San Saban ranch parents had hoped, "to be-

come a lady." That was the year of the Cheno Cortinas
raid from Mexico, when the dashing Cheno actually
held Brownsville for twenty-four hours. In the retreat
(when the rangers came) the red-haired Cortinas had
seen Stella Allison on the street. With Latin abandon,
the young general had seized the girl and carried her off
with his troops to Mexico.

The "romance" had been spectacularly terminated.

When she had been but three days the captive of
Cheno Cortinas, Apaches in force, raiding far out of
their country, struck the isolated camp of Cheno and
his staff officers, taking the white girl away in their own
retreat back toward the "great silent grass" from
whence they had come.

Wearying, on the retreat, of his white captive's wildcat determination not to be forced to the blanket, the
Apache jefe sold her for a number of fresh horses to
the *patrón* of a raffish band of comancheros. That is to
say, to the head of a nomad band of mixed-breed
Mexican Comanches who spent their lives following the
buffalo herds to hunt for the market.

In his surprised turn, the *patrón* discovered he had
wasted a lot of very good ponies on a virago and vixen
who would not bed him and who, indeed, caused him
several painful private wounds for his efforts.

But the *patrón* was a shrewd trader, and he convinced the very next party of war-riding Indians—these
were Mescalero Apache from the valley of the Rio
Grande, near Socorro—to take the Texan treasure off
his hands and to guarantee to transport her out of his
territory. He received some old Spanish gold coins and
three good repeating rifles for his property, a gypsy's
profit to say the very least.

Now followed the years of wandering and reselling,
jefe to jefe, tribe to tribe, territory to territory.

She had eventually and inevitably been "married" in
the bronco manner. Not one time but too many times
to remember, or to recount if remembered. With these
unions, mercifully, there had been no issue beyond the
first. These were twins, girls, and in the Apache custom
were killed, twins being a severe taboo. This shadow
also stayed with the mother. Less and less the dark-

skinned riders sought her as mate. More and more she was given over to the squaws as servant, pack animal, kicking post, and beating woman.

It was the Apache women who had given Stella Allison her myriad of wounds that would never smooth. The men were indifferent but the squaws exquisitely attentive. Stella hated the squaws and always would. This, despite her own full quarter of Comanche blood through her full-blood grandmother, and her being second cousin to the notorious Kwahadi Comanche raider, Quanah Parker. Somehow, the Apache were different.

In probable truth, the Comanche were as cruel as any Indian people alive. But Stella had not seen this in them, owing to the shelter of her grandmother's custody when among the Comanche on secret visits—against all parental warning—with her brother Ben.

Clint, her other "big brother," had no familial regard for the red cousins, being a Texan first, last, and, as he put it, "foremost." Her younger sister, Star Allison, was like Ben. Star looked and lived like an Indian. Unlike Ben, she was dark of hair, skin, and eyes. But in the heart they were both "Comanch." The remaining, small-fry brother, Arjay, was only six when Stella was taken, too young to have been visiting the fierce old Comanche lady.

It had been this "Indian hope"—of Ben Allison and the wild riders of Cousin Quanah Parker coming to rescue her—that had kept Stella Allison sane those first years of her epic captivity—sane and never surrendering her spirit.

By the time she knew that Ben was never going to come, nor Cousin Quanah venture so far into enemy Apache country, Stella Allison had grown more Indian than white woman and was able to survive and to keep from surrendering her mind, simply by her own strength.

By the year past she now finished her tale of wandering—she had lived with at least a dozen Indian tribes, mainly Apache and mainly of Mexico.

Then, at the close of that past year, last springtime it would be, she had been given as a gift to the wild people of Yaqui River. This by the Bedonkohe Apache of the ominous Geronimo; indeed, she came from the jacal of the chief himself. The gift was to seal an agreement of nonaggression with the Yaqui. This had become needful for the Bedonkohe in their ever-increasing flights to avoid American pursuit and entrapment by Mexican cavalry. The treaty permitted the Bedonkohe to come over the Sierra Madre and hide on the Yaqui side. In return, Geronimo vowed to stop killing Yaquis who might, for whatever need, enter his domain. Unless, of course, those Yaquis wanted to get killed and proved it by stealing Apache horses or women. The treaty had been honored, Stella Allison said, but not for her. The Yaqui had proved utterly pagan with her.

In fact, the sole reason she lived was that she struck the western slope savages as being so proud and such a *mujer dura,* such a woman of rock, that they made a game of seeing in whose camp she would finally die.

In this obscene succession of moves, the last one, but one night ago, had been to the camp of the dreaded Monkey Woman.

At this point, Flicker caught my eye. He nodded and tapped head with finger, as though to say, you see, hombre, what did I tell you; I knew there was reason we must hear her *fábula.*

I returned his nod, and Stella Allison continued.

When the ultimate ugliness of her fate—at being delivered into the camp of Monkey Woman—came to her, the end was plain to see. Here was the place where the *mujer dura* would break. When, the same night of her arrival in the Yaqui camp, Monkey Woman gave her as a "using woman" to a tribesman more wild animal than human being, Stella Allison determined to end the nineteen years of her living death among the Indians.

She would go that night. If they caught her, she had a knife and would kill herself with it. Should God, on the opposite hand, work a miracle and let her win away alive, then the world yet held some years of better days for Stella Allison.

Here, our storyteller paused, regathering composure lost to such vicious memories. Soon, she went on.

"I left the *campo* early last night; there was the

chance to go while the band was drinking Yaqui beer furnished by my husband to celebrate his new Yori woman.

"I ran all night long, coming north, trying to reach the Mexican settlement at Nacozari. Before daylight, I climbed into some high rocks and dug a hole in a bank of soft earth, up there, and hid myself in it. When the sun came, I looked far to the south and saw seven Yaquis following my track of the night before. I knew I was lost. I drew the knife.

"But, as I did, I heard the tinkle of mule bells. Below my high place in the rocks, I saw the packstring with its three Mexican drivers following the trail I had hoped myself to find with first light, that to the village of Nacozari. Now, also in the sun, I could see the town lying just over the next range of rocks from where I had hidden. By so near had I come to finding Nacozari before the Yaqui found me.

"But now there was still some chance. If I could reach the Mexican mule train and warn its drivers, we might, all of us, yet win to the settlement in time.

"I looked again for the Yaquis coming on my track, and now they had disappeared from it.

"With my last strength, I ran downward toward the mule train. God let me reach its haven but, once there, He deserted me, and the doomed Mexicans would not be convinced of my sobbing tale."

Here, Flicker interrupted her scowlingly. "Why not, for God's sake?" he asked Stella Allison. "Were they crazy?"

"No, they said I was," she answered him. "They insisted I could not have escaped from a Yaqui camp. They said I must mean Apache, bad enough certainly. But there were no Yaqui camps this high on Rio Moctezuma as the one I described, nor had there ever been. My mind would clear, they told me, when we were safe in Nacozari."

"But this is incredible, senora," it was my turn to object. "Do you say they did nothing to your warning?"

"Oh, yes. One of them climbed to a nearby point of high land and examined to the south, but he saw noth-

ing and came back down laughing to reassure me that
he had the eyes of a mountain sheep and that no Indians of any tribe were moving between us and Nacozari. As for Yaquis, well, I was not the first white woman to have a confusion of mind following long captivity
among *los bárbaros*."

"But the man was wrong." Flicker broke in to say it
flatly.

And Stella Allison nodded. "Yes. The Yaqui are like
rock wolves. No one sees them in such rough country.
They were there, where I said. And so was the village
of Monkey Woman where I had described it. She had
moved her *campo* into the country two months before, and no Mexican in North Sonora even knew she
had done so. That's how the Yaquis hide."

"We know it," Flicker said. "Go on."

"You know the rest. You and the Apache with you
over there." She pointed to the place of the massacre
along the Nacozari trail, and to the buzzards wheeling
above it, thick now as cornfield crows. "There was no
sight nor sound of Indians until the Mexicans made
their noonhalt. Even then the Yaquis waited until the
muleros had built a fire and were ready to cook their
midday food. Then they came out of the ground itself,
it seemed, right among the Mexicans. It was over in a
breath, even before I could turn to run again."

We both sat nodding but saying nothing. Gathering
herself once more, she forced on.

"The leader beat me senseless when he caught me,"
she said. "But that was a merciful thing. Just before I
lost consciousness, I saw what the others were doing to
the dead Mexicans; they were cutting out their buttocks
and ramming the flesh onto broiling sticks."

I paled at the horrible thing she had said, but black
Flicker never blinked.

"We have heard of this among them," he said. "It's a
ceremonial thing; they don't eat the flesh. You must
know that. But what is done to dead men doesn't count,
regardless. We're still alive and want to stay that way.
That's what matters. It's question time, white sister."

Stella Allison nodded her understanding, saying she
would do her best to be coherent and helpful.

"All right," the Negro Apache said. "Did we get all of the Yaqui that you know of?"

"Yes, I saw seven on the trail behind me. You killed six and took a prisoner."

"Ah, yes, that prisoner," Flicker said. "Let me see if I can answer my own question on him; he's your new husband, isn't he?"

"Yes."

"He damn near got you back, didn't he?"

"Yes, but for you and Father—"

She hesitated, looking at me, and I said to her quietly, "I'm Father Alvar Nunez. This is Robert Flicker." I stroked the sun-bleached hair away from the battered face. "These others," I swept the circle of our company that had gathered silently behind us, "are also friends. Do not be afraid of the Apaches; they are not broncos."

"That's right, ma'am," Flicker said in his deep voice. "We are all your friends here; you'll never be hurt again. We're going to take you home to Texas."

Flicker's emotion showed beneath the words. I was surprised by it. There was plainly for him, as for myself, some connection with the past in this pale-eyed white sister of Ben Allison. I ought to have guessed what it was, but I did not in that crowded moment.

We had other and surely more dangerous matters to attend to in that camp at Sycamore Water.

Shuddery proof of this came in the woman's answer to Flicker's very next question.

"Ma'am," he said, "what do you think we ought to do with your new husband, yonder?"

"Kill him," she said, the words calm as the quieted gray eyes that backed them. "You must kill him, don't you understand? You can't risk letting him get away."

"He won't get away, white sister."

"But if he did—!"

"If he did," Flicker said, "I would run him down for you—*just* for you."

"My God, you want him to get away!" She stared at my black chief of soldiers. "Don't you know who he is?"

Flicker stared her back. "We weren't introduced," he answered in his sardonic way, his strange gentleness

with the white woman momentarily abraded. "There
wasn't time, yonder, ma'am; I didn't get the name."

Stella Allison's gray eyes filled, her hands shook.

"I'm sorry," she said. "It's my fault. God, but it's
hard to forget. It doesn't yet seem real that I'm here."

Flicker took the trembling hands in his.

"*Ho-shuh,* lady," he said, using the old Apache
word to be easy, to be steady. "It can wait."

"No," Stella Allison said. "It can't. That's Niño Bonito tied up over there. He's the head of the Yaqui
broncos lobos. They run in a pack with those stolen
rurale uniforms to mark them as Pretty Boy's band."

"Niño Bonito," Flicker mused, "Pretty Boy."

"Yes," said Stella Allison. "He's the second son of
Monkey Woman."

Now the handsome face of Robert Flicker tensed.

Now there was no more musing, no more cynical
abrasiveness.

"The *what?*" he said unbelievingly.

Stella Allison repeated herself, and Flicker turned to
me and to those of our intent company behind me.

"My God," he said. "Santiago's brother."

34
HAND OF THE DEVIL

There followed a council of war.

That Monkey Woman's *campo,* or camp, was but a
night march distant had to be weighed. Flicker and
Kaytennae weighed it, decided our stock still must be
watered before journeying on. As well, the company
could still employ the time to organize itself for the
coming push for El Naranjal. Kaytennae estimated that
there remained some six to eight hundred miles to the
Tepehuane country, plus the unknown farther distance
to Ghost Canyon and the orange grove. The matter of
the "acquired" mule train—whether to keep it or

return it to Nacozari—presented a morality problem. Flicker decided it expeditiously.

"We'll take the mules and their packs," he said. "Father Nunez, here, will bless Nacozari in return."

I sputtered a bit but salved my guilt by promising myself that we would bring a share of the gold to the *alcalde* of Nacozari for distribution among the poor.

Flicker now made his assignments for the beginning of next day's drive through Yaqui land.

Young Grass would have charge of the picket line and the pack animals. Assisting her, learning the Apache trade, would be Charra Baca. Zorra was to be camp cook. Her assistant would be Stella Allison. (It had already been decided by the gaunt sister of my old *pistolero* that she would remain with us, rather than be left in Nacozari.) Campmaster, the Apache term for he who had charge over the entire baggage of the march, would be Packrat. Watchman of the camp would of course be the old dog, Loafer. His assistant would be Father Nunez.

This last was Flicker's African humor.

I suffered him to enjoy it.

After all, if the dog were guard of the camp and I commanded him, Nunez was in fact himself chief watchman.

Flicker and Kaytennae as a matter of course would be our scouts, the Apache specifically our guide, the Negro deserter our warrior outrider.

Upon this arrangement, we all retired to our various duties *del campo*. In a little time of the very pleasant desert afternoon, certain pairings of campmates commenced to evidence themselves. This is a peculiarity of the human nomad, of course, and will show itself among members of any traveling group in wilderness country. It was the nature of the pairings I observed that was of interest to my eye. And, yes, in a case or three, to my heart. Romance, even its first whisper of suspicion, had been my life's curiosity. And often its despair.

Flicker, completely without his own consciousness of it, I am certain, managed to circle in the vicinity of

Stella Allison. Zorra presently was seen to be spend-
ing time away from her cookfire consulting with our
American Apache campmaster. I heard her calling
Packrat, who was even less in stature than I, her little
Chaparra. This was a name translating into the Anglo
nickname of Shortie. Packrat seemed not to resent the
name, or the game, even if scowling furiously for camp
consumption.

The next pairing was the one that lifted the pulse of
Alvar Nunez. It was of my foster daughter Charra Baca
and the slender Warm Springs Apache, Kaytennae,
whom I had always regarded as a foster son. These
were my family. And, ah! what handsome savages they
both were. It was, I thought, a mating made in Indian
heaven, and also one that would work well in promot-
ing our Apache church—to draw in the wild Apaches.

I said nothing to them, fearing to frighten off the
painfully shy Kaytennae. But I did chance a knowing
wink and nod to Charra, who laughed aloud and deli-
ciously.

She was a creature of complete wile.

For a moment my own loins stirred to the mere sight
of her moving body, flame of long red hair, and slant
of luminous eye. Then I remembered my parishioners
at Casas Grandes and all the damnable lies they had
told of my lust for women, yes, and even plump girls.
That left me to watch only Packrat and the scheming
whore of Fronteras, and I found myself even savor-
ing the memorable lines of my former housekeeper's
derriere—upended in her present task of gathering fire-
wood.

Angry at my mortal clay, I cast about to join my
own assigned campfellow, only to find the rascal with
all four feet in the air and snoring to shake the sycamore leaves and unsettle the flies that buzzed about his
canine couch. This dereliction of his duty by Loafer
left me with only the Yaqui prisoner for company.

We had all been warned by Flicker to leave "Pretty
Boy" alone. He was not to be spoken to, fed, or given
water. The black leader had not decided yet what he
would do with Santiago's brother. Meanwhile, he knew
he wanted the Yaqui to suffer. If he strangled on his

gag, or his tongue swelled for water and choked him to
death, so be it. Such things happened.

Something drew me to the man, no matter.

I was standing watching him, while talking to his
present guard, Kaytennae. This was along quite late in
the day. Indeed, twilight was agather above the last
rim of the sun. I had only time to note that the neck
and face of the prisoner were terribly swollen from heat
and water lack and to think that he would surely die in
his bonds if not given to drink, when a distraction of
fateful simplicity hove near.

It was Zorra, who had just found a small sacklet of
fresh limes in the plunder of the mule-packs. She came
waving the lovely fruit and announcing that a cooling
ade of their juices would be made by her, forthwith. In
this same moment, Flicker chose to shadow up from
somewhere in the grove.

"Nunez," Flicker said, "I've been thinking of the
map. As you can remember it, what does it actually
show of the country about it? Was the scale in miles,
kilos, hectares, *varas,* what? Can you remember any of
it?"

"Before God!" I cried, "I won't have to remember it.
With the juice of those limes that the bawdy one has
just discovered, Nunez can restore the map itself. *Miran, Uds.!*" I waved, taking the limes from Zorra, as
Flicker and even Kaytennae crowded forward. "Watch
this."

I then quickly expressed some juice from the fruit
into a tin pan, brought forth the water-spoiled map,
and immersed it in the juice. I then said to my comrades, *"Esperan,* wait—"

Before their unbelieving eyes, then, the lime juice
restored each original dot, jot, line, twist, measurement,
and imprinted direction of the ancient map to the lost
Naranjal mine. For me, it was a small Franciscan miracle. For my Apache companions, unversed in priestly
arcaneries, it was very big medicine. As such, it restored my mystique among them.

The problem proved, however, to be one of the
wrong people being impressed.

As we all laughed and cried out in our various delights at the little magic of Father Nunez, I looked up, drawn by some instinct of uneasiness, and saw that the glittering eyes of the Yaqui captive had steadied in their wildness and were concentrating on the map in my hand, as though it were a doomed bird and the Yaqui the serpent in our brief paradise.

"What is it?" Flicker demanded, noting my startlement.

"Nothing," I said. "I just thought to see the Yaqui watching us—and the map—as if he understood what has happened. As if he knew the map had been ruined. And knows it has now been restored."

"How would he know anything of the map?" Flicker asked, scowling hard.

I frowned in my turn, also darkly.

"From Santiago Kifer?" I guessed.

"Jesus," Flicker nodded. "Maybe. If they've met since Santiago got around us, the bastard just *might* know about the map—about it having been ruined, I mean."

Kaytennae shook his head and said something in Apache to Flicker. It was that there should be no concern. For two reasons. We had done all our talking in English, a tongue as foreign to the Yaqui as Apache to an Anglo, and we still had both map and Yaqui under camp guard.

Where was any danger in that?

"Of course not," Flicker said. "You got it figured, Kite."

He then ordered Zorra back to the cookfire to get our supper served *más pronto*. I was told to get the hell away from the prisoner, while Kaytennae continued his job of sitting shotgun on the second son of Monkey Woman. "After all," Flicker finished, with one of his rare, quick grins, "we've got the map back. It shows great detail and covers much more area than I had thought, and it will take us to El Naranjal, *sin duda*. As for our friend Pretty Boy, if he can get away from Kite and my diamond hitch to that stump, I'm a Yori. Meanwhile," he waved, "we all owe a vote of thanks to the fine hand of Father Nunez."

"No, no," I objected. "It was the hand of God."

But we were both wrong.
It was the hand of the devil.

35
CHANGING OF THE GUARD

It was a fine lingering oil of a sunset. The purple dusk
that followed stole like a soft patina over the finished
painting. Then the early dark that came on was filled
with the heated redolences of the desert, a night to walk
apart from others with one of special choosing. Particularly after such a splendid meal as that prepared
from the packs of the mule merchants of old Nacozari
by our cook from Fronteras. This was the same cook
who, even now, was admiring aloud the magnificence
of turquoise necklace, earrings, and shirt-belt with
which the homely, small Packrat had adorned himself
from his Apache kit bag against whatever the evening
might bring of opportunity.

As for Flicker, he had already left the supperfire
with Stella Allison. "Need to talk to her some more
about the Yaqui *campo* she got away from," my chief
of soldiers explained to me, catching my cocked eye-
brow. "Got to learn all I can to get around that place,
eh, padre?"

I had mumbled something about learning to get
around something else, but he had only chuckled in
that basso profundo way he had and said, "Why, Father Nunez, what a thing to hint. Don't you know I hate
the White Eyes? Haven't you lectured me on it often
enough?"

But I was happy for my black friend.

He and Stella Allison were of an age, something in
their late thirties one would guess. Both had known
mean lives among the *bronco* Apache. Both had learned
from these lives that *now* was the only time for anything; in Apacheria as in *Tierra del Yaqui,* tomorrow
did not exist.

There was another thing between them, which drew them.

I had forgotten its common bond when first noting the black Apache's interest in the white woman, or at least his empathy for her plight. Flicker had known a great love among the Nednhi Apache of Chief Juh. This was a medicine dreamer named Huera, the Blonde. Huera had been of supposedly pure Apache blood, but she had waist-long hair, yellow as paloverde blooms, and a roseate glow of dark complexion indicating European blood or, perhaps, even descent from Cortez, the Golden Castilian. In any event, Huera had been the Apache love of Robert Flicker's lonely life. She had been all to him.

Then had come the pack of Santiago Kifer hunting Indian hair in the Sierra. The scalpers had caught the Nednhi band containing Huera in a night ambush of the Apache fire. All warriors had been killed and the golden-haired medicine woman pack-raped by the bestial Texans. Last and first astride her moaning terror of resistance was Santiago himself. The story that came to Flicker of the awful thing came from me, Nunez, and my then comrade, the tall Texan *pistolero,* Ben Allison. We had come upon the rape scene by accident, and Allison had very nearly lost his life in ambushing and attacking the Texas rapers in utterly gallant attempt to save the Apache woman.

From that day, Flicker had hunted Santiago Kifer.

Not until the breaking out from Tombstone jail had he ever met the scalper chieftain. Then had come the blinding of Santiago by the shotgun blast of Chongo. The hunt had seemingly ended in a thing worse than death for Santiago Kifer, and Flicker had abandoned his hatred.

Now came this Texas woman, the very sister of the *pistolero* who had tried with his life to save Flicker's Apache woman, Huera. And this Stella Allison that Flicker had rescued from the Yaqui *broncos lobos* of Pretty Boy had lived the same hell that Huera had lived.

She had been forced by a pack of men of another race, as surely as ever the white Texas scalpers of

Santiago Kifer had befouled Flicker's golden-haired Huera. And the primary lusters in both times had been half brothers!

Santiago Kifer for Huera the Blonde.

Niño Bonito for Stella Allison.

There was a blood debt owing here, I now could see in the actions of Flicker toward our new campmate.

He owed Ben Allison, this white woman's brother, for the life of his Apache sweetheart, Huera.

He owed Santiago Kifer for the terror that had ever after affected the mind of Huera.

And he owed Pretty Boy, the second son of Monkey Woman, for the blood and the shame on Stella Allison.

These thoughts of the past came to me in brief reverie while I lingered on at the supperfire, preparing to Flicker's order a dish of food to be taken to Kaytennae, where he guarded the prisoned Yaqui. It ought to have been Zorra's chore, of course. But the bawd was already vanished with her victim, Packrat, behind whatever trees would serve, and Father Nunez was again the butt of everyone. Well, almost everyone. The smelly camp guard, Loafer, lingered with me at the fire. Then he heard his inseparable friend, the tall bay horse, whickering from the picket line for him, and even the dog deserted me.

However, Nunez was of a sanguine disposition, always.

I went contentedly enough through the sycamores bearing Kaytennae's supper. Arriving at the Yaqui's tree, I discovered that Charra Baca had wandered over from her duty post with Young Grass at the picket line to pester Kaytennae with her thin campdress and all that it did not hide of her remarkable teats and buttocks.

And that face! My God, it would have tempted Jesus of Nazareth, let alone an ordinary Apache Indian. Before either Kaytennae or I might know in what manner she had worked her seduction, she had convinced the Apache youth that he could trust me to take his place with the shotgun guarding Pretty Boy, and she had brought me to believe the same thing.

The next situation I found myself in, I was standing

there in the new darkness with an *escopeta* I did not
know how to shoot, my anxious glance dividing itself
between the wicked-looking Yaqui prisoner and the disappearing figures, hand in hand, of my daughter Charra Baca and my son Kaytennae.

Ah, well, they were young.

And I doing nothing nearly so important with my
time as they might manage to invent for theirs.

"Bless you, my children," I whispered after them
and gave over my attention to scowling fiercely at the
Yaqui, lest the fellow think he had inherited some spe-
cies of churl or fool for a shotgun guard.

36
THE TRACKING OF CHARRA BACA

It went then like the rush of a river over a high place.
It thundered by and there was no stopping it.

The Yaqui, even as I first watched him, fainted and
hung loose in his bonds. He had, quite plainly, given
way to water loss. He must drink now, or perish.

I did not hesitate.

This was a human fellow, no matter how beastlike.
No priest of the cloth might stand by and permit him
to suffer unto death. It was unthinkable.

What was thinkable was that I, trying to give him
of water past his gag, conceived of placing a hollow
reed in his mouth in such manner as to pass the gag, so
delivering life to him. I attempted this by first sucking
a mouthful of water from Kaytennae's vessel nearby,
then expelling it by my own mouth into the reed and
thus into the mouth of the grateful Yaqui.

Grateful?

The first thing the brute did was to choke on the water I siphoned and spat into his drinking reed. Indeed,
such a show of strangulation did he display that I understood the gag must be let loose or his death would
swiftly ensue. Again, I waited not. My fellowman's life

was the responsibility of all my training in the Order of Saint Francis. Seeing Kaytennae's knife where he had placed it on a rock in preparation to eat, I seized up the blade and slashed the gag free of the Yaqui's mouth. He gagged, retched—all in strangely controlled silence —spat out the severed gag. Then, before I might remove my hand, and Kaytennae's knife, from its nearness to his face, an incredible thing followed.

His head struck toward my knife hand like that of a horned rattlesnake. The filed dog-sharp teeth closed with blinding pain on my wrist, and the head jerked itself back to draw my hand against the creature's chest. In this position, pain forced me to drop the knife. It fell along the front of his body down into—horror of horrors—his two strainingly cupped hands, which he had worked a few inches free of their ropings.

In a trice, Pretty Boy had cut himself entirely free.

In the second trice he had struck me a terrible blow on the head, dizzying me, and had bound me in his place to the sycamore stump. It was the ultimate ingratitude that he also stuffed into my mouth the same foul gag my Roman charity had removed from his treacherous jaws.

The last I saw of him was the ghostly flit of his squat body going through the sycamores toward the picket line. Next I knew, there was an uproar of horses neighing and mules braying and an old Mescalero squaw screeching. This outcry was almost instantly followed by the hammer of many hooves, and past me swept our entire remuda of pack and saddle animals, set free by the escaping Yaqui to prevent our use of them in any immediate pursuit of him.

Lastly among our stampeded livestock, here came the Yaqui himself astride the best horse in the camp, the tall bay from Tombstone.

That would have been enough, God knows.

But, as hell would have it, just at the moment the Yaqui ran his mount toward me, here came Charra Baca flying afoot from her trysting with Kaytennae to see what had happened to her picket line animals.

Pretty Boy uttered a growling war shout, leaned from the racing bay, seized up the slender girl in his apelike

arms, and vanished with her into the night and at a full
gallop away from the sycamore grove.

Now there was the belated rushing up of Flicker,
Packrat, Zorra, Young Grass, and the Allison woman,
with my adopted son Kaytennae in the lead.

Flicker was remarkable.

When told what had happened, he did not berate
either Kaytennae or myself.

All that he said was, "There is hell to pay now, and
we had best start counting out our money."

At once, Kaytennae insisted that we must go after
the girl, even to the camp of Monkey Woman. He
would go alone if need be, the young Apache said. It
was his fault, all of it. Moreover, the girl had captured
his heart. He would gladly die to get her back. What
had Mirlo to say to that?

Flicker answered that Kaytennae was right.

We did have to go after Charra Baca.

The only question was how? We could not wait to
regather our horses which Pretty Boy had so thoroughly
scattered. The Yaqui would be ten miles away.

We needed another of my miracles, the black Apache
said, and he turned to me with a bitterness for which
I could not blame him.

"Nunez," he snapped, "you let this rabbit loose;
where's your hound to run him?"

His words struck something in my memory. A spark
flew outward from this flint.

"God's name, Flicker!" I cried. "A hound you say?
Listen, we have such a hound." I wheeled about to call
Loafer from the darkness, and when the confused old
brute tottered up through the trees, I triumphed to
Flicker, "Remember which horse the Yaqui chose to
ride? Name that horse for me."

"You said it was the tall bay."

"It was. And this old dog will follow that horse to
hell, if that's where we're going. Quickly now, fashion
me a leash for our Yaqui rabbit hound."

They did so, no more talk then.

Within minutes, the attacking force was ready.

Young Grass, Zorra and Stella Allison were left behind with Packrat. Their orders were to round-up and

recapture our freed horses and mules, all that could be
found, and then ready the camp to move that same
night. A rendezvous on Rio Moctezuma—known as
Tanque Roqueño, and familiar to both Kaytennae and
Packrat—was agreed to by our Apaches. If our rescue
force failed to appear there the following day, Packrat
was to make his own escape, guiding our comrades safely from the country and seeing to it that Stella Allison
got home to Texas.

But the gray-eyed woman at once balked at this proposal for her special custody. She might remember the
way where Loafer could not find the scent, she pointed
out. Moreover, she must go with us. She *would* go. No
orders from Flicker or Kaytennae or, coming to that,
from Alvar Nunez, the Catholic priest, could stop her.
She *was* going with us to the camp of Monkey Woman.

If a crippled minion of the pope of Rome could
volunteer, a resurrected Hard-Shell Baptist from San
Saba, Texas, could surely do the same, she insisted.

There was no real argument to her point of her possible value as a trail-guide, should the old dog fail.
Flicker saw it, Kaytennae saw it, even Nunez could
understand it.

"All right," the black leader said. "Ride up here
with me."

We had two horses, Flicker and Kaytennae each having caught a mount instinctively as the escaping Pretty
Boy drove our animals out of the camp, to scatter
them through the night. Now Flicker took Stella Allison
up behind him on his horse and I, the master of the
pack, shook loose the rope that bound old Loafer.

"Hi on!" I shouted to the ancient dog.

The trail evidently smelled strongly, as it was heavily
indented by the tall bay carrying double. Loafer let out
one "whoof!" of discovery and charged off at the end
of his rope. I came after him, as swift afoot as most
desert men and despite my crippled form.

Behind me came the two horses with the three comrades.

Loafer made no sound running the track of the tall
bay. His wolf blood, and his training by Santiago to be
sentinal dog of the scalphunters' camps, made him a

silent worker. Before long the moon was up and we could sight-trail in many places. Here and there, Stella Allison did recognize pieces of country, enabling us to make several dramatic shortcuts to gain miles on our quarry.

As the night fled, so did we, silent beneath the Sonoran moon.

We came in the thick gloom of 4:00 A.M. to the low bluff of Rio Moctezuma, above the camp of Monkey Woman.

"Está allí," said Stella Allison, low voiced, "there it is."

"Muzzle the dog," said Robert Flicker.

I did so, and we all stood watching the darkened village below, seeing it as some ghost town of mud and juniper poles, apale in the last of the setting moon.

And now, finally, God showed his hand.

To the north of the village, along the riverbank trail inward-bound toward the shadowy huts, came two riders we knew, Pretty Boy and Charra Baca. We had beaten them to the Yaqui camp. God had thus granted us the chance to see where Pretty Boy would imprison his flame-haired Apache captive, or what the Yaqui would otherwise do with the girl.

And what Robert Flicker and Kaytennae could see, they could go and get back from the enemy.

I could hear both warriors sucking in their breaths at my side.

"Ussen is good to his children," the Apache said.

"Tell that to Nunez," Flicker advised.

"No, no," I said hastily. "Let Ussen have the hand from here; God has had it far enough: This is Indian work."

"Well, that takes care of Kaytennae's salvation," Flicker said. "Any last words for a poor nigger boy, Nunez?"

I stiffened, then said softly, forgiving him, "You know who your God is, Flicker."

But Flicker did not answer me. He crouched with Kaytennae at bluff's edge, watching Pretty Boy and Charra Baca come into the village below. The two watched, still, as the Yaqui camp came alive to the late-night arrival. Fires sprang up here and there about the encampment, while a council was called to convene at the central hut of Monkey Woman. Attending this excited gathering were Pretty Boy with Charra Baca, and a handful of tribal subchieftans. Presumably, Monkey Woman was within and conducting the closed meeting of war. During the ensuing tense half-hour, Flicker and Kaytennae said nothing to any of us on the bluff, only watching constantly below. Finally, Pretty Boy came out of the meeting-house with Charra Baca and surrendered her to a detachment of Yaqui guards. These squat fellows delivered the girl to another hut, separate from the others, and hard down by the fording place of the river. Here, Charra was imprisoned, a watchfire lit and guards mounted at the entrance.

At this point, black Flicker at last turned his eyes from watching below and spoke to slim Kaytennae.

"Are you ready, warrior?"

And the handsome youth answered in Spanish, *"Ya! lo creo,* yes, I believe it, Mirlo." Then, in guttural Apache, *"Ugashe!"*

Flicker nodded grimly and told me to hold the horses and to wait with them and with Stella Allison back down in the draw up which we had come to the blufftop.

"Keep the damn dog quiet," he said. "We will get back to you here if we can. Be ready to go."

37
ESCAPADA DE TANQUE ROQUEÑO

Flicker and Kaytennae disappeared, scaling down the bluff's face. We took the horses back from the bluff and tied them in the gully, leaving Loafer muzzled and tied with them. Then Stella Allison and I returned hurriedly to the bluff. Our two warriors had just emerged on the sanded bank of the Rio Moctezuma (Montezuma River, or West Fork of Rio Yaqui) below our vantage.

We could see them as shadowed doll figures in the waning moonlight.

Into the current of the stream they plunged. They moved in a way to let me know that Flicker had a military plan in mind. He was not just making a blind stab at freeing Charra Baca. I marveled that Kaytennae would go with the black deserter so easily. Apaches will not ordinarily submit themselves to the directions of another. But now we saw the two heads bobbing together down the stream toward Monkey Woman's secret village, and we watched to see where our swimmers would come out.

Stella Allison told me, as we waited, that the fording place of the stream being below the village was standard with the Indians. They always placed their camps upstream of a crossing, so that use of that place would not make bad water at campside. Flicker had known this, of course, but Stella had been able to describe the ford exactly for him. Particularly how the roadway on our side of the crossing went around the backside of the bluff to intersect the gully behind us. "I believe Flicker will try to get out that way," she now said to me, her English still halting from the near twenty winters in Apache rancherías. "He questioned me on it at length."

"Flicker is a marvel," I nodded. "A black genius."

"He's a strange man," Stella Allison answered quietly. "He's like me. Been hurt a lot. Maybe too much."

"No, my daughter," I said, "you will both be well again in your hearts. Nunez feels it."

"I feel something, too," the gaunt woman told me. "I can't think of Flicker as a nig——" She broke off the word awkwardly. "He doesn't seem like the colored men I've known. Most of them are so, *pues, hombres reducidos.*" She spoke, lapsing into Spanish to find the phrase she required. "You know what I mean, Father Nunez; their lives have been so cruel for them."

"They are broken in spirit?" I suggested.

"Yes, that's it. But Flicker——"

"Flicker is anything but broken in spirit, daughter," I laughed. "He is the damndest man I have ever known. He and your brother Ben, they are *los hombres más raramente que todo el mundo."*

"They *would* make a pair," she said, returning my laugh softly.

"They *did* make a pair," I told her. "Of enemies."

Quickly, as we scanned the river to follow the bob of the two heads toward the village, I told her the story of Flicker's life, before and after his ill-fated attempt to be a new messiah of the Apache, and of my adventure with Ben Allison in fighting Flicker over the ransom and rescue of the small son of the then governor of Texas.

When I had finished, she asked after her brother and the other Allison children—Clint, Star, and Arjay—and I had to remind her that my knowing of her Big Ben, as she called him, had been ten long years ago.

"The last I saw of Ben Allison," I said, "he was setting out to hunt down this same Santiago Kifer that we deal with now. That was in Casas Grandes, after Flicker ruined my mission with his damned Civil War cannon. Ah! those were grand days, child."

We fell silent; then she said quickly, *"Mira, padre.* They are landing now. See? There they go, bent-double and running to get into the shadows of the prison hut."

"Yes," I said. "I do see them. And thank God that those Yaqui guards are watching only the front of the hut. It permits Flicker and Kaytennae to make it thus safely to the rear of the prison. The Yaqui were not thinking of an approach from the river. That's the work of *Dios,* daughter. Nothing less."

I saw the flash of Stella Allison's teeth in the paling moonlight. "Yes," she smiled. "With maybe a little help, father." Then she wasn't smiling anymore and once again our talk stopped and the stillness extended itself.

For a long time it seemed nothing changed below. The gathering about Monkey Woman's *jacal* lingered awaiting the result of the council still going forward therein, or appearing to do so, and the minutes stretched endlessly.

Then, without warning, our two brave shadows broke from the blackness at the rear of the prison hut.

They dashed from thence to the sentry fire in front of the hut. And, even at such a distance, we saw by the fire's glow the flash of naked steel. It was our steel. And being driven by our shadow-men into Yaqui flesh. But the last sentry died noisily and his screaming alerted every tribesman in the camp. On the blufftop, Stella and I knew cold fear.

Now, belatedly, we saw our bigger shadow, Flicker, kill this damnable death-howler. In the same instant, we saw his slender companion-shade, Kaytennae, dart into the prison hut. The Apache youth was in there only long enough for Flicker, on the outside, to seize a certain very tall horse tethered at the fire. Then Kaytennae was back outside the hut with Charra Baca and the two of them were being forced by Flicker up onto the saddled back of the tall mount. We heard Charra Baca's high voice lifted in Chiricahua insult to the Yaquis, now running up from every quarter of the aroused camp. The girl's yell was echoed by a wild African scream from Flicker's black throat, as the latter struck the double-ridden horse in the quarters. The horse let out a shrilling neigh and charged off toward the fording place. He at once outdistanced the Yaqui foot pursuit, which then swung like a pack of yammering mongrels onto the track of the fleeing "big shadow."

But they could no more close on black Flicker in full warrior flight than they could on Kaytennae and Charra Baca double-mounted on the tall bay horse. So the tactic of Flicker going one way, and Kaytennae and Charra Baca the other, succeeded. It split the Yaquis in chase and in argument. All they caught that night were the further insults in fluent Apache hurled back into their filed teeth by a rolling bass voice with rich black American accents to its Indian tongue. By the time the Yaquis had returned to their camp and run in and saddled their ponies for a more relentless chase, it was too late for that fading night.

Flicker swam the Montezuma River high up where it bent to cut at the base of our bluff. He landed within ten feet of where he and Kaytennae had gone into the water. Five minutes later he was scrambling over the lip of the bluff, asking, "Where's Kite and the girl?"

I started to answer worriedly that God alone knew, when we all heard the sudden nickering of our horses tethered in the draw.

"Come on!" Flicker panted. "That might *not* be them."

But when we reached the gully, it was Kaytennae and a flushed and weeping Charra Baca who met us there. It was a reunion of greatest brevity but deepest emotion.

Nor was it one of human happiness only.

Old Loafer had recognized the puffing mount of Kaytennae and Charra Baca as his tall bay friend, and the old dog's wild gyrations of both bounding about and wagging of ragged tail led us all to laugh in great relief. At which Flicker said he thought it was all most touching, but he would a damned sight rather be making long tracks away from there than standing around laughing.

No dissent being voiced, we followed Kaytennae once more. He took us north from the Yaqui camp, following the river. We got into the shallows of the stream after a ways and waded five miles to break our trail from the Yaqui trackers—the very most feared in the Indian world. Then we left the river and struck inland, south by cast.

When the sun came, we could see no Yaqui pursuit.

But we could see something else.

Directly ahead was a clear-watered minor tributary of the Montezuma. It was down in a small canyon, well grown with cottonwoods and scrub pine. We could even see the meadow grasses growing in the flats of this beautiful riverlet and its widened canyon. And grazing those grasses and browsing the cottonwood buds and the willows' newest bark were several fine packmules and a remuda of good horses. I recognized the old white mare mule that was the belled leader of our stock and next moment heard the reedy voice of Young Grass inviting us to come on down the easy trail from mesa-top level where we were, breakfast was almost ready.

We rode down, happy as natural children.

This was Tanque Roqueño, Little Rocky Tank, and Packrat had found it as unerringly as had his friend

Kaytennae. We were all blessedly reunited, none were
wounded, and there had been no sighting of our retreat,
that we could determine, by the renegade Yaquis. For
that hour of that fresh new day, we were safe. It was a
time to sort out our gods and give them thanks for the
gifts of Flicker and Kaytennae.

This we did, inspired by the politician, Packrat, who
suggested, "Let's pray to all gods at once, including the
Yaqui. That way, no god will feel slighted, amen."

We bowed our heads in a small circle. It was a deli-
cate, a membrous moment. The thing I remember of
it most poignantly was that Flicker and Stella Allison
had their hands touching.

Oh, there was one other thing I noted, cheating a
glance as the others did not. Zorra was wearing the
most exquisite set of turquoise earrings, with necklace
and shirt-belt of the same blue stones, that I had ever
seen. Except, of course, upon the pudgy person of El
Ratoncito.

I said a separate little apology for the shameless she-
merchant of Fronteras.

Even if I had to interrupt my chanting of the *e'ra
pro no'bis,* the refrain of the Litany to the Virgin,
whose burden translated into "pray for us."

I thought it all right under our circumstances to include a prostitute with the Virgin, just the once.

After all, there was the example of Mary Magdalene.

Perhaps Zorra also might reform.

38
REPORT FROM THE CAMP OF
THE ENEMY

The *reunión* at Tanque Roqueño was permitted to go
forward one hour by Robert Flicker. Then my chief
of soldiers called us to council. His words startled us.

In the aroused village of Monkey Woman, both before and after being thrown into the prison hut, Charra
Baca had overheard some things.

Santiago Kifer had come to his mother because of his eyes. Monkey Woman had treated him and a miracle had followed. Santiago could see again. More, he knew from Pretty Boy—just as I had feared—that the map to El Naranjal had been restored. It developed that not only had Santiago's brute half brother understood what he had watched of the actual citric acid restoration of the ancient map, he also understood every word of English we had spoken in front of him.

There remained no question what the Yaquis would do.

Pretty Boy and his *broncos lobos,* those outlaw *rurales,* would go immediately on the trail of the Franciscan priest's small band of treasure hunters. With them would ride, also, Monkey Woman and her firstborn bastard son, Santiago Kifer, he of the inexplicably restored eyesight. These Yaqui vulture troops would not directly attack us seekers after El Naranjal, but rather they would harass and track us until Kaytennae had guided us to the portal of the great lost mine. Then the butchering would proceed. And the first to die would be the cursed black Apache who had killed four of the six men of Pretty Boy's war party. And captured Pretty Boy's fugitive wife, the Yori woman. Yes, and humbled and made a dog of Pretty Boy into the bargain, had this black one.

So much had Charra Baca learned in the camp of Monkey Woman. She had heard what she had heard only because Santiago spoke *en Español,* and the others replied to him in like tongue. Of the Yaqui language, the runaway wife of the shoemaker of Casas Grandes comprehended not a syllable nor lingual accent. Flicker said not to worry over what she may have missed, but think only of what she hadn't missed.

"God knows," he finished, "what Charra's told Kite and me is more than plenty. They mean to dog us like buffalo wolves and cut out the weak or slow ones of us by hamstringing when we fall behind or are caught apart from the others. They will herd us toward El Naranjal, and, when Kite has us going into the wings of the orange grove corral, they will close the gates on us and the beef shoot will begin. They can easily check the carcasses for which one has got the blood-soaked map on it. Any one of us that doesn't understand what I've just said can ask for a translation from our friend, the padre."

He paused to sweep our intent circle with those piercing dark eyes, and, in that moment, seeing him there in the early sunlight of the meadow at Tanque Roqueño, I had again to think of his physical magnificence.

Robert Flicker was perhaps six feet and two or three inches in height, as tall almost as the great Texan gunfighter, Ben K. Allison, but a man of thicker thew and sinew. Flicker had no fat on him but did not look lean and gaunt in the manner of my old *pistolero,* or, indeed, of his gray-eyed lost sister who rode with us now. He, Robert Flicker, drew the eye with different magnets.

His costume was a combination of Apache *n'deh b'keh,* high soft boots; thigh-tight Mexican vaquero pants; and an American cavalry jacket with bright brass buttons and sergeant's chevrons on the sleeves.

He wore no hat, summer and winter, save that one composed by nature of his thick and savage hair. This hair held, if not an Apache straightness, then only a sort of slight, flat wave in its otherwise wild shag. The effect of Flicker's leonine face, extremely handsome by any race's definitions of the male human animal, surrounded by this cocklebur of fiercely untamable hair—which Packrat told me Flicker barbered with sheep shears each spring and autumn—was one of the most powerful and forbidding impression.

As with Allison and other tall men of the horse, this black American soldier and gentleman-almost, Robert E. Lee Flicker, became of doubled power and beauty when astride a favored mount.

But even afoot and, as I watched him now, poised and waiting for any of us to query him, the Negro renegade fascinated the imagination.

As the Spanish say, he "drew the eye."

In that moment I knew that here was the warrior to match Niño Bonito, Santiago Kifer, Monkey Woman, *and* whatever number of their *rurale*-clad wolf pack might now come yowling with them on our track to El Naranjal.

It was I, Nunez, of course, who had to answer his demand for challenges to his judgment.

"There are no questions," I said to him, when the others held their silence. "What is it that you will now do, Soldado Negro? Have you decided?"

"I have," Flicker said. "We're going to run for it."

"Run for it!" I cried, astonished. "You mean that we shall flee? Run away? You, Flicker, afraid at last?"

He looked at me, white teeth bared in that grimace of his that was a smile only if black-maned lions smiled.

"I mean," he said, "that we will run for your orange grove, Nunez. We will bust our butts running for it, *comprende?* Now get your horse, Father Hunchback. When a nigger runs, he *runs*. Get moving!" He wheeled on the others. *"Mismo al todos, compañeros; montad en vuestros caballos. Al instante!"*

At the order to mount up at once, the *compañeros* raced to throw saddle or surcingled blanket on riding animal. The women cinched tight the packs, ordered the mules into line. In minutes, Young Grass came to Flicker, saying, *"Nosotros somos listo,* we are ready;" and Flicker grinned.

"Well, *niña linda,"* he said, "when a beautiful woman says she is ready, a man must take her at once."

"I didn't say I was ready, I said we were ready," the old Mescalero snapped.

"No matter," granted Robert Flicker gallantly. "I still know a beautiful woman when I see one."

"Gracias to you and God," the old lady mumbled.

"Por nada," Flicker bowed. "Start your mules."

39
THE RUN FOR EL NARANJAL

Young Grass shouted *ugashe,* go! at the bony white bell mule. She struck the obstinate creature a tremendous whack with her knobby walking cudgel. The mule squealed, kicked, tried to bite, and, defeated, squatted

and blew urine out at the old lady. Whhaackk! Again
the Mescalero squaw welted the brute's haunches. As if
by magic, Cosa Dulce, that was the white mule's name
—Sweet Thing—altered her argument. The musical
bell about her scrawny neck commenced to tinkle in the
tempo of a gaining trot. The other mules came rapidly
to its rhythm. The riders of the camp followed in the
order of their readiness. Altogether, it was not the
quarter part of one hour after Flicker gave order to
break bivouac that we were once more on the march.

I sat with Flicker at trailside watching to see that the
company got by in good pace and proper position behind the wary Kaytennae. When the last of them were
past, old Loafer, my watchguard of the camp, came up
through the dust to bark at me and say that nothing
had been forgotten, nothing left behind that would profit the enemy. I turned uncertainly to Flicker.

"I wish to God," I said, "that I knew what we were
doing."

"You mean you wish you knew that I knew what I
was doing, don't you, padre?"

"*Pardiez!*" I said. "By damn, that may be it."

"You have company, Nunez. I wish the same."

"My God, you don't know?"

"I haven't known since Huera died."

It was the first I had heard that his Apache wife was
departed. I had naturally thought many times to ask
him of the woman, for whom I had myself hungered.
But always I had stopped short. Flicker was a man of
utmost inner dwelling. I knew little if any more of him
now than when I had helped him escape the Texas
Rangers ten years gone.

"I am saddened to hear of Huera," I told him now. "I
always imagined that you two went to live apart from
the Nednhi. To be alone. I had imagined happiness for
you."

"There was no happiness," Flicker said. "Huera
never recovered from what the scalpers did to her."

"*Quita,* God forbid such sadness."

"When she was gone," Flicker said, as if not hearing me, "I made the vengeance vow to kill them all."

"Surely you haven't done this senseless thing?" I said, aghast.

"I have done nothing else the past eight years. Some I followed a year. There were twelve of them. Now there is only Kifer left, number thirteen."

"You killed twelve men? You gave eight years of your life to that, to murdering twelve white men?"

"They happened to be white, padre."

"No, Flicker, I don't think so. Would you have hunted them all down had they been Indians? Mexicans, even?"

"I would."

"No," I said. "You would not. You still hate the white man, Flicker. You deserted your God over it, blaming Him for what the whites had done to you."

"Bullshit. Papist bullshit. I never knew that God you talk about, Nunez."

"Another lie. You told me your father prayed on his knees every day of his life, and you beside him."

"My father was praying for me."

"But of course!"

"He was praying for me to get a better God than he had. He didn't live to see how his God answered that prayer. Thank God."

"Thank what God, Flicker?" I said. "Don't you know yet there is a devil? You serve Satan, hating as you do."

"More Roman bull manure, Nunez."

"No, think. Who sent you to steal the ammunition from Fort Huachuca? Did you do it to get ammunition for Nana and Victorio, as you claimed, so they might fight free of the white man? Don't you see that, doing so, you only guaranteed more white men would die?"

"That's a damn lie. I thought only of helping the Chiricahua get back to Mexico, to go free."

"Well, what truly happened then, Flicker? Think about that. You did *not* get the ammunition. Nana and Victorio went out as planned, depending on you. They were slaughtered by the Mexican and American troops alike. You yourself told me Tule Moon and Go-ta-chai told you of this."

"They did. Victorio lost a hundred people. His own son Washington fell. I don't know how many Nana lost."

"You see?" I nodded. "The Chiricahua broken, running for their lives, and who was it failed them—God?"

Flicker looked away from me.

"Are you saying it was me, padre?"

I spread my hands. "You must answer that," I said.

But Robert Flicker did not answer it. Instead, he made a pretense of standing in his stirrups to peer back toward the valley of the Moctezuma, looking for Yaquis.

"We've got to go," he said. "No more talk, Nunez."

I at once put up complaining hand.

"Hold—damnation!" I insisted. "One more question."

Flicker checked his restive horse.

"No, by Christ," he said. He gave me a final mean stare. "And here's a new war I'm going to make for you. If you open your ugly little half-breed trap one more time, I will add *mestizo* backslider priests to my White Eye list. *Comprende,* Father Bullchips?"

To this day wherein I set down these memories of our journey, I do not know if he would have harmed me.

He may have.

Robert E. Lee Flicker was a stranger to us all, and mostly to himself.

For that moment, I told him *lo entiende,* meaning that I understood him, and backed my mount nervously away from his.

But again I did not know my man.

"I'm glad," was all that Flicker said.

And the air about us cleared of more than the dust of our company's departure. The shaggy-maned badman of Mexican Apacheria leaned over from his horse, patted me on the head as if I were some small saddle-trained dog, and said, "Come on, padre, we've got a gold mine to find. Last one to catch up to old Kaytennae is a nigger baby."

We both laughed and away we went shouting on our horses and kicking them in the ribs to make them race

the wind, and that is how the run for El Naranjal began.

How it ended we shall now see, and with a terrible
swiftness no one of us could then dream.

It remains that man merely gathers the storm unto
himself.

God still delivers the lightning.

40
GHOST GUARDS OF THE TEPEHUANE

The journey from Tanque Roqueño (near Nacozári)
to the country of the Tepehuane Indians (between
Durango and Culiacán, Sinaloa), where the legend held
that the gold of the Franciscans lay buried, was in itself
a sufficient hell to fill a separate journal. Suffice it for
this tale that we forced desert, mountain, jungle, raging stream, sandstorm, cloudburst, freezing cold, and
broiling heat, twenty-three days unabated. On the
dawning of the twenty-fourth day, we came to the base
of rearing 10,335-foot Cerro Huehuento, the great
monolith from which, the legend said, the country of
El Naranjal must be located.

In the entire march thence we had not seen one Yaqui behind us nor had a glimpse of Santiago Kifer and
his two deputies, Crench and Belcher, much less a
frightening view of Monkey Woman and her mad son
Pretty Boy.

Again suffice it, however, that Flicker and Kaytennae
swore to us that they were "back there." It is to be
believed, amigos, that this silent stalk of nearly seven
hundred torturous miles put more fray to our poor
nerves than any amount of the predicted harassment of
Yaqui "buffalo wolves" herding us by cutting down our
strays.

The secret was of course that Santiago wanted the
gold. It happened that he herded us more to protect
us—and our map!—than to decimate us.

Our other fear, that of the savage Tepehuane, proved equally as delayed. We had seen not one Indian of that reputedly fierce band who, again as the legend went, were the bronze guardians of all Catholic-stolen gold mines in Mother Mexico. That is to say, of that part of Mexico lying north of Zacatecas and south of Sonora and Chihuahua. Even so, and in the same way that the invisible *broncos lobos* of Pretty Boy haunted us to our final campfire, so, too, did the unseen Tepehuane Indians stand increasing guard of our presence in their forbidden land.

As we made camp that night below Mount Huehuento, we were all in a state of apprehension compounded by weariness and a growing fear of the unknown. One could *feel* the ghosts of the Spanish and Indian past. They were all about our fire. Just out there beyond the light of its flames, waiting. Was it revenge they sought? Justice? Some accounting for the crimes of Cortez?

We did not know.

One must know that ghosts cannot leave footprints. And the footprints that Flicker and Kaytennae and Packrat found next morning out beyond our fire most assuredly must have been those of Tepehuane Indians. Yet we had not seen those Indians. And did not see them now in the sunlight.

As a priest, I had one explanation for this strangeness which I did not voice to my comrades: Those Tepehaunes out there in the dark may have been very old, may have been even two hundred years old, as was El Naranjal itself. They may have been the same Tepehuane Indians who slaved in the torchlit pits and abysses of the Spanish mines, burrowing out the golden metal that made their whipmasters wealthy beyond the dreams even of Don Hernán and his Conquistadores—those rapers of my red ancestors who confessed to the Aztecs that they were sick with the disease that only gold might cure.

Ghost guards for ghostly gold?

A priest would never deny such things. He would only clutch his *cruz* a bit more tightly and be ready to use it in exorcism of bronze avengers from the dark past.

But Flicker cheered us over the breakfast fire and said that this day we would go up the mighty Huehuento and, from its snowy loft, draw our course for the land of El Naranjal.

"Hombres, mujeres, compañeros," he said, *"no hay tiempo que perder,* there is no time to waste. *Vamos!"*

We climbed the mountain by the old mule trail that Kaytennae somehow knew was there. From a place on the shoulder of the vast peak, Flicker made his calculations from consultation with Kaytennae's memory of the Apache directions. We set out in a northwesterly path, a course that would take us more toward Culiacán than Mazatlán and would bring us in any event to the tropic jungles and vast *barrancas*—yawning chasms—of that strange land.

The path must be recounted for future legend-seekers.

In three days, following a trail as faint in places as milkweed hair, we came into this canyon jungle country. We could scarce believe that Kaytennae would so many times lose but always refind the ancient roadway committed to him by memory alone from the old Nedn-hi Apache keeper of the secret. There was something ethereal about the young American Chiricahua's performance. We all felt more powerfully even than we did when high on El Huehuento the mystic and frightening "something" that was in the very air.

We went on. The nature of the terrain was that of a barranca-cut wilderness where frequent rages of floodwater washed away entire mine dumps and caved in the tunnels behind such tailings of the gold and silver ore. Even whole sections of the ancient trail itself had been undercut by barranca water and had been reclaimed over its dislodged surface by the verdant jungle (so near the mighty Pacific Sea) that seemed to grow almost while the canyon slides were still moving. How in the name of the great God might we ever find least trace of El Naranjal in such a place?

Well, the answer was in part Kaytennae's uncanny ability to smell out the renewal of the trail beyond these monstrous disturbances of the old land—of the way that it lay two and more centuries gone, when the Franciscans were there. There was also some help, I blush to say it, from my trained priest's mind and its sharp eye for history's footnotes.

In this regard, our Apache guide's instincts and tribal memory were virtually useless. Even Flicker was on the point, that fifth day of terrible travel through the jungled canyons, of giving up. The trail had vanished totally, and we were now convinced that the instructions of the legend, both Apachean and Franciscan, were false, perhaps deliberately so. But then it was that Father Nunez saw the rock.

I had crept off to one side of the halted company to sneak the last dram of encouragement from my many times refilled hollow Bible. I was about to drain the flask when I saw something on the rock face of the barranca wall just beyond my resting rock. *Espíritu Santo!* What was this?

I went to the place, but three paces distant, brushing aside the superficial moss and lichened growth that covered what I thought to have seen on the face of the barranca wall. Ah! *Cristo dulce!* Yes, there it was, the road-sign rock of the Franciscan legend: *the* rock! And, upon its oblong man-hewn surface, there was an unmistakable *cruz* of the church, rendered in the equally identifiable Franciscan style of Far Eastern orthodox origins. And more, before God. Beneath the cross were words cut into the oblong stone in a manner to absolutely determine the nature of this marker: It was an ancient directional sign posted by the Department of Roads, over two hundred years ago.

It appeared thusly to my incredulous eye:

☨

**Departmento de Caminos
Camino a las
minas de Arco
y Naranjal
A.D.
1673**

Trying to be calm, I understood that I was gazing at a sign put up by the Mexican Department of Public Thoroughfares, which sign read, *"Road to the mines of*

Arco and Naranjal." Por Jesús y María, this *was* the true way to the treasure of my order. For one of the persistent anchors of the legend in Franciscan accounting was that El Naranjal lay nearby another great mine, the Juana Arco—the Joan of Arc—abbreviated for stone carving into ARCO.

My mind was not in this instant so much boggled as bedazzled.

I let out a great *chillido,* a screech or scream of superhuman kind, for Flicker to come running. *"Nombre Dios, hombre,* I have found it. *Aquí, aquí—!"*

Not alone black Flicker but all the others charged up through the thick barranca bottomgrowth.

"By God, padre," the big Negro said, deep voice stirred to a growl of excitement, "you have stuck your thumb in the real pie this time. You can pull out a plum and call yourself a good boy."

"Gracias, jefe de soldados," I saluted him. "God has only selected me. It means He is with us."

But was He?

We went on, utterly restored of energy and the hunger for gold now. All about us the jungle thickened. Everywhere we saw the birds and beastlings of the land. On all sides of us flashed the startling colors of the gorgeous imperial woodpecker. Its cries echoed from as far as a mile distant, seeming directly to hand. Finches, parrakeets, small great-billed true parrots, even, were seen. The barranca constantly deepened.

Late in the twilight of that day we heard the thunder of rushing water. It seemed the very walls of the canyon shook about us. "Far enough," Flicker said. "We camp here tonight." He paused, staring with the rest of us into the gathering gloom and toward the roaring of the nearby—yet unseen—river. *"We may be here,"* he said softly. "The sun tomorrow could show us Rio Naranjas."

All of us were too whelmed over by the darkness and the power of the past to answer him.

We slept little that night.

41
RÍO DE LAS NARANJAS

We were all up and huddled to the fire before the sun came. "Did you hear anything last night?" Flicker asked us.

"Some wolves howling," Kaytennae answered him. "Only that."

Flicker grimaced, nodding. "Doesn't that say a peculiar thing to you, cousin?"

"What is that, Mirlo?"

"There are no wolves that we have seen in this barranca country."

I interrupted. "What are you saying?"

"The Yaqui have caught up to us," Flicker replied.

"*Santa!* How could that be?" I asked. "We ourselves cannot find even our own trail five minutes after we have made it."

"Could be you're right." Flicker conceded the point, as anxious as any of us to be off to where the strange river roared. "Everybody look sharp today. Holler if you see a wolf—a real one. Let's go."

"I don't know." Kaytennae hesitated. "We have seen only foxes and a few coyotes, far off. Nothing down in this barranca. What would wolves hunt here?"

"Us," Flicker answered him succinctly. "*Vamos, amigos.*"

We went then rapidly around where the barranca turned abruptly inland, to our right, as we went northerly. There before our astounded gazes, a second barranca, enormously greater than the one we followed, entered from the east. Where it joined our barranca, the combined chasm angled again to the left, westerly, and so to the Pacific Sea. Down this new cleft roared the stream that came out of the great dark canyon we saw yawning before us. None of us could speak, only gape and stare.

It was Kaytennae's moment.

The slender Apache, sweeping his bronze arm toward the issuance of the water from the towering cliffs, announced a single name into our silence.

"Rio Naranjas," he said.

And the inward sucking of our breaths sounded like the hissing of human snakes.

Flicker recovered first.

"Wait," he said. "If that's River of the Oranges, where's the trail? There's no road going into that chasm, friends. Look at those rock walls. Right up from water's tide. Sheer. And they rise a mile. No break in the first thousand feet that a cliff-darter could build a nest on. It's black as the pit in there." He pointed, as dramatically as had our Apache guide, into the yawning maw of the river's canyon. "And God alone knows where that pit leads to. Naranjal, you say, Kite? You will have to prove it to me."

Naturally, our letdown of the spirits was considerable. What Flicker had pointed out was indisputable: No human thing could enter the black canyon and live. Not from this barranca bottom that Kaytennae's legend and my discovered roadway sign said was the trail to El Naranjal. In any and certain event, it seemed our grand expedition and great expectations were both come to road's ending, so near and yet so far from the legendary orange grove and its *Mina del Naranjal.*

As I mourned, Kaytennae did not.

His dark eyes had never ceased their search of the inland canyon and its rushing green tide of clear mountain water that thundered opposite our halting sight.

"Mira, hombre!" he cried suddenly to Robert Flicker. *"Naranjas, naranjas—!"*

Not alone black Flicker, but all of us weary comrades of the ended march to Nunez's dream, glanced resignedly across the waters. Instantly, our resignation vanished. Our tired bodies held the strength of youth. Our defeated spirits arose in flight once more.

Three round and golden globes had bobbed out of the black canyon on its flooding tide, and they eddied now in the backwash pool of the pebbled and rocky beach before us.

Milagro de Dios.

Those were fresh and fragrant oranges bobbing in the eddy at our feet.

Kaytennae was right; that was Ghost Canyon yonder, and he had found the River of the Oranges.

42
BLOWUP IN NORTH BARRANCA

"The map, padre," Flicker commanded me.

I gave it over to him. We were regathered at our breakfast fire around the turn of North Barranca from the issuance of Rio Naranjas.

Studying the wrinkled paper, the Negro once sergeant of the United States Cavalry frowned. He put the document on the earth at our feet and copied from its lines a much larger map in that same fireside earth. Suddenly, we saw him brighten.

"I've got it, padre!" he cried. "Look here where I've expanded it." I leaned to peer at the larger map in the dirt, and the others pressed in. "You see?"

"No, it looks like the scratchings of the mission chickens in my garden at Casas Grandes. What do you see there, Flicker?"

"When the Franciscans built this road," he answered me, the gold fever burning within him, "it was to lead on whoever might come this far looking for El Naranjal. Then they would be left 'northed,' just as we were, staring up yonder hell-deep canyon, convinced that the road to the orange grove had once led through it but had since been washed away." He looked at me, dark face afire. "Well, bullshit, padre," he said. "It never did lead in there."

He glanced toward the higher walls of North Barranca.

"It's up there somewhere," he said. "And I think, by Christ, that I know where. Padre, remember back yonder where you found the stone sign? There was a side barranca coming in from the east."

"The east!" I exclaimed. "The direction of El Naranjal."

"Exactly," Flicker nodded. *"That* was the road to the orange grove."

My heart bounded, then settled. "Impossible," I lamented, recalling the jungle-choke of the side-cleft. "An ordinary dog could not find passage of that eastern barranca."

"You're wrong, padre. That's why the Franciscans put that damn road sign just where they did. They alone knew what it really meant: *Turn right here for El Naranjal.* It's the other mine, the Juana Arco, that must lie on down North Barranca."

The vision of possibility in the black soldier's reasoning rekindled the fever in me, also. "What must we do, Flicker? " I said, trembling.

"What we must do," Flicker replied, "is get our people and packmules up that damn vised-in slot, back yonder. Start praying, Nunez. We will need the extra shove." He whirled from me to Kaytennae. "Let's go, Kite!" he shouted. *"Vamos al Naranjal!"*

But the Apache guide did not go.

Instead, he held up a hand, staring over our heads. "There is a problem," he said quietly.

"The Yaquis," Flicker groaned, not even looking up.

Too late, we all wheeled from our map-drawing and grand planning at the breakfast fire in big North Barranca. Too late, we saw what Kaytennae had discovered and Flicker guessed at so intuitively.

The *broncos lobos,* a filthy company of twenty in their besoiled *rurale* uniforms, stood up-barranca not fifty feet from us. A rock rat could not have squeezed past them to come again to the stone sign and the true road to El Naranjal.

Yet a worse sight stood in the van of the Yaqui wolf pack.

The gaunt figure in torn, trail-fouled coat and gray-striped trousers of the sheriff of Tombstone, Arizona, removed his wide-brimmed hat. He swept it in a gallant

bow that bent his belly to the horn of his double-
cinched Texan saddle. The gesture went to our women,
where they had gathered with Stella Allison resolutely
to their fore.

"Good day, ladies," said the remembered flat and
deadly voice of Santiago Kifer. "I trust that we are not
too late for coffee." His eyes ran past the women. "Gen-
tlemen," he added, hatred writhing the leaden pock-
marks of the shotgun pellets buried in his face, "would
you be so kind as to join me? I believe we have some
business to arrange."

We all looked to Robert Flicker.

Our black chief of soldiers permitted the stillness to
extend itself.

Think of our situation, now.

Even though the enemy outnumbered us four to
one, they could not ignore our armament. But for Zorra
and myself, each of our company was heavily armed
and must be considered quite dangerous. Five of us—
Flicker, Kaytennae, Packrat, Young Grass, and Charra
Baca—were of Apache quality. The sixth, Stella Allison, would be the unquestionable superior of most
frontiersmen with rifle, knife, or pistol. It was, in the
classic sense of the *monte,* a Mexican standoff. Kifer
knew it; Flicker knew it; we all knew it.

The Negro deserter was the first to break.

I, Nunez, could not believe it.

Flicker afraid?

It was impossible, yet there he was palming the
pinks of his black hands to Heaven, smiling in defeat at
Santiago Kifer, and betraying us.

"Well, now, friend scalper," I heard him say, "we do
have a map for sale, and you, I believe, possess title
to an important roadway, passage of which we require
to reach our real estate."

"True enough," said Santiago Kifer, and he held
there.

Again Flicker let the silence multiply itself.

As he did, I studied the remarkable twain of sub-
commanders flanking Kifer. Niño Bonito, the beautiful
child, we already knew of course. But this was the
first time to see the fabled Monkey Woman, *Dios* for-

bid the sight. Not to squander charity, she appeared to be a human simian. A female ape in the trappings of a Yaqui Indian squaw. She looked even to sit her runted pony like some dressed monkey. Indeed, in the uneasy moment I had to examine her that morning in North Barranca, she was engaged in picking fat gray lice from her rancid hair and cracking them in her teeth. To note that the creature then munched on the unspeakable body vermin—as one might on seed of sunflower or pine nut—seemed but expectable. *Qué mujer mugrienta,* what a vile and greasy woman. And worse, God save Nunez.

At the very last, catching my eyes remarking her, she, in fair return, examined me. Doing so, she clapped her monkey's paws in delight and barked something in Yaqui to son Santiago. I could not translate her speech, but Kifer could.

"She wants you for her jacal pet, priest," the scalper told me, clearly pleased. "She's just made it a condition of our bargain with your nigger."

"Oh, my God," I said, startled. "Flicker!"

I had thought to see the renegade Negro flinch when Santiago called him nigger, but I quickly knew I must have been mistaken. "I can't help you, priest," he coldly said, mimicking Kifer's address. "Just do your little dog's best by the lady. Don't let your comrades down."

I could not even then believe that Flicker meant this treachery, but there remained no time to worry about being the Catholic jacal plaything of Monkey Woman. Flicker and Kifer were going to the breakfast fire: Our surrender was to hand.

Riflemen mounted guard for both sides. For us, the negotiators were Flicker and Packrat, Kaytennae commanding our rifles. For them, Santiago and Monkey Woman sat to the bargaining over the coffee tins. Pretty Boy stayed with his *broncos lobos* and their twenty cocked guns.

In moments, only, the traitorous deed was done.

We could destroy the map before they might seize it from us, true. But they could hold us in the barranca until we starved to death. Or shoot us all down in a prolonged rifle fight. For alternative, Santiago proposed

that we all go on together to El Naranjal. That we
divide equally whatever we might find there of Franciscan gold. And that we then go our separate, peaceful
ways in the gentleman's truce and soldier's trust that he
was prepared to offer here. Why, in sanity's name,
should we kill each other, and no one find the gold?

There followed some brief, weak argument from
Flicker, but then, plainly defeated, he signaled me
over.

I went to him and he drew me aside so that no one
might hear us. "Tell our mining expert that Mirlo says
it is time for him to change his mount and ride the old
white bell mule. Say it in precisely that way, Nunez,"
Flicker emphasized. "Packrat will understand."

Seeing my dumbfounded frown, he became *más
severo*. "Don't you back off me now, damn you,
padre," he snapped. "Listen. Remember when Packrat
took the old white mule at my order into the big
American mining camp at Cerro Ventana? I said I
sent him in for some good American cigars, remember?
Well, that was a business trip. And Flicker knows his
business. Especially when it's monkey business. Believe
it, hombre, he didn't buy cigars in Cerro Ventana!"

"But—"

"But *nada!*" Flicker glared. "Remember just this one
thing more: When I sent Packrat for those cigars, it was
immediately after we had found out that Santiago and
the Yaqui *rurales* had not given up, as we thought, but
were right behind us again. Think about *that*."

He gave me a pat on the back and called aloud to
Santiago Kifer and Monkey Woman that all was settled
with Father Nunez, the last of our side to require understanding of Santiago's generous terms.

Kifer then went to Pretty Boy, talked quickly with
his ugly half brother, returned to the fire, and announced the final agreement from his side, as well.

The shameful bargain was put to immediate effect.

We traveled broken into three groups. First went
Kifer, Monkey Woman, and Robert Flicker, with Kaytennae again as Apache guide. Then came my company, including all our women guarded in its middle by
Loafer and myself, with Packrat in outer command.

Behind us, who were thus really hostage to the damnable plan, came Pretty Boy and the *broncos lobos*. In this way, it was claimed, the maximum of security would be obtained, the minimum opportunity for treachery provided.

The map, *de seguro*, rode with Nunez in the middle of his brave little company.

Thus we set out, back through North Barranca, to come to where the road to El Naranjal went into East Barranca.

In our central group we were depressed in the extreme. Stella Allison, riding knee and knee with me, confided her well-learned fears for Yaqui treachery. For my part, I cursed Flicker's cowardice. Or at very least his foolhardy trusting of the scalper's word. One knew that some planned crime of betrayal was included in the terms.

In truth, it was.

But not by Santiago Kifer and the Yaqui.

When our cavalcade neared the site of the ancient stone sign, I noted Packrat riding the old white bell mule so that she lagged behind. I reprimanded him sharply and ordered him to keep up, but he told me in Apache to mind my part of Soldado Negro's business deal and let him get on with his.

Next, I noted he was riding the white mule nearly back into the Yaqui *rurale* troops. As I remarked this, I saw him pull from his pocket, bite the end off, and light with flourish of large sulfur matchstick a most impressive but peculiar looking *cigarro grande*.

He put this great cigar in his mouth to wet the end for smoking.

Evidently, however, Packrat did not relish the taste of the big smokes that Flicker had sent him to purchase at Cerro Ventana. He made a wry face and, removing two more of the offending cigars from his pocket, wrapped them in a bundle with the first cigar. He then flung this packet contemptuously—but most forcefully —over his shoulder toward the trailing Yaquis. The three-cigar bundle made a fine high arc above the narrow pathway of North Barranca and fell squarely among the brute-faced *rurale* troops of Niño Bonito.

Only it was not a bundle of three cigars that Packrat had "bit and lit," as Flicker later put it.

It was a packet of three sticks of the very best United States–made giant blasting powder. And what Packrat had bitten off so short as to sputter no more than six measured clock-ticks was the hard twist of black fuse that ran into the first of *los tres cigarros*. Small wonder that the rotund Apache so unmercifully whipped the old white bell mule away from the puzzled Yaqui *rurales*.

The following explosion, held so tightly close by the crowding walls of the barranca, literally knocked me off my mount—and I was one hundred *varas* away from it.

Dirt, rock, jungle limbs, clots of fernery, and bits of Yaqui soldier and *rurale* uniform rained down upon our hunched shoulders for what seemed eternity. Then Packrat was yelling for us to whip on our horses and the packtrain of our mules. Up ahead, I could hear the vicious cursing of Santiago Kifer and the unearthly simian screaming of his mother, Monkey Woman.

I vow that I heard also, above everything, the rich, deep laugh of Robert E. Lee Flicker.

Ah! Flicker. Gentleman, scholar, almost officer of the United States Army. Decent and honorable black human being of superior character, unquestioned virtue, absolute trust of given word and sealed contract.

Also, thank God, unmitigated rotten traitor to his Yaqui bond.

Flicker had met the enemy and blown him nigh out of North Barranca.

El Naranjal lay before us.

43
CLIMB FASTER AND DON'T LOOK BACK

Ahead, we could hear Flicker yelling, *"aquí, aquí,"* meaning for us to "come this way." Kaytennae was up there, too, shouting in Apache, *"ugashe,"* or, "come on, let's go!" Rallying my people, I led them through the still-hanging dust toward the voices. We had abandoned our horses now but still had our mules. About us, as we went, I could see Yaqui bodies, both moving and not moving. Some were half buried in the debris brought down from the barranca walls. I did not see their leader, Pretty Boy. Nor was I looking for him. Or any of them. I was looking to save the life of Alvar Nunez, naturally in company with those entrusted by Flicker to my shepherding. The fact that I beat them all to East Barranca, and to the rocks that hid Flicker and Kaytennae at that point, had nothing to do with it. I was their leader. Did I not have to go ahead of them to be sure the way was safe? *Por supuesto.*

Even so, my selfless act in preceding them nearly cost me my life. Yet some still say that Nunez ran like a rabbit that day in North Barranca "when the walls came down." Such is charity among the tiny of mind.

What really happened is that I blundered out of the dust into the very middle of some hot rifle fire that commenced just as I arrived there.

Fortunately, my keen eyesight rescued me.

To my left, I saw, belatedly, Flicker and Kaytennae firing from their rocks in the throat of East Barranca. To my right, all in the same eaglelike glance, I observed a cavern in the wall of the northern barranca, just opposite the entrance of the eastern branching. Inside the lip of this cavern were Monkey Woman and Santiago Kifer and then two others who, in all the stirring of alarm, we had entirely forgotten—Crench and Belcher, the two deputies of Tombstone. Later we were to learn that Santiago had left them behind as rear guard while he probed on down the North Barranca after us. For the moment, I saw only that Belcher, the hairy lank devil, had reared himself up to one knee and leveled his weapon—another shotgun—full into my body, where I had, quick as a panther, gone to my abdomen in the dirt. Out of the same eye-corner, I saw Crench, the great lurching oaf, reach with his arm and knock aside Belcher's gun barrels. The weapon discharged as Crench moved, its heavy load of buckshot whizzing over my head and blowing out the belly of a poor mule that stood beyond me. Ears ringing from the powder blast, I heard Crench raging at Belcher, "Hyar, damn ye! Leave the little crunchback be. He ain't done you no hurt."

Belcher's reply was obscene, but Santiago's voice from the cavern was merely blasphemous.

"Shoot the padre, goddamn you, you two dumb bastards!" he screamed at his deputies. "He's the one's got the map on him. Get him down!"

With the same shout, he shouldered his own Winchester to kill me. Belcher also recovered and rammed two more shells into the shotgun. But Crench, the supreme fool that he was, lunged out of the cavern, scooped me up like a barnyard chick, and raced with me over into East Barranca's rocks. There, he dropped me among my own people and just stood there, fully exposed to the fire of his friends who were trying now to kill him from the cave.

Flicker it was who reached out from behind his rock and knocked Crench's great flat feet out from under him, bringing the hulking deputy down among us like the felling of some forest giant.

"Lay low, deputy," the Negro Apache advised. "Your amigos yonder got it in mind to do you scant good."

Crench first said, "why, thanks," then blundered back to his feet and yelled across the barranca, "Hyar, damn ye, ye bastards. It's me, Crench. What the hellsfire you trying to do?"

Flicker felled him again and just in time.

"Stay down, you idiot," he said calmly. "We can use a mule like you. You can carry the packs of that one Belcher blew the bowels out of."

The lumbering mind of Deputy Crench strained to catch up to this idea. Flicker patted him on the head. "Good boy," he said. "Don't fret it. Welcome to the dream of Father Alvar Nunez. And thanks for coming."

"Huh?" Crench frowned. "Thanks for what?"

"Thanks for helping us out," Flicker explained, throwing a shot into the cavern across the barranca. "We appreciate it."

"I ain't done nothing," the deputy objected.

"You saved the padre's life," Flicker told him. "We call that something. Not much, of course. But something."

"I like the little fart," Deputy Crench defended.

"Sure enough," said Flicker. "And that isn't easy."

He turned to me.

"Nunez," he said, "get your people together. You'd best persuade Crench to stay with us; Kifer will kill him, sure. Be ready to go when Kite and I open full fire. How many mules left?"

"Five. They have all gotten into the barranca brush behind us. My people are in there with them, also."

"You mean in East Barranca, where we're going?"

"Yes, praise God. Young Grass got the mules and everybody in there."

"Goddamn Apache."

"Yes, *gracias a Dios.*"

"Mierda," Flicker grimaced. "If you see God, give him a Winchester. Tell him to hold low and not get his barrel too hot."

"Forgive this black sinner, dear Savior!" I pleaded.

"Hand dear Savior a Winchester, too," Flicker growled. "You ready, Kite? You got ammo left?"

"Anh, yes," Kaytennae nodded.

"All right," Robert Flicker said. *"Ugashe."*

He and Kaytennae commenced, as one, to lever their repeating rifles. Their fire went into the cavern opposite. There was no halt in its thunderous roll. Powder smoke and the stink of powder smoke clotted the outer barranca. Beneath its cloud, I went with the women and ex-Deputy Crench on up into the brushchoke of East Barranca. Packrat stayed behind with his rifle to join Flicker and Kaytennae in the blasting of Kifer, Monkey Woman, and Deputy Belcher.

As abruptly as it had begun, the barrage broke off.

Flicker and the two Apaches came running and dodging through rock and scrub. Behind them, the weapons of the enemy were silent. That stillness but lent the wings of fear to our steep climb up East Barranca.

"God knows if we hit anything," Flicker panted to me. "But Santiago's too smart to get winged by luck.

With his kind you never say they're dead until you dig them under. Then you sit shotgun on the grave for a week."

"I didn't see Pretty Boy down where I was," I puffed. "He might be dead."

"Where was he when the sticks blew?"

"Let's see, he was with his men. No, he was lagging behind them. Talking to that one he calls Buzzard. That's his second, his *ayudante*."

"How far behind the men were they?" Flicker said.

"Ten *varas*, perhaps."

"Damn, that's far enough."

"You think they escaped?"

"I don't want to think about it," Flicker grunted. "Climb a little faster, padre. And don't look back."

44
THE ROAD TO THE ORANGE GROVE

The barranca gained elevation constantly. After the first few hundred *pasos* of jungle-grown lower course, we broke into an open vastness of barren rock. Here, great excitement seized us.

In rock, a trail will show if it be five hundred years old. Or five thousand. We saw unmistakable evidence of ancient mule traffic now. In places, the old track was worn six inches deep in the soft sandstone. I knew from the Franciscan literature that El Naranjal had been mined through parts of two centuries. Such a deep track had to mean that Flicker was correct. East Barranca was the road to the orange grove.

"Jefe," I flattered him, while we still panted behind the rump of the last packmule, *"dispénseme.* You seem to have guessed right. Such a trail as this one must be the road to a very rich mine—*only* a very rich one, eh?"

"It has to be El Naranjal," he answered, face flushed not alone by the heat of the climb. "Padre, I've got an apology, too. We're closer to that Apache church of yours than ever I believed we would be."

"Gracias a Dios," I murmured, crossing myself.

"Him and old Kite," he corrected.

"And old Mirlo," I amended.

He laughed. It made a good sound there in the sun-glare of the barranca.

We took a quarter-hour noonhalt in a small saucer of rocks that contained a spring. There was just room for our five packmules and nine human beings and one exhausted old camp dog to stand in the basin. We made no fire. It would be foolish to let any possible pursuers know our location where we could not see theirs.

Then, as we went on, we noted the air thinning.

"Damned high," frowned Flicker. "Strange, too."

"Yes, we must be a mile up."

"And still going straight up," Flicker said.

"We could see only the rim of North Barranca from down below," I recalled. "Perhaps there is no mesa above us, as we have been assuming, but a mountain, rather."

"We couldn't know," Flicker said. "We've been in that damned big barranca the last three days. We could have come to a mountain."

"Very big one, I think," I said. "Its name will be El Quebradero. Eleven thousand feet, nearly, and not showing on any modern map."

"The hell," Flicker said. "Not on the maps?"

"It's on one map," I said. "This one."

I held up the Franciscan *carta,* and Flicker frowned and said he didn't remember any El Quebradero on that map. I gave him the document. He looked at it, then me.

"That wasn't on that map this morning," he said flatly.

"Perhaps that is why they call it El Quebradero," I smiled.

"The Enigma. Hmmm."

"Yes, or the mystery. It's part of the legend."

"Yeah," said Flicker. "Since about five hours ago."

"Sabe Dios," I shrugged. "I remember it being there

all the while. Perhaps you were looking always at the
tracings of the mine itself."

"The hell," said Flicker again.

The way became so steep shortly that actual stairsteps had been cut into the living rock—for mules that
would now be two hundred years old. Our own pack
beasts placed their hooves in these stepholes with some
uncertainty at first. But then old Cosa Dulce, old Sweet
Thing, our white bell mule, took the lead and had no
trouble at all. Surely it was only that she was brainy
enough to figure out the stairsteps, the others then
imitating what she did. Still, it disturbed me somehow that she would seem to know the way.

"Well, look at it like this," Flicker said, when I
sought reassurance from him. "Either it's her brains or
her age."

"Her age?"

"Yes, you know; maybe she *has* been here before.
Like two hundred years before."

"Preposterous," I waved.

Flicker eyed me. "To an expedition that has maps
that grow mountains," he said, "what the hell is a two-
hundred-year-old white mule?" Again, he cocked dark
eye at me. "Matter of fact," he said, "you're beginning
to look a little ancient yourself, Nunez. I wish we had a
good priest here. We could use some exorcising about
now."

"I can still pray," I reminded him stiffly.

"Yes, but who listens?" he said.

I replied to his insulting with silence.

At sundown, we still had not come out of East Barranca, and we had to make a cold camp. Very cold.
Flicker and I and our Apaches, all old mountain men,
guessed our altitude to be seven thousand feet. Eight,
possibly. Teeth chattered, bones ached, bladders
cramped. But Flicker would permit no fire. Neither did
we see any fire in the night below us. If the Yaqui
survivors were coming on, they played their game as
craftily, and shivering, as did Flicker.

We had not gone an hour next morning, however,
when we broke out of the narrowing barranca. Halting,
we gasped at the mighty Sierran panorama.

East Barranca had led us within one thousand feet of the crest of a tremendous old man of a mountain. The great mass dominated the country that spread before us fifty miles in all directions. Yet there was a single direction that we all seized upon, as one. Kaytennae put a name to our wonderment, pointing in hushed awe.

"*Mira,* look," the Apache said. "*Cañon Espectros.*"

We all saw it. It lay off to our left, to the north. It came from the west, cutting inland to the east. An impossibly deep and wild chasm, five miles distant.

"*Santa!*" Zorra cried. "The Ghost Canyon."

"Listen," Kaytennae admonished. "Do you hear that?"

We all held intently still, and we did hear what the Apache had heard—the unmistakable muted thunder of big water falling swiftly. "*Rio Naranjas,*" Kaytennae whispered.

"Jesus!" Flicker breathed, the fever in him.

"Wait, listen some more!" I implored them. "Don't you hear that other sound? The bells! Can't you hear the bells far off?"

They all cocked their heads, paling. And all heard it as had I: the distant ghostly ringing of the mission bells, far, far off, and as the legend told it.

"God," Flicker said, "we're there. Come on, amigos. We can be at the rim yonder in two hours. She's all down hill from here." He shaded his eyes against the morning sun. "My God, padre," he said to me, "I can see where the packmule trail goes over the edge!"

"Prepare yourself for a sight perhaps no other man has seen before us in these two centuries," I told him. "Below that point, where the mule path goes down the face of the cliff into Ghost Canyon, lies the hacienda. It will be on the canyon floor, on the far side of the river. Behind it will be the mission and the mine. The legend describes it. I could tell you where every orange tree stands. How each *acequia,* each irrigation ditch, runs from the river. God's name, feel the history, Flicker!" I cried. "We are five miles and two hundred years from the house of Don Blasco Salazar. The hacienda, Flicker. The Mission of the Bells. The orange grove. Sweet Christ, the mind dizzies!"

Packrat, standing by my side with Zorra the whore, yawned in my face. "Are you done with your speech, Padre Jorobado?" he asked. "I've got to empty my bladder pretty bad."

"*De ahí,* rascal!" I cried happily. "Come on, *compañeros.* Five miles to the gold of El Naranjal—!"

We laughed like loons on a lost lake. All of us raced ahead of the packmules, crazily. Loafer ran around in circles wheezing his ancient bark. The women chattered in the manner of so many mountain jays robbing the eggs of other birds. The men joked mindlessly. Brainless Crench let out a roar called a "rebel yell," which could have been heard, given the right wind, in Culiacán. Even Mazatlán. No one cared. Flicker himself threw back handsome black head and echoed the shrill American *chillido* of the lead-witted deputy. We were all crazed.

And, before Christ, why not?

We had found the lost Naranjal!

45
AND A RIVER FAR, FAR DOWN

As we neared the great rim that had been visible from high on El Quebradero, the trail went into a cleft in the solid rock. It deepened and narrowed constantly. Soon, the packmules could not go forward without unloading. We sent them back out of the cleft, with Young Grass, telling her to wait for us "on top." The old squaw was happy to go. She was feeling the spirits. So, indeed, were our other Apaches, but they went on with us. As did another, unasked, member of the company: the old white bell mule.

For some reason, this disturbed Flicker. He didn't like being followed, he said. The old white devil made him spooky. But, while I shared some of the same uneasiness, I saw no great harm in it. Sweet Thing carried no packs and could scramble among the rocks like a marmot born to these heights. I believed she came along out of an attachment for Packrat, our campmaster.

This didn't convince Flicker, but the gold fever was upon him. Nothing mattered now save to gain the edge of the great canyon ahead—to gain the edge and get to its legendary switchback mule trail down the sheer face of the canyon of the River of the Oranges.

At last, after what seemed a far longer time in the cleft than we expected, we saw ahead a glimmer of light.

"The rim!" Flicker shouted hoarsely, and he began to run. All followed him. Men cursed at rocks that cut them. The women fell and were trod upon if in the way. We elbowed one another to be first out of the cleft, to be first to rush to the fabled "rim above Naranjal" and to see over it, far, far down, the white adobe hacienda and the mission with their ghostly grove of golden citrus. It was a madness, of course. The same sickness that had afflicted Hernán Cortez and his plumed Conquistadores. As with his time, so with ours; there was no cure for it.

None but the gold itself.

I remember, strangely, in this headlong stampeding to break out upon the rim, not the human figures of my comrades pushing and shoving all about me, but the old white bell mare coming along behind us. I can still see her there. The homely head bobbing. The ragged ears at measured flop. The rheumy brown and ancient eyes seeming yet to smile at our insanity. The music of the bell about her neck tinkling its eerie rhythm to her unhurried pace. It was as if she knew each separate stone and footing place. Had made her way among them not one time, but many. As if she knew, above all, that there was no hurry to reach the rim that lured us human fools, and as if she knew why there was not.

The thought disturbed me, but I put it from my mind.

Ahead loomed the U-notch of the trail's opening out upon the canyon's rim. My silhouette pursued the shadows of my comrades, racing to be free of the dark cleft. I remember that I was not last to reach the over-

look of the great canyon. Only Flicker was there before me. Together, we flung ourselves on our bellies, the
better to hang over the dizzying height and peer below.

Nombre Dios, there it was!

Four thousand feet straight down the wall of the
canyon went. The mile-wide flat of its verdant bottom
was a mixture of roughly jumbled stone, native trees,
and wild grasses, through which looped the Rio Naranjas. Against the base of the far canyon wall, enfolded
entirely in a wide circle of the stream, we saw what no
living man before us had seen. Or, what no man of our
time, before us, had lived to tell of seeing. It was
Naranjal.

There was the rectangle of different, brighter green;
that must be the Valencian orange trees. There, the
walls of slave-cut stone and white-plastered adobe that
were Don Salazar's storied hacienda and the mission
beyond it. There, the geometric traceries of *acequias,*
dug to water the grove two centuries gone and appearing to do so still. It was a sight to steal the breath, to
isolate the mind in warp of time and space beyond human imagining.

It was there, it was all there.

Except for a single thing.

A thing that Flicker was first to note and Nunez to
realize only when the black man's deep voice cried out
the agony of his discovery.

*"The trail, padre! The mule trail down the cliff. It's
gone; it isn't there anymore—!"*

We stared in common disbelief into the abyss.

Where once ran the switchback packmule trail of the
legend, the trail up which had climbed ten thousand
mule loads of the fabled orange-balled ore of El
Naranjal, there was nothing now. The ancient rock of
the great cliff had split away, as the slice from the loaf.
Below us lay nothing but four thousand feet of straight-
down.

Naranjal was there, and would remain there for all of
the days of our years. Neither mortal man nor living
mule would reach it by that cliff.

We had found the lost Naranjal, yes.

And lost it still.

46
WHERE NARANJAL WAS

Our immediate reaction was to rush about the rim seeking another way down into the great canyon. Flicker reasoned there must be such another way. I insisted the good God would not have given me the map and not have conducted us safely all this way to find only a blind four-thousand-foot drop-off. "Keep looking!" was our company shout. But we did not find any other way.

Indeed, the only thing we found, on returning to the issuance of the cleft upon the rim, was that our old white bell mule had disappeared. "She's gone back up the cleft to the other mules," Flicker said. "And we might as well do the same."

No one disagreeing, the disheartened company turned to depart the rim. But only turned.

There, in the mouth of the cleft, stood Santiago Kifer and his evil survivors of North Barranca. With him, in addition to the half dozen Yaqui *rurales,* were both Monkey Woman and the abysmal Pretty Boy.

"Amigos," said Robert Flicker very quietly to our group, "there is going to be a dogfight to see who goes over the edge."

We did not need to ask him what the edge meant.

We had all just been looking over it.

And he was right, of course. Even as his words fell among us, Santiago gave an order in Yaqui, and the *rurale* wolf pack rushed snarling upon us.

We had laid aside our weapons, the better to explore the rocks and brush of the rim for that "other" way down to El Naranjal. These same weapons were in fact leaning on the rock of the wall of the cleft's opening, much handier to Santiago's people than to our own. The Yaquis all had, as was the custom of the Western Slope natives, huge machetes. These two-foot-long blades were of the ultimate viciousness in fighting arms.

191

Run and dodge as we might, in the narrow confines of the rocky rim, we would be cut to stew-meat pieces within moments.

But, God be knelt to, I had hired the proper and magnificent chief of soldiers.

As the *rurale* pack charged, led by Pretty Boy's *teniente,* Buzzard, our small flock was huddled in some rocks to one side of the trail's approach to the rim. Flicker instantly roared out an Apache mother-of-insults directed at the Yaqui, which they plainly understood. He then leaped into the trail and ran limpingly for the rim. The Yaqui uttered a chorus of their wolf howls, altered course to go after him. Their fury to bring Flicker down was not reduced by Santiago shouting to them that the black man was the devil who had made the plan to blow apart their brothers in North Barranca.

More than that, though, they went after Flicker, bypassing us, for the fact that our poor leader was so badly crippled. We had not ourselves seen him take the wound, but now we assumed he had hidden his pain as any good Apache would. Quarry and pack were but a stride from the rim, and we knew Flicker must double hard to right or left, or plunge over into eternity. To our horror, over the edge he went.

Also to their horror, the howling Yaquis went over the edge after him, assuming that where the black devil would go, there would be a good trail for them to follow him. We all heard the fading eerie screaming of their four thousand feet of falling. Then there was the most terrible of silences, until I heard a hissing whisper from "eternity" and ran to the edge to find Flicker cursing my name and reaching up one black hand for me to haul him back from the yawning death below.

What he had done was to remember that a few feet down from the lip of the chasm, where the broken trail ran over it, grew a small but stoutly gnarled cedar bush, the sole sign of plant life on the cliff's riven face. To this he had clung while his pursuers leaped over the rim hot on his black quarters. So rapidly had all this occurred that, glancing below as I pulled Flicker back to the rim, and to life, I could see the diminishing, fly-

small bodies of the Yaquis falling still toward the canyon floor nearly one mile down.

Now Santiago understood that tragedy had struck his forces. He knew, with those instincts of hell that were his, that he must kill or be killed himself. He raised his rifle. Monkey Woman and Pretty Boy did the same. "Stay where you are, all of you," he said.

We did as bid, black Flicker nodding and in his so-quiet manner advising us to obey the mad scalper.

"Priest!" snarled Kifer, "hand over the map. If you harm it, or throw it over the edge, you will follow it."

Even in the image of death that stalked there, I could barely suppress a priestly smile. What good was the Franciscan map to anyone now? Santiago was welcome to it. But I must give him something more with it.

I slowed my walk toward the monster, making a business of getting the map carefully from my travel pouch. Then, when I drew up to him, as I extended the map and he reached to take it, I seized the brim of his wide hat and pulled it down over his eyes. At the same time I kicked him in the cojones and leaped to escape into the nearby rocks. It was sufficient of maneuver that both Pretty Boy and Monkey Woman missed their shots at me. And sufficient also of tactic that, with one of his great lion's bounds, Flicker was able to come at Pretty Boy.

In the same moment, our women descended in a screeching pack on Monkey Woman. There was hell's own scramble there against the rock faces of the cleft, and Zorra the whore of Fronteras single-handedly battered the head of the screaming Monkey Woman so hard on the rocks that the Yaqui squaw was helpless but to lie paralyzed and moaning on the rim. Charra Baca, Apache blood up, was going to "boot" Monkey Woman on over the edge to join her loyal departed troops, but I—a priest of God yet, remember—forbade her on point of purgatory, and she desisted for the moment.

Flicker was having his hands full with Pretty Boy. They were rolling on the ground locked in a blurred ball of white teeth, fanging and gouging; ripping with fingernails; fighting like bears or wolves.

Stella Allison had seized a fallen machete and, followed by Zorra and Charra, run with it to stand over the furious combat of Flicker and Pretty Boy, seeking opening to swing the deadly knife into the leader of the vanished *broncos lobos*.

This left me alone with Santiago. Or rather left Santiago alone with Father Nunez, a far more sinister event.

I made here the lethal error of hesitating to shoot him with the Winchester rifle I had picked up. I thought the sombrero jammed over his eyes and my sandaled foot driven into his aching manhood parts should be sufficient to hold him helpless. At least until Flicker or our Apaches might come to my succor. Well, at very least, until the two Apaches would race to save me. *Quita!* the rascals.

I saw Packrat scurrying promptly to seek political refuge in the nearby rocks, and I observed brave Kaytennae to have chosen to rush, with Ben Allison's sister, to Flicker's aid, there trying to get in a rifle shot that would release the battling Mirlo from his deathlock with Niño Bonito.

Suddenly, then, I realized my utter aloneness.

We had sent Crench back to stay with Young Grass and the mules. All my comrades, stout and cowardly, had deserted me. Santiago had the sombrero ripped away from his blazing eyes and had straightened from holding his wounded crotch. With a foul obscenity, he wrested the rifle from me and struck me a terrible blow with its barrel. Sick with pain, I went to my knees, dropping the map, which I still held foolishly extended in my hand.

Santiago recovered the map and seized my fallen body up in one continuing swoop of his long arms. He had the map now, and I, Nunez, represented all of the ill that had befallen Santiago Kifer since I uncovered his true identity to the good folk of Tombstone, Arizona.

Unmindful of all save revenging himself on Alvar Nunez, he whirled me high over his head and tottered with me thus upraised toward the brink of the awe-some chasm.

It was then—actually it was in the moment that he struck me down with the rifle—that the forgotten member of my beleaguered flock flew into rightful rage.

Limping out of the rocks, where he had taken the refuge of long experience when the fight began, now came the old crippled dog, Loafer. It was my cry of pain that alerted him, that lit the fires of vengeance in his own noble heart. He owed me his life, and he owed Santiago Kifer for a lifetime of brutal mistreatment.

It was only in the last eye-flash before Kifer flung me into the abyss that I saw old Loafer coming in his wobbling charge to rescue his friend and fellow cripple.

His single snarl of warning was heard by Kifer.

The scalper whirled about on the brink.

The ragged old wolf dog launched himself at the scalper's throat. All that Kifer had to defend himself was the small priest of Casas Grandes still in his grasp. He hurled my body then into the face of Loafer, and the old dog and the hunchbacked black robe collided and went down, as one.

The black robe stayed down, dizzied from the impact.

The old dog did not stay down but staggered once more to his remaining three good feet. On these, he charged Santiago Kifer, just as Kifer took first stride to flee the rim's dizzying edge. The sight yet burns in memory.

The dog caught him full in the chest, driving him back the one step to the edge. Then, as Kifer hurled the old dog once more from him, Loafer came in a last writhing effort from the rocks where he fell. And his yellowed stumps of canine fangs caught the twisting Kifer in the hamstring of his right thigh, ripping that vital tendon apart.

With a lingering scream, Santiago Kifer took one lurching crippled step—backward—into the ages that awaited him four thousand feet below.

Somehow I found myself lying bellied on the rim with the panting old dog, watching downward as the tiny form of Santiago Kifer turned over and over in the clear air of that sunbright morning. We watched thus together until the body struck the outward bulge of the cliff at two thousand feet. It bounded outward, then vanished forever from our view, hidden by the outbulge for the last two thousand feet of its fall. But we knew where he must land.

At that point Rio Naranjas ran at the very base of the cliff of the legend and in a course as shallow and studded with impaling rocks as any pitfall of a just and avenging God.

I turned from the sight of Kifer's death-fall only in time to see Kaytennae bleeding and motionless on the ground where Flicker and Niño Bonito still fought. And worse, even. Flicker himself had been blinded by his own blood flowing from a tearing of his scalp above the eyes by the filed canine teeth of the brute Yaqui. The black Apache was still on his feet but staggering in a helpless circle, groping for his enemy. Niño Bonito, growling in his throat, was crouching in toward Flicker, slavering for the easy kill.

Thus intent, Pretty Boy did not see our women gathering behind him. He bent and gathered a great skulling stone from the rim of the bench, raising it above the proud head of his sightless foe. In that second's pause, I cried out a warning to blind Flicker and he turned toward the sound of my voice. The move caused Pretty Boy another moment's pause to alter the blow with which he would crush the black man's skull. It was in this second hesitation that our women killed the Yaqui.

Zorra and Charra leaped in behind Pretty Boy and grasped his two arms. Their inspired strengths, with the heavy weight of the killing stone and the Yaqui's weariness from the fight, brought Pretty Boy to lose balance momentarily. His upraised arms bent rearward with the killing stone before they might straighten for the final thrust. In that moment, Stella Allison fronted him with the waiting machete.

Uttering a singular Indian war cry that I knew to be neither Apachean nor Yaquian, but must have been from her own quarter-blood Comanche origins, she drove the great blade downward.

The blow went in a median line of her Yaqui husband's face. It carried through the brainpan, divided the broad nose, separated the narrow eyes, cleaved the heavy bone of the prognathous jaw, and came to grating halt only when encountering the thick gristle of the breastbone.

Niño Bonito died without a sound.

For all I know, he lies there yet on the great rim of the Ghost Canyon of the River of the Oranges, a machete of his own *broncos lobos* buried in his split and bleaching skull. *Sabe Dios*. We did not linger then to dwell on such things of death.

Preparations were ordered to leave the rim at once.

While Packrat, reappeared from hiding to see to this work, and the women tended to the wounded Kaytennea who, thank God, was but lightly unconscious, I was drawn to the rim a last time by the whimpering and digging there of the old dog Loafer. I joined him and saw that he had found the Franciscan map where it had fallen from Santiago's hand and lodged between two stones.

I took the ancient *carta* from Loafer with but a careless glance. I would save it for a memory piece for telling lies when I was old. But something impelled me to look at it again. I did so and grew pale.

There was nothing on it. All signs of drawing and directions had vanished, and this time I knew no juice of lime nor other earthly arts of Franciscan cryptology would restore it.

I did not signal my find to my comrades. Instead, I crumpled the empty parchment, letting it drop from my hand over the rim. It was as I followed its downward flight that the second thing of God's eerie will caught at my eye.

There, far, far below, where El Naranjal had been, there now was no alabaster hacienda, no mission belltower, no orderly grove of glistening green trees, no webwork of straightly dug *acequias*. There was only a rubble of gray stones to call a house or a mission's chapel, and these may have fallen from the canyon wall. The irrigation ditches were no longer truly-drawn but seemed now to be random coyote or deer trails among the lesser brush of the river's loop. And the beautiful green of the orange grove was but a snarl of twisted ancient stumpings more liken to mesquite forest ruins than to orange trees of old Castile.

I looked to Heaven and crossed myself.

Nor did I ever, then or in all the years of my life, say to my comrades what I had seen that they had not.

Rather, I busied myself with the others in preparation to leave the cliff. All went swiftly well, except for one odd absence. When we came to search for the paralyzed Monkey Woman, the Yaqui hag was vanished. Some of the company believed she might have regained use of her limbs and scuttled up the passage ahead of us, hence escaping us. I did not contend this benign explanation with my fellows, other than to give a hardened look toward Charra Baca, who merely laughed at my scowl and murmured, "Father, you have a dark and suspicious imagination; come, now, the old lady's simply gone."

Again, I accepted the company view outwardly.

But I always thereafter believed that I knew "how" the old Yaqui devil had "gone." And so, too, did Charra Baca.

Still, it was time that we must depart the cliff. And so, with Charra supporting the recovering Kaytennae, and Stella Allison guiding the still-blinded Flicker, we made our way quickly up the dark cleft to where feeble-witted Crench, Young Grass and our faithful pack-mules waited to bear us back to the outer world.

47
BLACK ROBES' GOLD

We came forth upon the mountainside from the cleft.
There, some final surprises awaited.

Young Grass lay bound and gagged beside our only two remaining packmules. We freed the old lady and got her story. Kifer had left Deputy Belcher and Deputy Crench once again as rear guards, Crench having made his peace with his old friend Belcher. The moment Kifer and the Yaqui had gone down the cleft, the two deputies had taken the other mules and fled for East Barranca, and the return to civilization. Any belief they had in Naranjal, or any hunger for its gold, were both long forgotten in the urge, as Young Grass had heard hairy Belcher put it, "To get shut of Kifer and them crazy Injun kin of his, 'fore one of us, or both, gets kilt."

We made little of this flight of minor thieves.

"Forget them," Flicker advised. "We'd better take a leaf from the same book, padre. We can walk out. We've got two good packmules left, and the old bell mule can carry Young Grass."

He glanced around, "Where's the white mule, *anciana?*" he asked Young Grass. But the old Apache squaw peered hard at him and answered that the white mule had been with us, not with her. And, no, it certainly had not come back ahead of us, through the cleft.

"Do you think, Mirlo, I would not know that old devil of a she-ghost? She has tried to bite me or urinate on me for seven hundred miles. *De ahí!* She's gone."

"Yes," Kaytennae added uneasily. "And let us be also gone. I feel a heaviness of spirits in this place."

"*Anh, ugashe,*" agreed Packrat.

They all started to go, but I had heard something.

"Wait!" I called out, holding up a hand. "Listen—"

There was a silence then and we all heard it—the eerie thin tinkling, coming up the cleft, of the mulebell hung about the neck of old Cosa Dulce, the white and bony leader of our packmule string.

"Christ," said Robert Flicker. "It can't be."

The black soldier's vision had cleared now; he turned with the others of our company to stare at the dark opening of the cleft. A moment later, the old white mule emerged into the sunlight of the topping-out place.

For the first heartbeat, none of us noted the peculiar thing about her. Then Flicker said, "Wait a minute, that mule didn't have any packs on her." And, as one, our eyes dilated and our breaths whistled sharply inward.

Slung on the lather-caked sides of the panting animal, heaving from a climb the length of which no mortal man might know, were two ancient ore-carrying panniers of leather. They were of a design not known nor made for two hundred years. And both were bulged to spilling over with an ore embedded by nuggets as large as Majorcan hens' eggs and of a blazing deep orange color and clustering of odd, ball-like globules of the mother gold known only from one mine in Mexico's history.

"*Jesucristo!*" I said aloud, staring at the ore of El Naranjal. "What is this that God has sent us?"

And Robert Flicker, taking the hand of tall Stella Allison and answering for the others, said quietly to me, "It's your black robes' gold, padre; we all found some of it here, one way and another."

It was true. Glancing about me, I could see that it was. Zorra and the pudgy Packrat had found one another. So had slim, shy Kaytennae and bold, ripe-busted Charra Baca. Even I had found a friend where I had none before, the wheezing old and smelly camp dog, Loafer. And Young Grass had the old white bell mule to curse at and be beshat upon by, and so she was no longer alone, either.

Yet there remained something missing, some one thing incompleted, undone, forgotten even.

Then I struck fist into palm.

"The church!" I cried. "My church for the Apache. It can be built now!"

Flicker nodded, but he looked at me questioningly.

"Where will you build it, padre?" he asked. "In the Sierra Madre, still?"

"But of course," I started confidently, then frowned. "Why, I don't really know, Flicker," I admitted. "Where else would you build it?"

"I would build it where it's always been built," he answered. "In your heart, padre."

The words filled the void that had disturbed me. I

knew at once that he was right. A man cannot build a church with golden bricks, no matter where. Love is the only mortar that will cement the soul to salvation.

"You have answered me, Flicker," I confessed. "The gold shall go to other good causes, as the company in communion may agree. Let us leave it thus, as it was sent us, in God's will. Can you say amen to that?"

Robert E. Lee Flicker looked long at me.

Then the black head inclined soberly.

"Soldado Negro says 'amen' to it," he murmured. "It is the will of God, padre. I know that now."

And so we all went back over the mountain, followed by the tinkling glad bell of the old white mule and her ancient-panniered load of clustered gold. But I cared not for that treasure in the final thing of it.

I had found my black robes' gold where Robert Flicker had at last found his.

In our hearts, where God had come to dwell again for Flicker as for Father Nunez.

Return to Casas Grandes
A CONCLUSION

They tell it in old Chihuahua in this manner.

When Nunez announced to the compañeros *that he would return to Casas Grandes to serve his punishment for his church and for the God he had rediscovered at Naranjal, a touching thing happened. The comrades voted to go with their little crippled priest. They wanted to stand by him and to speak for him before the Franciscans.*

They did this, but their loyalty found that yet more "gold" of Naranjal awaited Nunez.

The bishops' committee from which the hunchbacked cura *of Casas had fled had not come to arrest or charge him. They were sent to confer the blessings of the order on him for his long and dangerous work among los bárbaros del Norte, the wild Apache of his parish. A change had come in the regimes of the church; evil Bishop Galbines and his protector Cardinal Mendoza were deposed. The new "scarlet prince" of the church was Jimenez Bustamante, a cousin of that Bustamante who was the alcalde of Casas Grandes. And even more, the new cardinal was a seminary mate, in the long-ago monkhood of their youth, of Alvar Nunez himself.*

Not only was "Father Jorobado" pardoned and restored fully of his robes and his parish, in the kind letter he received from Jimenez Bustamante informing him of this reaffirmation, a postscriptum was attached inquiring how rang in the ear of his old monastery cellmate the name of Bishop Alvar Nunez?

Typical of Nunez, he declined his bishopric. Rather, he would rebuild his mission at Casas Grandes and labor therein to bring all skin colors of men together in God.

Stirring news awaited other members of the famous little band of heroes.

A courier from the governor of Texas arrived in Casas the same day they did. He bore a full pardon for Robert E. Lee Flicker from the state of Texas and also from the Department of the Army covering all charges against him. The white officer guilty of the crimes charged to Flicker had confessed. Robert Flicker could go home again.

Moreover, the courier was a man known to several of the little band. He was very tall with notably pale eyes and a mane of flaxen hair. His name was Ben K. Allison, fabled Texas gunfighter, favorite pistolero of Father Alvar Nunez, brother of long-lost "white Indian," Stella Allison.

The grandsons of the monte *who still tell such olden tales say that when tall Ben learned of Flicker's role in saving Stella from the Yaqui, he offered the Negro wanderer full partnership in the San Saba ranch and asked that he and sister Stella come and live there with him.*

The couple tried it, but both had been too long with the wild red brothers. It is remembered that, in the blaze of one certain night of a full Comanche moon, Robert Flicker and Stella Allison rode out and away, forever, from the land of the white man.

Kaytennae found waiting for him in Casas Grandes a delegation of American Chiricahua from Warm Springs. These people said that the government of the United States wanted Kaytennae to head an Apache farming program to save his Apache kinsmen from being sent to Florida or other bad places. Kaytennae accepted the position and rose to documented fame among his long mistreated people.

A footnote: In the delegation from Warm Springs was a handsome squaw named Born Again who had recovered from a seeming death-wound. It was learned that the woman had lost an infant child in this very town of Casas, having left the child for succor on a church doorstep. Nunez questioned the squaw and, yes, she did prove to be the mother of Charra Baca. Charra's Mexican officer father was dead, and the flame-haired child-wife of the shoemaker went at last to live with her own, her mother's people.

A further footnote: When Charra confessed to Father Nunez that Kaytennae's baby was already growing in her belly, the good cura *blessed the couple by back-dating their wedding banns and the final papers of their marriage, as well. "A small enough sin," he said, "given the temptation."*

Packrat and Zorra opened a cantina in Fronteras, hometown of the onetime fallen sparrow. It had, as they said in Fronteras, "a second floor and a back door," and it proved a better gold mine than Naranjal.

Old Young Grass was given charge of the barnyard at Father Nunez's new mission, a responsibility including the two packmules, the old white bell mule, and Nunez's prize flock of purebred Majorcan chickens.

As for the dog, old Loafer, and Bayo Alto, the tall bay horse of Tombstone, the two were adopted as town mascots of Casas Grandes and were inseparably seen in the dusty streets and grassy plots of the ancient settlement for muchisimos años.

Loafer died in 1888, at an estimated and unusual age of twenty-three years. Villagers say that the tall bay horse was dead within the same hour that the old dog wagged his tail and whined his last.

As for the gold of El Naranjal and the old white bell mule that bore it away from Ghost Canyon this near century gone, well, quień sabe?

The old mule disappeared one dark night and was never seen in the flesh again. There are those who see her every anniversary of the return to Casas of the Naranjal comrades, but such ones see ghosts at the bottom of every bottle. The only problem with denying this story of the ghost bell mule of Mission Casas Grandes is that, every time it is told, fresh mule tracks are found leading into and then away from the now-abandoned mission.

The gold itself?

Ask God.

All that is known is that, for a simple priest of the people, Nunez lived better than any cardinal in Mexico and most happily ever after.

Biographical Summary

The following appeared in the *El Paso Daily Outpost,*
October 23, 1868, under the by-line John Brown
Stokes, later a noted New York feature writer. Copy-
right © 1874:

My true name is Robert E. Lee Flicker. I believe
that is where the troubles of my life began, bearing
that famous name.

My father, James Alvin Flicker, known as old
Black Jim, was a slave—one of the slaves—freed by
General Lee when he went away to fight for the
Confederacy. Black Jim would not accept the eman-
cipation and served Lee as personal body servant
from Sumpter to the end.

With the eventual surrender at Appomattox, Lee
once more insisted my father take his freedom.
Black Jim agreed but in his parting told Lee of his
one wish, that his son Robert, now nineteen, could
attend the United States Military Academy at West
Point and graduate an officer and gentleman, "the
same as any white man's son."

Lee, to the consternation of his advisors, obtained the appointment. Robert E. L. Flicker, born
a slave and son of a born slave, became a black
cadet at West Point.

The times at the academy were despairful. The
body of appointees was still made up of Southerners
in no sense prepared to accept the reality of equality
with a black boy. The memory of my father's wish
sustained me, but I was not to win the victory in
the end.

The final night of graduation week, a white girl was
sexually assaulted at the Point. Incoherent at the

time and failing of subsequent emotional recovery, the young woman was never permitted to testify. Her affidavit stated only that her attacker had been hooded and wearing gloves, thus identifiable by cadet uniform alone. A suspect, however, was not long in being provided.

Each cadet was accounted for, save one.

Robert E. L. Flicker could find no cadet to testify to his whereabouts at the time of the attack.

Indeed, the only testimony was from his cadet roommate, the young Alabamian, Jefferson Flowers III. Said Flowers: "I could not imagine where Bob was, and still stoutly maintain he could not be guilty of this heinous crime against a white woman. Yet circumstances compel me to confess that he was not in our quarters during that time when I pray to Almighty God that he had been."

The precise opposite, I testified, had been the case. I had been in the room; Flowers had not. My charge was never followed up.

The prospect was unthinkable, in any case, as the victim had been Flower's own betrothed. This one "fact" exonerated the white cadet, of course.

As for the black cadet, almost-lieutenant of the army, R. E. L. Flicker, I could thank a generous Lord that I had been appointed by General Lee. By virtue of this condition, I was offered a sergeant's rank, permanent enlistment, and my academy records were sealed. The public would be told the course had proved beyond my capacities, providing I agreed to the lie. As any other action by me would have involved General Lee and my father, I accepted the lie and have lived with it.

The army promptly sent me far.

I arrived at this post (Fort Bliss) early in 1868 and was further isolated by special assignment.

Owing to a command of languages, I was made a scout of cavalry. These troops were engaged in illegal forays into Mexico in pursuit of raiding Apache parties and in gathering intelligence against further hostile incursions of U.S. territory. My Spanish was most useful. Many of the Indians spoke it, and I acquired their difficult tongue through this ability to communicate with them. I have since been reasonably content in my duty and have recently become even happy in my personal life here.

I met and fell in love with Miss Luana Thompson, daughter of Albert Thompson, who is the post sutler. But my color caught up to me once again. Luana was ordered by her father to stop seeing me. I heard Thompson quoted as saying he would be damned if his girl was going to marry a black "nigger" horse soldier. We both were heartsick, and we refused to obey Thompson. A new happiness as well as problem had come to us: We had learned Luana was to have our baby. But fate was stalking me yet. The very officer of my past sorrows was transferred here at his own request five days ago. Yes sir, he had found me; it was Lieut. Jefferson Flowers, my old roommate at West Point.

Flowers, first hating me for the lie he had fabricated to ruin my career, hated me still.

He began deliberately to court Luana Thompson. She is a young girl and defenseless. He is a Southern dandy. I understand her being flattered, swept along. I could even accept her seeing Flowers. But yesterday, when her father announced her engagement to Lieutenant Flowers, dismay invaded me. I pleaded with Luana to meet me in our trysting place at the river. She finally did so last night in the early evening. She asked me to forgive her and said that she wanted everything between us to be as it had been before. I said this would be so, and we embraced. I can still hear her soft weeping . . .

At this point, reporter Stokes tells of emotion overcoming the black cavalryman, and of Flicker then continuing "only through a soldier's stern discipline."

As you now know, from the discovery of the body, there is evidence of forcible rape. Yes, I expect to be put in arrest and charged with the crime. You understand that I am already confined to quarters here and am fearful of what will follow now.

Yes, I have been told a board of officers will sit at 10:00 A.M.

Yes sir, I will be given the opportunity to appear and be heard, they say.

But you know what they are already really saying: "The girl was found where she and the nigger soldier have been meeting right along."

You also know what a Fort Bliss board of hearing will make of that.

I thank you for taking my story and I hope it may serve to one day let the people know who told the truth of this tragedy.

No sir, I do not know what I shall do.

Escape, sir?

How might that be? The night is gone. It is nearing 5:00 A.M. The day is growing and there are troops everywhere out there.

No sir, I do not hate these people. But this is Texas and I am a black man. What verdict would you expect in my place? You nod, yes, you know what I say. Thank you for that. At least, you do not lie.

Will you say then, also, that you do not believe that Sergeant Flicker lied?

This ends Stokes's piece for the *Outpost,* but there is a footnote to it. It is contained in the closing sentences of Flicker's unpublished *Memoirs of a Black Apache,* and it provides the only known account of the Negro trooper's actions following his predawn interview with reporter Stokes:

When Stokes had been gone some minutes, an elderly Apache janitorial worker at the post arrived for that day's duty. He had heard a story that morn-

ing, he said, coming over the bridge from Ciudad
Juárez, where he lived. The army was already building a scaffold on the east parade quadrangle. He
did not know if the story were true, but I went immediately to a window and listened to the east wind;
I clearly heard hammers and sawing.

I thanked the old Apache and went out the un-
guarded high rear window of the noncommissioned
officers' barracks. It was about 5:15. The weather
was misting and gray. I was able to reach the river
and get into the brush. Making upstream for an
hour, I crossed into Mexico. There, I stole a horse
and rode the entire day, south by south.

With that nightfall, and the failure of my brave
mount, I was seventy miles inside Mexico. Still, I
knew I was not safe. Stealing a second horse and
guiding on the stars as the Apache had taught me,
I rode that night through.

Just before dawn, I stole yet a third horse.

Now using landmarks I had memorized in my own
scouting, with the United States Cavalry, of the
Apache in Chihuahua, I reached Casas Grandes
without incident. There, I had been given the names
of certain mestizos del campo, poor half-breeds of
the countryside, by the old Apache janitor at Fort
Bliss. With the help of these faithful ones I was en-
abled to find the wild band of Nednhi Chiricahua
under Chief Juh. The Nednhi accepted me, their past
enemy, as a brother. For the next ten years I dwelled
with them in Juh's Stronghold, in the deepest reaches
of Sierra Madre del Norte.

I went to Texas but one time after that, but I did
not stay. My white wife and I agreed. Our wild
brothers were our true brothers.

They still are.

"REACH FOR THE SKY!"

and you still won't find more excitement or more thrills than you get in Bantam's slam-bang, action-packed westerns! Here's a roundup of fast-reading stories by some of America's greatest western writers: